Friendly Fire

RESCUE & RETRIBUTION #1

MORGAN JAMES

Claire

Grayson

Qutdes

Moments funny sad happy

One

CLAIRE

My fingers skimmed over the windowsill, resting in the empty space that had once housed one of my favorite pictures. It wasn't the first time something had been moved recently, but now it was just... gone. The cleaning crew came through a few nights a week, and occasionally they'd moved things slightly as they'd dusted and performed routine maintenance. But the picture of my sister and me after graduation was nowhere to be found.

I'd even checked to make sure it hadn't fallen in the trash. That'd be a stretch, considering the bin was several feet away from the window and tucked beneath my desk. Perhaps one of the crew had broken it while cleaning and they'd been so embarrassed or worried that instead of coming forward, they'd gotten rid of it. That, I could understand. I wasn't angry—I just wanted the picture back. I'd have to address the issue with Principal Sutton to see if he'd heard anything.

"Looking for something?"

I whirled toward the deep voice floating through my doorway and dropped my fingers from the sill. My gaze swept over the young man standing just outside my office, and I forced a professional smile to my face. Trent Jones was no stranger to my office, but was his expression just a little more smug than usual? I couldn't tell.

"Not at all." I gestured to the chair in front of my desk. "Have a seat."

His expression didn't change as he sauntered through the doorway and practically threw himself into the chair. His backpack hit the floor with a loud thud, and I pressed my lips into a firm line as he slouched insouciantly, one eyebrow cocked toward his hairline as he studied me, a challenging glint in his eyes. His behavior had gotten worse recently, and he'd been caught fighting yesterday afternoon after school—hence his visit to my office first thing this morning. As guidance counselor for Cedar Springs High School, it was my job to help students. And Trent was screaming for help more than anyone.

Donning my emotional coat of armor I glided back to my desk and took a seat. "How is everything?"

He shrugged. "Same shit, different day."

"Language," I admonished, but there was no heat behind my words. Trent didn't have it easy. He was incredibly smart—probably one of the smartest kids I'd ever met—but he had a horrible home life and a giant chip on his shoulder. His parents were in the middle of a very brutal and messy divorce, each flaunting their new affair in front of the other. For the past two years they'd dragged Trent through the proceedings, using him as a pawn. It was divorce ping pong at its best, played with children and emotions instead of sports equipment. I wished I could smack both of them.

"Heard there was an incident after school yesterday," I said as I settled back in my chair and crossed one leg over the other.

Trent clenched his jaw, then wiped his expression clean. "It was nothing major."

"I think giving Matt Cruz a black eye is pretty major," I said softly.

"He's a dick."

I pressed my lips into a flat line and studied him for a second. Having met Mr. Cruz, I couldn't exactly disagree. He was obnoxious and rude, and notorious for provoking other students. Unfortunately, he never got caught in the act, so he was rarely disciplined for his actions. I personally thought he needed to be knocked down a couple pegs. It would be incredibly unprofessional of me to admit that out loud, though, so I kept my opinion to myself.

"Tell me what happened."

It was as much an order as an invitation, and Trent rolled his eyes. "He was running his mouth about my mom again."

My stomach twisted with dread. "What did he say?"

Anger flared in his eyes. "Basically that she was fucking every guy in town except my dad."

I didn't bother to correct his foul language this time. Cruz's words were a low blow, considering everyone knew his mother had slept with Trent's football coach last year just to spite her soon-to-be-ex-husband.

"We both know fighting's not the way to solve anything." *Even if the kid deserved it.* "Just do your best to ignore him," I said. "You'll be out of here soon enough and won't ever have to see him again."

Trent's gaze skittered away. "I'm still stuck in this hell hole for the next eight months."

He absolutely hated school, primarily because of the students like Matt Cruz. "Why don't you look into testing out? You could get your GED or join a work program. That would get you out of here, and you could get your foot in the door somewhere."

"And give them the satisfaction of running away with my tail between my legs?" His lip curled. "No thanks."

He could be so stubborn sometimes, but I had to admire his grit. "Don't let them determine your future. This is just the beginning for you. Prove them all wrong and make something of yourself."

He snorted. "Who the hell would hire me anyway?"

"If you're a hard worker, I'm sure there would be a ton of places willing to give you a shot."

"Right. Then they'll fire me as soon as the year's over. Assholes only care about themselves."

Trent had no reason to trust adults; he'd grown up with the two of the worst examples known to mankind. I decided to level with him. "You know what? You're right. People suck and they can be assholes sometimes."

His eyes widened fractionally with surprise, then immediately narrowed suspiciously. "What the hell would you know about it?"

"My parents did the same thing when I was twelve. Their divorce was long and messy, and all they cared about was hurting the other person. My sister and I never even registered on their radar. We bounced from house to house, counting down the days until we could leave." I leaned forward. "Kids always have it the hardest, especially during divorce."

"You don't know what the hell you're talking about." His mouth set into a hard line.

"Your parents have a responsibility to make sure you're getting what you need," I continued, "and so do I."

Trent jumped up, his face red. "I don't need your help!"

His anger didn't surprise me, but his huge form hulking over my desk sent my pulse skittering wildly. I slowly rose, clamping down on my control. "Trent…"

"Shut the hell up!"

He snatched up his backpack and stormed from the office, leaving me standing there, knees shaking. As my heart rate returned to normal, a sharp twinge moved through the muscle. Trent wasn't a bad kid. He was lonely, misunderstood. And mostly, I just felt bad for him.

I shrugged off my unease and fought to control my pulse. I couldn't wait until he finally graduated. I hoped he did just as I suggested and took off as soon as he could. The best thing he could do was get away from his parents' toxic environments. I'd met them on a handful of occasions, and I could honestly say I didn't like either one of them.

Despite Trent's misgivings, I knew he had the potential to do anything he wanted to do. He was a talented football player, though he'd quit as soon as he found out about his mother's affair and refused to join the team his senior year. I wished for his sake that so many things were different. I'd give him the weekend to cool down, and I would use that time to check out a few local work programs. I was certain that someone would be more than happy to have him.

By the end of the day I had several prospects lined up. My personal favorite was a local construction company who was willing to take him on part-time. I'd spoken with the owner for nearly an hour this afternoon, and I thought it would be perfect for Trent. He could work with the crew in the morning, then use the afternoon to finish his coursework online. I sat back in my chair, pleased that we were able to find some options. Getting Trent to agree to it would be a different story, but I'd cross that bridge when I came to it. He was like a wild stallion sometimes; you had to make him think the idea was his before he'd agree to anything.

My phone chimed from inside my desk, and I opened the middle drawer to retrieve it. A message from Gray lit the screen, and I couldn't help but smile. Gray had been my best friend for the past two years, ever since I'd moved here to take the position as guidance counselor at Cedar Springs. One of the teachers had convinced me to attend a barbecue with her, and she'd introduced me to her family and friends. It was there that I'd met Grayson Thorne. Newly appointed to Chief of Police, Gray was smart and handsome, and he knew it. He'd immediately hit on me, and I shot him down. He'd laughed it off, thrown an arm around my shoulders, and we'd been inseparable ever since.

I scanned Gray's message. **Steak tonight?**

I loved that he just assumed I was free on a Friday night. A normal person would be out on a date or doing something fun. But not me. I was the predictable homebody, and he knew it.

I quickly tapped back a response. **I'll make a salad.**

The bell rang, sending teachers and students alike flooding from the building. I gathered my things then locked up my office. I wasn't taking chances this time. I waved to a few remaining teachers before climbing in my car and heading home. The football team had an away game tonight, otherwise I was sure Gray and I would have ended up there instead of hanging out at my place. I left the front door unlocked knowing that Gray would be there soon anyway, then made my way up to my room. I stripped out of the jeans I'd worn today and tugged on the comfiest sweats I owned. After all, I wasn't trying to impress anyone.

I cringed as I skimmed my hand along my calf. How many days had it been since I'd shaved? Too many, undoubtedly. Not like I had a man who even cared about whether my legs were hairy or not. It had been years since I had dated anyone, let alone had sex. The memory of my college boyfriend pinched my heart. Even though years had passed, in so many ways it still felt like yesterday. Once upon a time I thought he'd be my forever. But fate had other plans, and he'd been taken from the world all too soon.

For so long I'd held myself away from people, afraid that the same thing would happen to them. But all that had done was get me to twenty-seven, alone without even a pet to keep me company. I'd never had a dog or cat growing up. My mother didn't like animals and my father had traveled too much, even before they split up. I should probably start entertaining the idea of letting my sister set me up with one of her husband's friends from work. Jane had suggested it more than a few times, but I'd always resisted. Wasn't Tinder the new place to meet people? As much as I hated the idea of online dating, setting up a profile and at least trying it might not be the worst thing in the world.

The front door opened, and Gray's voice reverberated through the house. "I'm here!"

A tiny smile curled the corners of my lips. Punctual as usual. That was exactly the type of man I needed. Someone driven who would give 100% in a relationship. Gray was such an amazing person on so many levels, and he'd shown me over the last couple of years what a man could be. He'd set the bar high, and every man I'd even contemplated going out with had fallen short. I wanted someone loyal and trustworthy, someone I could always count on to be there when I needed him.

I sighed. Finding a decent single man was like looking for a needle in a haystack. Forget Tinder, I should probably start with the Humane Society.

GRAY

The back door stood wide open, affording me a view into the kitchen through the screen door. Half-hidden by the lid of the grill, I peered over the edge at Claire. I flipped the steaks, my eyes barely straying from the woman just a few feet away. This was my favorite view; I loved standing outside staring in, just watching her. It didn't matter what she did, I was absolutely fascinated by Claire Gates.

She moved efficiently around the small kitchen as she grabbed ingredients from the refrigerator to add to the salad, pulling bowls and plates down from the cupboards. She wiggled her hips to some mysterious song in her head, and a smile lifted my lips. She'd pulled her hair into a messy ponytail, and the ends brushed her shoulders as she moved. It didn't matter that she was clad in a pair of baggy sweats and a tank top, she was the most gorgeous woman I'd ever seen.

I checked to make sure the steaks were done then set them on a plate to settle while I cleaned off the grill. I'd bought it for her last summer, claiming it was a gift since she said she'd always wanted one. Truthfully, it only made sense since we had dinner together more often than not, and I preferred to grill over using the oven. She'd complained that it was too much, too expensive, but I didn't care. I loved doing things for her, loved taking care of her and treating her like a princess.

The moment I met her, I knew she was different. I'd dated dozens of women, but none of them could compare to her. She was smart and independent, the type of woman who didn't need a man to support her. But that only made me want to baby her even more. I wanted to be her rock, her shoulder to lean on when things got tough. I wanted to be her everything.

I carried the plate into the kitchen where I passed it to Claire, who traded me for a bowl of salad. I made a little face, and she threw a teasing smile my way. "Have to balance out all that red meat you eat."

"Real men eat red meat," I returned.

She hip-checked me as she rounded the counter. "So, chicken tomorrow night, then?"

It took a second for her implication to sink in. "Brat!" I lifted my voice in mock outrage. Good thing I knew she was kidding, or I'd almost be offended. "You're lucky I have my hands full, otherwise I'd put you over my knee for that."

Claire just laughed, that tinkling, happy sound I loved so much. I shook my head as I watched her go, that perfect ass swaying enticingly as she practically bounced toward the living room, incredibly pleased with her snappy wit. Smart aleck. She had no idea how serious I was. I'd love nothing more than to pull her into my lap, steal those snarky words and replace them with kisses. God, I wanted her so bad it hurt sometimes.

I could only imagine what she would say. I'd considered telling her a hundred times how I felt, but I always chickened out. I wasn't afraid we would ruin our friendship; Claire wasn't like that. She was the most level-headed, steadfast person I knew, and not even the awkwardness of attraction would change that. What bothered me most was that I wasn't nearly good enough for Claire, and we both knew it.

Hitting on her that first day had been strictly impulse, one I couldn't control. I'd approached her at a friend's cook out after she'd caught my eye from across the yard. I'd been attracted to her, drawn in by the sunny smile that lit up her face. I still remembered exactly the way she looked in that blue strapless sundress, the sun enhancing the reddish strands of her hair and turning them to fire. I hadn't even considered what I was doing as I walked right up to her and asked her to go out with me.

She shot me down, of course. As she should have. She didn't know me from Adam, didn't trust me, and I respected the hell out of her for turning me down. As a cop, I preached on the mindset of avoiding strangers and always being aware of one's surroundings. She'd politely turned me down with that same sweet smile, but I knew at that very moment that Claire was special.

We spent the rest of the afternoon talking and hit it off. With a few well-placed inquiries I'd discovered she wasn't dating anyone, and apparently didn't have any interest in doing so. So I did what any man would have done and moved seamlessly into the role of best friend. I was the one she called when she needed something or just wanted to talk after a long day. We spent our evenings together more often than not, and we had a standing appointment for breakfast at The Village Café each Saturday when I didn't have a case to work. It was the one day I always tried to take off work so I could spend it with her.

Over the past two years since I'd come to know her, I'd learned everything there was to know about her. She was funny and smart, beautiful and caring. I loved her so much it hurt. And she had no idea. We did nearly everything together but I'd somehow managed to hide my feelings for her, because having her in my life in that capacity was better than not at all. Though she never explained exactly why, she'd never dated anyone else. And the more time we spent together, the more I found myself falling for her.

For the past eight months or so I'd been doing my best to put myself in front of her, to make her see me as more than just her best friend. I wanted to be the man in her life who could give her everything—the security she needed, and a love stronger than anything she'd ever known. So far it hadn't worked. But I wasn't giving up. I'd wait forever for her if it took that long because Claire was worth it. She was my best friend, my everything, and I wanted her with a ferocity I'd never experienced.

"What's on tonight?" I asked as I settled on the couch, then scooped up a bite of food.

Claire was a sucker for home renovation shows, so I knew it would be something along those lines. She picked up the remote and the TV flickered to life, bringing up a show about a couple who flipped homes for a living. I particularly despised the vapid female host on this one, and I rolled my eyes. "Oh, God, can't we pick anything other than this?"

"I like this one," Claire protested as she settled on the couch, legs crossed, the plate situated in her lap.

The woman was fascinated by granite, for whatever reason, and couldn't resist remarking about it any time they found it in a home. I changed my voice to emulate the TV host's. "Ohhhh! Look at that granite! It's soooooo beautiful!"

Claire rolled her eyes with a grin. "She's not that bad."

On the screen, the woman strolled into the kitchen and gasped, dramatically pressing one hand to her chest. "Oh, look at this! Granite countertops! We won't even need to update those!"

I rolled my head to glare at Claire, who stifled a laugh. "So she's a little obsessed with granite. Who can blame her? It's a nice house."

"Still wouldn't pay what they're asking," I countered.

For the next half hour while we ate, I zoned out and watched Claire from the corner of my eye. Once we were done she grabbed our plates and carried them to the kitchen.

I snatched up the remote before she could make a grab for it and turned on a sci-fi movie I liked. "My turn."

Claire groaned from the doorway. "This one is so cheesy."

"I know." I grinned. "That's why I like it. Plus, you owe me for insulting my masculinity earlier."

I threw a look her way, and Claire laughed. "That was pretty good, if I do say so myself."

"Mhmm... I see how it is. No respect around here." I settled back on the couch. After a long day I didn't want to think about anything. I just wanted to sit here with Claire and enjoy myself. She settled on the couch next to me, a pout on her pretty lips.

"Please." She rolled her eyes. "We both know that's not true. Besides, that's no reason to torture me with the least realistic movie ever produced."

"Come here, let me make it up to you." I grabbed her feet and pulled them into my lap.

Claire lay back and stretched her legs over mine. "Well, if you insist. Don't let me stop you."

I snorted and rolled my eyes, but I couldn't help the little smile that played along my lips. She let out a little moan as I pressed my thumb into the arch of her right foot, and my cock swelled. Christ, I loved that sound. I wanted so badly to pull her into my lap and tell her how I felt, spill everything I'd bottled up for the past two years. I clamped down on my control and nudged her foot slightly away so she wouldn't feel my desire for her.

The movie I'd chosen had been strategic because I knew

her total lack of interest would allow her to relax and tune it out. Claire's eyes closed as I massaged her calves, then finally she was out. She was the deepest sleeper I knew. Once she was out, she was out for good. I sat there for several long minutes just studying her. God, she was so beautiful. I knew I was biased, but I didn't care. Claire was the most perfect woman in the world to me. I loved moments like this where I could just sit back and watch her and she wouldn't get suspicious. I needed to tell her how I felt, but the idea sent a tendril of anxiety curling through my stomach.

Tomorrow was the day. I'd been thinking of nothing else for the past few weeks, and now it was time. I wanted to take her to breakfast tomorrow and lay everything on the line. I hoped she wouldn't freak out, but I never could tell with Claire. She hadn't shown any real interest in dating, so my heart raced at the thought of getting shot down. Either way, it would be worth it. I wanted Claire to know how special she was to me, and I'd do whatever she wanted. If it was just friendship, then I'd deal with that even though I'd be heartbroken. But I needed Claire to know everything; I couldn't hold it back anymore.

Keeping my touch feather-light, I brushed a strand of hair away from her face and traced the contour of her cheek. Her chest rose and fell with deep, even breaths, and my heart swelled as she turned her head slightly and nuzzled my hand. I stroked softly over her hair, loving the silky texture beneath my fingertips.

Careful not to jostle her too much, I shifted on the couch so I could lay next to her and tucked her in close to me. I never stayed the night, though God knew I wanted to. I wished I could carry her upstairs and slide into bed next to her, feel her skin next to mine. I wanted to run my hands over every inch of her, learn each dip and curve and swell of her body. For now, though, I had to content myself with this moment right here.

I'd get up soon, but for now I just wanted to hold her close and imagine doing this every day for the rest of our lives.

Pressing my lips to the crown of her head, I buried my nose in her hair and breathed deeply. The essence of fresh cut flowers from her shampoo mingled with the eucalyptus from her favorite body wash, filling my nostrils and making me ache. She smelled like sweetness and sin all wrapped into one, and I'd never wanted anything more in my entire life. Wrapping one arm around her waist I pulled her gently into me and pressed a kiss to the top of her head. She brought a calmness to my life, made me whole in a way no one else could. My heart expanded as I held her close. Tomorrow I was going to tell her everything and hope for the best.

Three

CLAIRE

Heat enveloped me and a delicious, decidedly male scent filled my nostrils. A giant hand slid up the side of my neck, then cupped my chin and tilted my face upward. My heart slammed against my ribs, and a gasp lodged in my throat when Gray's eyes came into view. His hazel irises were dark, full of lust and desire. He'd never looked at me like this before, and it sent my heart galloping in my chest.

I swallowed hard as I blinked up at him, pulse racing. "Gray?"

His intense gaze cut straight through me, making my knees weak. "Yeah, baby?"

"What... what are you doing?" I bit my lip, and his thumb brushed over my mouth, pulling the flesh free of my teeth.

"God, you're gorgeous." His words came out low and throaty, and heat pooled in my core. His head lowered, his warm breath wafting over my cheeks. "I've waited so long for this."

Before I could process his words, his mouth covered mine. My lips parted in surprise and he delved inside, tongue sweeping over mine as he explored every inch. I let out a little whimper,

*and he pulled back the slightest bit, just long enough to speak.
"I've got you, sweetheart."*

*Then his mouth was on mine again, teasing me as he
alternated between soft, sensual kisses and playful nips. He
kissed his way over my cheek and chin, leaving a trail of fire in
his wake. I melted into him, loving the smell and feel and taste
of him. I moved my hand under his shirt and slid my fingers
over his scorching flesh. I wanted to strip the fabric over his head,
feel every inch of him against every inch of me. His hand
dropped to cup my bottom, and I pressed further into him with a
little moan. His erection pressed against my stomach, and heat
pooled in my core. I'd never been so turned on in my life.
"Gray..."*

The sound of his name leaving my lips pierced my
subconscious, and Gray's broad form shimmered like a mirage.
I shifted restlessly, clutching more tightly to him, not ready to
let him go just yet. His face wavered then dissipated as I
abruptly came awake and my eyes popped open. I was met
with a stark blackness, and my pulse thrummed wildly, the
blood rushing rapidly in my ears.

Holy shit.

A flash of intense heat followed by a frigid chill swept over
me as the reality of what had just happened sank in. I'd had an
erotic dream... about *Gray*.

I bit my lip and clenched my eyes closed once more. This
couldn't be happening. I'd had a dream about my best friend
in the whole world. One who happened to be incredibly sexy
and sweet and kind—not that any of that mattered. It was
wrong. The hairs on the back of my neck prickled, and I
silently cursed myself as shame swept over me.

This had never happened before, not in the entire two
years we'd known each other. Aside from my sister, he knew
me better than anyone in the world, but never once had I ever
imagined us like this. Everything had always been perfectly

normal, just two friends spending time together. Not sexy at all. Of all the people on this earth, I'd dreamed about my best friend. And worse... I *liked it*.

I felt shaken, rocked to the core. It was like a veil had suddenly been lifted. Because now I couldn't unsee the way he'd looked at me in the dream. I couldn't *unfeel* him. I could taste him on my lips, feel his hands running over my skin, warming me from the inside out. I'd never felt anything like that before. It was... incredible. My heart raced and every nerve ending felt like it was on fire. I bit my lip to stifle a sigh. It felt so real, so good. And, unfortunately, it was all just a dream. A wonderful, perfect, amazing... terrible dream.

I couldn't begin to process what my subconscious was trying to tell me right now. Did I have a crush on Gray? I found him attractive, of course, and I loved his honest and caring nature. I respected his integrity and need to always do the right thing. But I could *not* lust after him; I just couldn't. If he knew... What would he say? Thank God he'd never find out.

I blew out a breath and shifted slightly. All of a sudden I became aware of a heavy weight draped over my hip, curling around my bottom. My eyes popped open and the same blackness filled my vision as I took stock of my body. But it wasn't dark out as I'd originally thought. The folds and creases of Gray's black tee shirt stretched across my field of vision, and the distinct smell of his cologne tickled my nose where it was buried in the soft cotton.

Oh. My. God.

What was happening right now? I blinked to make sure I wasn't still dreaming or suspended in some crazy alternate reality. But no. When I opened my eyes again, he was still there, his huge body wrapped around mine like a vine.

What the hell happened last night? We'd eaten dinner, watched a movie... and apparently we'd both fallen asleep.

Gray had never stayed the night before, let alone cuddled me like this, my face pressed to his chest like I was trying to crawl inside him.

I realized with startling clarity that one side of his shirt was hiked up. Trepidation snaked down my spine as I dropped my gaze to where my hand was splayed over his stomach. He was so solid, so warm. The dichotomous sensation of his silky soft skin stretched over the hard ridges of his abs tempted me to drag my fingertips across them, trace them with my tongue, press my lips—

No! God, what was wrong with me today? I momentarily squeezed my eyes shut and shook off whatever crazy hormones had taken over my brain. It had obviously been way too long since I'd been with a man. And now not only had I had a seriously sexy dream about my best friend, but I was practically feeling him up in my sleep. How the hell was I going to get out of this without him finding out?

Holding my breath and sending up a silent prayer that he was a deep sleeper, I shifted ever so gently away from him. My hand was still pressed to his stomach, and I reluctantly retracted it. My left leg was draped over his, and his hand...

Sweet Jesus. His hand was curled around my ass cheek, his long fingers perilously close to, well... *there*. His hand twitched and his fingers brushed along my cleft, sending heat curling through me.

Mortification washed over me, and I sucked in a breath as I reared back. The motion carried me backward, and I flailed in midair for a moment before sprawling on the floor, knocking the last tiny bit of air from my lungs. For a second I just lay there staring up at the ceiling, praying the floor would open and swallow me whole. Noise from above startled me into action, and I rolled awkwardly to my hands and knees. I felt completely off-kilter, like my whole world had been tipped upside down. Holy shit, I couldn't let him see me like this.

"You all right?" Gray swung his legs over the edge of the couch as I popped to my feet and hastily brushed my hair out of my face.

"Fine, fine. I'm... fine."

One brow arched toward his hairline as he studied me. "Okay..."

I felt flustered, ridiculously nervous as I eyed him. Had he been awake? Did he know I'd had my face pressed to his chest and one hand up his shirt? But... his hand had been on my butt. Was that a mistake or...?

"You never sleep here," I accused. He blinked at me, but I couldn't stop the word vomit as it exploded from my mouth. "Why did you stay? You never stay. I thought you would leave after the movie was over."

Shut up, shut up, shut up.

Gray eyed me warily, his shoulders stiffening the tiniest bit as he shifted toward the edge of the couch. "Sorry?"

Sorry? That's all he had to say? Inside I felt frantic, horribly off-balance. I realized I was lashing out at him, but I couldn't stop it. "You could have at least laid the other way."

He blinked. "And wake up with your feet in my face?"

Every cell of my body froze, and I felt the blood drain from my face. God, how awkward. I was mad at myself—for the dream, for allowing myself to get so close to him. This was Gray, who'd never looked at me with any interest at all. Of course, he didn't know what I'd been thinking. He hadn't given a second thought to falling asleep next to me while I was dreaming of him kissing me and... Oh, God.

Heat swept over my chest and neck. "I need to take a shower."

I practically sprinted to the bathroom and slammed the door, my lungs heaving as I fought to bring myself under control. How was I ever going to face him again? We were supposed to go to breakfast, but how could I sit across from him knowing I'd envisioned him shirtless, my hands skimming over his pecs and lower...

I lightly banged my head on the door. *Think, Claire. Get it together.*

I needed some kind of diversion. Drawing a deep breath, I cracked the door a couple inches. "Gray?"

"Yeah?" He definitely sounded wary, and I grimaced.

"Can we skip breakfast today? Jane needs me to stop by today for a bit. I don't know how long I'll be there, but it might be kind of an all-day thing."

I held my breath, pulse thrumming erratically.

There was a long pause, then, "Sure."

Those three seconds of tense silence spoke volumes. I'd made him uncomfortable, and he was probably ready to run out the front door. "Thanks. I'll talk to you later."

"Okay."

I closed the door again and scowled. Damn it. Why'd I have to go and ruin everything?

Dejected, I climbed into the shower and languished under the hot spray until I couldn't drag it out any longer. Carefully wrapping the towel around me, I tiptoed from the bathroom and peeked down the hallway. So far, so good. I didn't hear any noises, so I assumed Gray was gone. I poked my head into the living room just in case, and my gaze landed on my cell lying on the coffee table. I let out a groan. Great. No doubt Gray had seen it and known I was lying. So now he probably thought I was not only crazy, but full of shit too. Freaking perfect.

I stomped off to my room and yanked on a sundress and sandals before grabbing up my purse and phone. I climbed into the car and checked the battery level on my cell. Naturally, it was almost dead from sitting out all night. I plugged it in and fired off a text to my sister to let her know I was coming over. I desperately needed some sisterly advice.

Four

GRAY

I COULDN'T BELIEVE I MADE A JOKE ABOUT HER FEET. The way the color had drained from her face, her eyes going wide with shock and humiliation, grated on my last nerve. How fucking stupid could I be? I'd been so caught off guard, disappointed by her reaction at waking up next to me, that it had taken me several minutes to regain my composure. I said the first thing that came to mind, and it had completely backfired.

Nice job, Gray. Just what every woman wants to hear.

The weights slammed together with a harsh clang as I released the handles on the machine. As soon as I got home, I came straight down to the basement to work out. I had already put myself through a rigorous five-mile run, and now I was attacking every weight machine I owned with a vengeance.

None of it had done anything to temper my piss poor attitude. My skin still burned with shame, and I was beyond furious with myself for mishandling the situation so epically. When I woke up this morning with her face pressed against my chest, her hand resting on the flat of my stomach, it had seemed like a good omen. And in ten seconds flat, it had tanked like a fucking missile. I was 99% sure I'd blown my chance with her. I could've said something, anything, different. Instead, I'd opened up my big, stupid mouth and the worst possible thing had come out.

With a growl, I swiped up the towel lying next to me on the bench and ran it over my face. The lights in the basement flickered, and I twisted toward the stairs in time to see my brother. Fucking great. Just what I needed today. He'd always been able to read me like a book, so there was little chance I'd be able to hide what had happened this morning.

"What are you doing here?" I asked.

"Saw your truck in the driveway when I came past, so I decided to stop. Kind of surprised you're home," he said. "Isn't this your breakfast day with Claire?"

He knew damn well it was, and I could sense that he was fishing for information. "She's gotta swing up to see her sister today, so we decided not to go."

"Uh huh." My brother nodded slowly, but the expression on his face told me he didn't believe a word. "And why aren't you with her?"

I tensed. "You make it sound like we're attached at the hip."

Drew lifted a brow. "Your words, not mine."

"What does that mean?" I threw the towel around my neck and wrapped my hands around the ends, clutching the fabric so tight that my knuckles turned white under the strain.

Drew shrugged. "Just saying, you guys spend all your time together."

"Not that much," I gritted out.

"More than I spend with a woman I'm not sleeping with," he pointed out. "Y'all have a fight?"

"What the fuck is with the interrogation? Jesus." I stood up and stormed toward the mini fridge in the corner, practically ripping the door off its hinges in my haste to pull out a water bottle.

"You did," my brother said, his voice tinged with incredulity.

I took a long drink, hoping he'd take the hint and drop it. He didn't.

"What happened?"

I recapped the water and leveled a glare at him. "What the hell are you talking about?"

"You two had a fight."

I threw my hands up in exasperation. "We didn't fucking have a fight!"

"No?" My brother crossed his arms over his chest. "Because you only get this defensive over Claire."

Deep down, I could admit that he was right, at least in part. With most everyone else, I was chill and laid-back. But only Claire stirred up a possessiveness that turned me into a caveman. I wanted to throw her over my shoulder, carry her to my bed and never let her out. And I made a joke about her feet. Oh, God. I scrubbed a hand over my face then closed my eyes as I dropped my head back.

"That bad?" he asked.

"Probably worse," I confirmed.

Drew's arms dropped to his side, and he tipped his head toward the stairs. "Tell me over a beer."

"How do you know I have beer?" I groused as I pulled the towel from around my neck and tossed it into the laundry basket near the washer.

"Because I brought you a twelve-pack months ago, and you only drank a couple of them."

That much was true. It was just one of the ways Claire was making me a better man. She didn't drink, and in turn, I hardly drank at all anymore, either. Unfortunately this was one of those instances where I almost wished I had something harder on hand. "You know it's not even noon."

"Never stopped us before."

I let out a sigh. "Fine."

My brother started up the stairs and I trudged along behind him, flipping off the light as I passed. Drew headed straight for the fridge, and I sank down in a chair at the kitchen table.

He handed me a frosty glass bottle, then cracked the top on his before dropping into the chair across from me. "Spill."

I cracked the top and took a long swig before launching into the events of the morning and telling him exactly what had happened.

When I was done, he gave a slow shake of his head. "I don't understand you two. You've been dancing around each other for years. Why don't you just tell her how you feel already?"

I ran one hand through my hair. "You know what's fucking crazy? I was going to. I was going to take her out for breakfast, then come home and lay it on the line." Instead, I had to go and imply that her feet stink. They didn't, but still. Now she'd probably be self-conscious about it forever.

"Fuck." I dropped my head to the table.

My brother laughed at my expense. "Yeah, that's pretty bad."

"Thanks, asshole." I sat up and tossed the bottle cap at him. He batted it out of the way, and it pinged off the cabinets with a metallic clink before spinning onto the floor.

Honestly. "Why?" I asked out loud. Of all the things I could've said, why that?

"Because she makes you stupid." I threw a hard look at my brother, and he lifted one hand in supplication. "It's true. You've been hot for her forever, and it's messing with your head."

I didn't have anything to say to that because he was absolutely correct. It was no secret that I enjoyed women's company. Or, at least, I had. Before Claire. Almost as soon as I met her, I knew we were meant to be together. She was like my other half, the sun to my moon. I was attracted to her, lusted after her hard. She was smart and sweet, everything I'd ever wanted in a woman, and every day that passed only made me crazier about her.

"Look, you know I like Claire." I bristled at my brother's words. "But maybe—"

"Don't even start," I growled out. "Whatever you're going to say, don't."

He studied me for several seconds. "How long has it been since you've been with a woman?"

I refused to dignify that with a response. All he got was a cold glare, and he rolled his eyes. "Seriously. You haven't been on a date in, what? Two years?"

I ground my molars together. He wasn't far off the mark. "You interested in my love life now?"

"I just worry that…" He trailed off, then sighed. "Claire's a great girl, and you know I'd do anything for her. But have you considered that she might never be ready to be with you?"

My entire being revolted at the idea. I refused to believe that. I knew I'd fucked up this morning, but we could go back to the way things were. I hoped.

"Is that what you want?" he asked, as if reading my mind. "I know how much you care about her, but I don't want to see you stuck in the friend zone, waiting on a woman who won't ever be able to commit to you. You deserve better than that."

I didn't care. Maybe it was stupid of me, but I didn't want anyone else. I hadn't even thought about another woman since I'd met Claire. They never registered on my radar, and I never once entertained the idea of going out with anyone other than her. I shook my head. I knew my brother didn't understand, but that was fine. When he found a woman like Claire one day, he'd get it.

"She's it for me," I said quietly. "I would ask her to marry me right this second if I knew she'd say yes."

My brother was quiet for nearly a minute. "I hope it works out for you."

"Me, too."

"Well, I should go." He pushed up from the table. "See ya later."

I sat there long after he left, staring at the empty brown bottle in my hands. I felt strangely numb, a little on edge, an itchy sensation building between my shoulder blades. For the past two years I'd waited for Claire to come around, to really see me. I could only pray that I wasn't wasting my time waiting for a woman who could never love me the way I loved her.

Five

CLAIRE

THE SOUND OF RAISED VOICES REACHED MY EARS before I made it to the front door. I lifted my hand to ring the bell, but the door was flung open before I had the chance.

"Don't you dare drip water all over my floors!" my sister yelled over her shoulder before turning back to me and rolling her eyes. "Come on in."

I stepped inside just in time to see my niece slipping silently up the stairs. She sent a pleading gaze my way and pressed one finger to her lips, begging me to keep quiet. Water streamed from her swimsuit and dripped from the ends of her hair onto the carpet as she silently sprinted to the second floor. I bit back a grin and turned my attention to my sister.

"God save me from teenagers," Jane lamented. "Allie invited her friends over to go swimming, so it's like a freaking zoo here today."

I tossed a quick look at the steps as my sister closed the door behind me, but Allie was gone. Jane led the way through the great room to the kitchen, and I trailed along behind her. High-pitched voices arose from the patio out back, and I paused by the sliding door. Nearly a dozen teenage girls clad in bright swimwear were splashing or sunning themselves by the pool, and I couldn't help but smile. "Yeah, I'd say you've got your hands full."

"Right?" Jane rolled her eyes with a shudder. "I'm just glad Allie didn't ask to have any boys over. I'm not ready for that yet."

"Where's Dex?" I wondered if my brother-in-law was home to help wrangle them.

"Hiding in the basement. He'll probably make himself scarce until I scream for help."

I smiled as I watched Allie re-enter the pool area from the gate at the side of the yard, a book in hand. I couldn't see the cover from where I stood, but I assumed it was something racy if she was trying to sneak around with it. She carried it to a chaise lounge where the other girls gathered round. "I don't blame you."

Jane rounded the island situated in the middle of the large U-shaped kitchen. "Have you eaten?"

I shook my head, then slid onto one of the high stools. "Not yet."

My gaze was drawn to the granite countertop, and a tiny smile played at the corners of my lips as I traced a finger along the smooth stone. The memory of Gray's words last night came filtering back, the way he'd mimicked the TV host on the renovation show. He always made me laugh, and everything seemed to remind me of him. A sharp twinge moved through my heart.

Jane tossed a quick look out the windows behind me to check on the girls, then cocked her head to one side as she studied me. "Isn't this your breakfast day with Gray?"

I barely managed to bite back a groan. After this morning, I wasn't sure we'd have those ever again. "Yeah... We, uh, decided not to go."

Her brows drew together as she leaned forward and rested her forearms on the island. "Okay, so what's going on?"

I propped an elbow on the counter and dropped my chin into the palm of my hand. "I don't think you'd believe me if I told you."

"Try me."

I lifted my gaze to meet hers, trying to figure out exactly where to start. I hadn't told her much this morning, only that I was coming over.

"Does this have something to do with why you're not having breakfast with Grayson?"

I rolled my eyes. Leave it to her to cut straight to the chase. "Kind of."

"He working?"

I shook my head.

"Dating someone?" she tried again.

"Not yet," I murmured, forcing down the pain at the thought.

"So...?" she prodded, and I sighed.

I drew in a deep breath through my nose, then slowly let it out. "I had a... dream."

"A dream," she parroted, one brow arching toward her hairline. "What kind of dream?"

I flicked a glance around the kitchen to make sure no one else was hovering nearby. "The sexy kind," I admitted in a low voice.

"Okay..." Jane drew out the word, and I huffed out a breath.

"About Gray."

"Oh!" Her eyes widened with surprise. "That's new."

That was an understatement.

"So..." Her mouth twisted into a smirk. "Is he good?"

My mouth dropped open and mortification swept through me as I stared at my sister. "Jane!"

"What?" She flipped her hands up in a shrugging gesture. "You've been friends for years now. Honestly, I'm kind of surprised it didn't happen sooner."

"I haven't slept with him," I muttered. Why did I sound so disappointed by that fact? He was my best friend—my very platonic best friend. I wasn't supposed to feel that way about him. I wasn't supposed to lust after him like some teenage girl with her first love. And judging from his reaction this morning, he very obviously didn't feel that way about me.

"But you want to sleep with him," my sister supplied.

I leveled her with a glare. "No."

Maybe.

"So you're upset about the dream?"

The dream I could handle... mostly. It was the fact that, seemingly overnight, I'd become suddenly, acutely aware of him. We'd known each other for two years. Why was this happening now? "I'm... confused," I finally admitted.

My sister pushed off the counter and turned around. She popped up onto her toes and reached into the cupboard over the fridge, then pulled down a bottle of wine. I watched as she uncorked it and poured a healthy amount into a stemless wine glass. She flicked a look at me. "You want one?"

For the first time in years, I almost said yes. I hadn't drunk a drop of alcohol since college, but I was sorely tempted this morning. I bit my lip, then slowly shook my head. "No, thanks."

"Okay." From the fridge she grabbed a pitcher of sweet tea and poured me a glass. She slid it my way, then lifted the glass of wine to her lips.

I raised a brow as I wrapped my hands around the glass, enjoying the coolness of it. "It's not even noon."

She shrugged one shoulder. "I've got ten teenagers in the house. It's five o'clock somewhere."

I couldn't argue with that. She drained the contents in one

long swallow, then poured a second time, this one slightly more reserved than the first. She popped the cork back into the bottle and set it aside, then rounded the island and slid onto the bar stool next to me.

She tossed another quick look out the window, then turned her focus back to me. "Start from the beginning, and don't leave anything out."

Where to even start? Heat swept over me as the dream came back full force. His hands and mouth trailing over my skin, stirring a fire low in my belly. The way he'd looked at me, like he wanted to devour me whole. The way I'd fallen into those hazel depths, flecked with green and brown and gold. I loved the way he'd held me close, loved the way he teased and kissed and touched me. I loved—

Shit.

I loved *him*.

I sucked in a breath as the realization slammed into me. I was in love with my best friend.

Beside me, my sister clucked her tongue. "Just figured it out, huh?"

I turned to her, eyes wide, my heart racing. "W-what?"

"I know that look." She lifted one eyebrow as she studied me. "You're in love with him."

"Oh, God." I dropped my head to the counter. When had *that* happened? And what the hell was I going to do?

"It's going to be fine." Jane spun in her stool so she faced me more fully. "Just out of curiosity, what would you do if he told you he felt the same way about you?"

I shook my head. "He wouldn't."

"But what if he did?" she persisted. "Flip this around and look at it from his point of view. If he was in love with you, and he told you he was having erotic dreams, what would you do?"

I bit my lip. "I... I don't know."

I'd like to say I'd come out and tell him how I felt, but I wasn't sure I would. The truth was, I was scared. Being friends with him was safe. If we moved beyond that and things fell apart, I would be devastated. I'd lost too many people in my life; I couldn't afford to lose Gray, too. But could I afford to stand by without telling him how I really felt? Could I watch him move on one day and settle down with someone else?

My stomach clenched, and I placed one hand low on my abdomen. Jane was five years older than me, and it felt like a lifetime ago that she'd married Dex. They'd been so young then, fresh out of high school. How had they made it work? "How did you know Dex was the one?"

Jane glanced out the window at the girls, but her gaze was far away. "That's a complicated question. When Dex and I met in high school, I was immediately attracted to him. He was always so calm and easygoing. He didn't need to stand out to get attention.

"After our parents split, I needed security. I was so tired of the tug of war, tired of the constant fighting. It was natural to be drawn to him." She paused for a second. "But there was more to it. There was something between us—something I felt only with him, like we were somehow connected. It might not seem that way sometimes," she said wryly, "because I swear that man doesn't listen to a damn word that comes out of my mouth."

"But you still love him?" I found myself holding my breath, waiting on her response. Anyone could put on a show when others were around, but Jane and Dex had always seemed like the couple that would be together forever.

"More than anyone. It's different now, of course. It's not the starry young love we used to have, but more an appreciation for being steadfast and reliable. He's an amazing father and husband, and I respect everything he does for us. It hasn't always been easy, but I wouldn't change it for the world."

I could see those exact same traits in Gray, could see us being happy together. But would he see us the same way? To him we were just friends; I was changing the game. Years ago I'd shot him down and told him I didn't want to date. I hadn't gone out with anyone else, and he hadn't either. That was a good sign, right? I could admit that I was in love with him. So now the question was—how the hell did I tell him?

Six

GRAY

I DRUMMED MY THUMBS AGAINST THE WHEEL AS I turned into my parents' driveway and pulled to a stop behind my brother's truck. As much as I loved my family, I was already dreading the conversation ahead. Everyone would want to know where Claire was. And I didn't know what to tell them.

I hadn't gathered the courage to text or call her yet, and it had been radio silence on her end, too. Twenty-four hours had passed since I'd left her house, and each minute that ticked by was more excruciating than the last. I was pretty certain this was a record; we never went a whole day without at least checking in with one another.

To make matters worse, she'd lied to me. The story she'd concocted about her sister was obviously false. After I insulted her, Claire had sprinted from the room like her ass was on fire. She'd secluded herself in the bathroom, leaving her cell phone behind on the coffee table. So when she told me something had come up and I'd seen it laying there, I knew she hadn't spoken with Jane. At least, not by that point. I was certain she'd called Jane the moment I walked out the door to complain about my stupidity.

I'd embarrassed the hell out of her, and guilt pinched my heart. Fuck. Why the hell had I fallen asleep with her? I knew better, damn it. Granted, I'd planned to tell her how I felt... but not like that. She'd woken up to me grabbing her ass, for God's sake. She probably felt dirty, used. The only tiny bright spot in the whole situation was her reaction to me while she was sleeping.

I tipped my head back and closed my eyes, the memory of yesterday morning turning my blood hot. I was customarily a light sleeper, so I felt the moment she moved. I wasn't entirely sure what she'd been dreaming about, but damn... She'd slid her hand under the hem of my shirt and splayed her fingers over my stomach, trailing them over my skin like she couldn't get enough. I should have stopped her, but it felt too damn good. I'd been frozen, shocked and turned on, unable to peel myself away from the woman I'd lusted after for two damn years. And then she'd moaned.

Oh, God. I'd never forget the way my name sounded floating from her pretty lips. Even now my blood pooled in my groin, turning my cock to steel. I shifted in the seat, fighting against the confines of my jeans. She'd arched into me, her breasts pressing into my torso as she dragged her leg over mine, opening herself to me.

I hadn't been able to resist. I'd cupped her ass and ground myself into her. Christ, I wanted her so badly. Every little whimper and moan gave me the courage to continue. But I knew the moment she'd woken up. Her body went entirely rigid, like someone had shoved a steel rod down her spine. Her fingers had slowly retreated from my stomach, almost reluctantly. And it was then that she realized I was still gripping her ass like a man clinging to a life preserver.

And then she'd done what any woman in her situation

would have done: she'd thrown herself off the couch in her haste to get away from me. It didn't matter that she'd been dreaming; I was awake and fully aware of my actions. I'd taken advantage of her, and we both knew it. I swallowed down the bile that rose up, burning the back of my throat. I never wanted her to feel cheap or disrespected, but that was exactly what I'd done. I wasn't sure if I'd ever be able to make that up to her, or if she'd even give me the chance.

I sighed as I heaved myself out of the car and trudged up the front walk. "Hey, ma," I called out as I shoved open the door and stepped inside.

My mother had an open-door policy, much to my chagrin. I knew the likelihood of someone messing with my parents was slim to none, but things were different these days. She was old-fashioned in her ways, and my preaching only fell on deaf ears. All I could do was keep an eye on them as best I could to make sure they stayed safe. The sound of drawers slamming reached my ears, and I followed them down the hall to the kitchen.

"Hey, baby." My mother paused long enough to brush a kiss on my cheek, and I opened the oven door for her to put the tray of garlic bread in to heat. She turned to me with a smile, her gaze skittering over my shoulder before returning to me. "Just you today?"

An itchy sensation started between my shoulder blades. "Yep."

"Oh." Her face fell. "Is Claire busy?"

"Yeah." I tensed as my brother's voice floated over my shoulder.

"Hey, man." He stared at me, a challenging glint in his eyes. "Where's Claire?"

I threw an aggravated look his way, silently warning him not to start shit. "She's at her sister's."

"Two days in a row?" He lifted a brow, calling me out on my lie, and I gritted my teeth.

I blinked hard. "Guess so."

He smirked, but my mother cut in before he could speak. "That's okay, honey. Maybe next weekend."

I hummed noncommittally and made a mental note to make sure I was busy with work next Sunday. My mother shoved a giant bowl of pasta my way. "Take this to the table, will you?"

"Sure, ma." I scooped it up, then grabbed a beer from the fridge and headed into the dining room, Drew hot on my heels.

"Still haven't talked to her, huh?"

I glared at Drew. "Not yet," I gritted out.

"You should pony up and head over to her place later."

I swiped my tongue across my teeth and drew in a deep, calming breath as I settled in my chair. I loved my brother. Really, I did. But sometimes I really wanted to stab him with a serving fork.

"If I were you," he continued, "I would—"

"Don't you have something to do?" Like, anything other than comment on my love life—or lack thereof?

"Not at the moment," he replied cheerily as he threw himself into the seat next to me.

"That's enough." My mother bustled into the room, and I accepted the bowl of sauce and meatballs as she threw a disapproving glance at Drew. "Leave your brother alone."

"Yes, ma'am." My brother turned to me and rolled his eyes. *Favorite*, he mouthed.

There were definite perks to being the oldest. My mother loved all of her children equally, but it had been a running joke in our house for years that I was her favorite. And who could blame her when compared to a knucklehead like Drew? But at least he was a cop. We playfully joked that our youngest brother, Luke, was adopted since he'd chosen to become a firefighter instead of going into law enforcement like our father and grandfather before him.

"Come and eat!"

My father and Luke came sauntering in from the living room still discussing the game. Izzy followed just a few seconds later. Her head was bent over her phone, and my mother tsked. "You know the rules."

"Yes, mama." Her fingers flew over the screen before she tucked the phone in her back pocket and slid into the seat next to me.

"What have you been up to, trouble?"

Izzy turned and smiled brilliantly. "Same shit, different day."

"Language," my mother admonished as she set the bread on the table.

My baby sister rolled her eyes. "School, that's about it."

"You behaving yourself?"

Izzy smirked. "Of course I am. Why would you think otherwise?"

There was a collective eye roll from everyone at the table. The only girl and the baby of the family at just twenty-one, Isabella was spirited and outgoing. Thanks to growing up with three older brothers, she wasn't afraid to speak her mind, and she loved to have fun. As a child, she'd followed us boys wherever we went, and she'd always tried to prove she could do whatever we did. She was wild and smart and strong, and I hoped nothing ever dampened her zest for life.

Despite our age difference, Izzy and I were extremely close. Maybe it was because she was the baby of the family, or because she was the only girl, but she and I had a special bond that didn't exist between our siblings. Growing up, I was the one she'd come to if she needed something or if she wasn't comfortable talking to our mom or dad. It didn't matter whether she wanted to talk about friends from school or how she had a crush on some boy, she knew she could always come to me. I hoped that never changed.

"There's a guy in my biology class whose family owns a ranch near Fort Davis," she started. "We've been out a couple of times. Might be something serious."

As one, my father's and brothers' gazes slid toward Izzy, silently assessing her interest. We were a protective lot, especially when it came to Isabella. I glanced at her from the corner of my eye, but she continued to eat like nothing had changed, and my gaze narrowed. Judging from her lack of expression, she probably wasn't even interested in this guy romantically. It was just a way for her to get a rise out of us.

"That's nice," my mother interjected before any of us could grill her on the kid in question. "Maybe he can come to lunch next time."

"Maybe." She smiled that secret little smile of hers and turned her attention back to her plate. I bit the inside of my cheek as I studied her. I swore, sometimes she just said shit to get everyone riled up. I gave my head a slight shake. I had enough of my own shit to worry about. I listened with half an ear to the buzz of conversation around the table, losing myself in thoughts of Claire.

Once everyone was finished eating, my father and siblings disappeared to the living room to finish watching the game. Instead of joining them I moved into the kitchen to help Ma with the dishes. "How's everything with you?" she asked as she dunked her hands in the soapy water and scrubbed at a pan.

"Same old." I crossed my arms over my chest. "Staying busy with small town drama, but nothing major."

"That's good," she acknowledged as she passed the pan to me to dry. "But I meant with Claire."

Heat flared up my neck and across my cheeks, but I kept

my gaze glued to the pan as I wiped the towel over it. "She's good."

"Good lord." My mother tossed down the sponge and turned to me. "You're as bad as your father. Getting either of you to open up is like pulling teeth."

I smiled a little at that. "You raised me to be strong."

"But not to hide from your feelings," she countered. "Does she know you love her?"

I stood there, stunned. "Ma!"

"What?"

"I don't—"

"Don't give me that." She leaned one hip on the counter and regarded me. "You're my son; you can't hide these things from me. I see the way you look at her."

"Too bad it doesn't go both ways," I grumbled.

"I'm not so sure about that," my mother said softly. "I think you might be underestimating her feelings for you, too."

After the last twenty-four hours of silence I wasn't so sure about that, but I forced a smile anyway. "I guess we'll see."

Izzy wandered into the kitchen a few minutes later, and I gently flicked her with the dish towel. "Coming in to stir up some trouble?"

She grinned. "Never. Just wanted to come talk to my favorite brother."

"Ha." I tossed the towel on the counter, then dropped an arm over her shoulders. "Let's go sit outside."

Izzy was quiet as I led her out to the porch and settled on the top step. Sinking down next to me, she leaned her back against the post and turned her gaze out over the back yard. I studied her for a second, pondering her reserved demeanor. "New guy not cutting it? Need me to beat him up for you?"

A tiny smile curled her lips as she shook her head. "No, he's actually pretty nice."

"That's good." I could tell from her tone that something was bothering her. "But..."

She was silent for several seconds before speaking. "It's kind of complicated."

"Hit me." I placed my hands behind me and leaned back. "I've got nothing but time."

"What if this guy is older than me?"

I tipped my head from side to side and considered her question. Was this the same guy from her biology class, or someone different? God, I hoped to hell she wasn't involved with a professor. I took a second to gather my words. "He's not... married, is he?"

"No, it's nothing like that." Izzy shook her head adamantly, and I breathed a little sigh of relief.

"Well, then I guess it depends on the age difference and how much you have in common."

"We like a lot of the same things. He's funny and nice, the kind of guy people go to when they need help." As she talked, her face changed completely, taking on a dreamy quality. "I've liked him for a long time, but..."

"The gap worries you?"

"A little." She pulled her knees up and wrapped her arms around her legs. "But it's more like... I'm worried I'm not right for him."

My brows drew together. As much as I teased her for being wild, Izzy was the sweetest person I knew. "Why not?"

The corners of her lips turned down in a frown. "I feel like sometimes he doesn't really see me."

"Then he's an idiot."

Izzy rolled her eyes with a smile. "You have to say that; you're my brother."

"No." I shook my head. "I'm saying that because any guy would be lucky to have you."

She snorted softly, and I sat forward. "I'm serious. If he

doesn't want to give you the attention you deserve, then fuck him. He's not worth it. Find someone who will love you with his whole heart and won't ever look at another woman the way he looks at you." Her eyes widened, but I wasn't done. "Don't settle for someone just because you think it's the best it's ever going to get. Tell him how you feel and if he doesn't feel the same, then cut him loose. Because life is too short to spend it with someone who doesn't love and respect you."

She stared at me for several seconds, then swallowed hard and blinked away a tiny bit of moisture that had gathered in the corners of her eyes. "Thanks," she whispered, her voice breaking a tiny bit on the single word.

Impulsively, I wrapped my arms around her and pulled her into a tight hug. It was as much for myself as it was for her, because somewhere during that conversation, I'd finally discovered exactly what I needed to do with Claire. And the thought of what might happen already ripped a hole in my heart.

Seven

CLAIRE

I SMOTHERED A YAWN WITH ONE HAND AS I SLID THE key into the lock, then opened the door to my office. I felt completely drained, and my exhaustion seemed to run bone deep. I'd felt out of sorts since Saturday, ever since Gray walked out. We hadn't talked since then either, and it grated on my nerves. I missed him, damn it, and I was terrified I'd ruined everything.

I slammed my purse down on my desk and dropped my chin to my chest. Stupid dreams. Stupid libido. What a hell of a time for my body and heart to finally decide it was time to lust after a man. And lucky me, it had picked the one person I could never have.

I groaned under my breath and sank into my chair. I needed to get my shit together. The dream had come again this morning, just before dawn, and I couldn't get it out of my mind. It seemed so real, I could practically feel him lying there next to me. I knew my subconscious was trying to tell me something. Probably to suck it up and clear the air already, convince him I wasn't some sex-crazed lunatic trying to grope him.

Although I might have to lie a little. But if it salvaged my relationship with him, so be it. Gray was my best friend, and I couldn't stand the thought of not having him in my life. I needed to figure out how he felt, whether he was open to more, or... not. And if he wasn't interested in anything more serious, then I'd just have to keep my emotions in check, shove them down deep so he'd never suspect how I really felt.

The sound of voices and laughter echoed down the hallway as students filtered in, and I forced myself to focus. I stowed my bag in my desk, then headed to the staff lounge for a much-needed coffee. I'd been so preoccupied this morning, drowsy from lack of sleep and emotional turmoil, that I'd woken up late and had to forego my morning cup of coffee.

Several haggard teachers were already milling around inside, and I offered them a weary smile as I moved toward the coffee pot. I doctored my cup just the way I liked, then turned to head back to my office. I was brought up short when a woman about my age bumped into me, causing my coffee to slosh precariously.

"Oh, gosh!" She stretched one hand out like by doing so she could stop the coffee from spilling. "I'm so sorry," she apologized. "I wasn't paying attention at all."

"No problem." I offered her a smile as I studied her unfamiliar face. "I don't think we've met. Are you subbing today?"

"No." She shook her head. "Actually, I started last week, but I'm still crazy nervous, in case you couldn't tell."

She huffed a mirthless laugh and lifted one hand to tuck a strand of curly blonde hair behind her ear. "I swear, I'm making a hash of things already."

"No, you're not," I assured her. "It's always stressful being in a new place. But I promise everyone is really nice."

Not exactly the truth, but I wasn't going to burst her

bubble. I wondered why I hadn't met her yet, and I held out one hand. "I'm Claire Gates."

She slipped her fingers into mine and shook. "Melissa Kramer."

"Nice to meet you. So what do you teach?" I leaned against the counter, watching as she poured herself a cup of coffee then added a liberal amount of sugar.

"I'm high school math," she replied.

"Oh, right!" The pieces of the puzzle fell into place. She was covering Kayla, who'd just started maternity leave this week. I assumed she'd been in last week getting everything prepped and ready to take over. "Have you taught anywhere else before, or is this your first job?"

"My first," she admitted. "I just finished school in the spring, and it was a stroke of luck that I applied here right when Kayla found out she was pregnant."

"Definitely," I agreed.

"I don't know what I'll do next year," she said, "but I'm just happy to be here."

"I'm sure you'll do great." She turned her bright blue eyes on me. "Are you a teacher, too?"

I shook my head. "I'm the guidance counselor. But feel free to stop in anytime."

"Thanks, I will." She smiled, then her gaze slid toward the clock positioned over the door. "I should get going," she said, "but I'll definitely come see you again soon."

"Sounds good!" Coffee in hand, I headed back to my office and booted up my computer. I had a stack of stuff to get caught up on today, so I dived right in.

The bell at the end of first period rang, startling me. I opened my desk for a piece of gum and started to reach inside. A yelp suspended itself in my throat as I jumped up, knocking my chair backward and sending it crashing into the wall. Six beady eyes stared back at me from inside the desk drawer, the tarantula's hairy body twitching as he moved defensively.

My first instinct was to run from the office, but I stopped myself just in time. If I left the drawer open, the damn thing could crawl out and disappear. I refused to spend the foreseeable future wondering when it would show up in some random place. Like inside the closet, or in my purse. A shudder racked my body, and the spider and I stood in a silent standoff for another minute as I waited for my heart to slow.

I hesitantly stretched my fingers toward the drawer. The tarantula moved, and I jumped. Damn it! How the hell had this thing gotten in here? My fear morphed into anger as I steeled my spine and closed the drawer as quickly as possible, hopefully confining the creature inside.

Trent's infuriating smirk popped into my head, and heat raced over my skin. First my picture, now this. He'd gone too far. I stomped out of my office then down the hall, making a beeline for the principal's office. I stepped inside the front office and smiled at the secretary, Mrs. Knowles. "Is Jeff in?"

"He has Trent Jones with him," she said.

My eyes widened slightly. Apparently he'd already been caught doing something else. Couldn't this kid stay out of trouble for a single day? I rubbed my temples and sank into the chair across from Mrs. Knowles's desk.

She slid a look my way. "Long morning?"

I repressed a snort. "You have no idea."

I was tempted to go straight back and join Trent during his meeting with the principal, but I decided not to interrupt. Less than ten minutes later, the door flew open and Trent stormed out, followed by the high school principal, Jeff Sutton. "I'll be back in just a minute," the principal said to Mrs. Knowles as he passed.

He flashed a quick look my way, face creased with frustration, then followed Trent into the hallway. I shared a look with Mrs. Knowles, who lifted one shoulder. It was barely nine o'clock. Which meant...

"Suspension?"

Mrs. Knowles made a little face. "Can't say I didn't see it coming."

Me either, but a small part of me felt bad for the kid. His home life was crap, and I understood why he acted out. Not that it excused his behavior, but I got it. Mr. Sutton returned several moments later, then tipped his head toward me. "You need me?"

"Please."

He gestured for me to precede him into his office. "Come on in."

I took a seat in the chair across from him and watched as he ran his hands over his face. "Can I ask what happened with Trent?"

"Two weeks out of school for this last stunt." His lips flattened into a thin line. "It's always hard, but... there are only so many things we can do."

I nodded. I'd tried on multiple occasions to speak with Trent, but he wouldn't let anyone in. He seemed to always get the short end of the stick, and no one was really willing to give him a chance to prove himself. "Actually, I wanted to talk to you about him."

I explained the situation from last Friday, then told him about finding the spider. Mr. Sutton rolled his eyes with a slow shake of his head. "Kid doesn't know when to stop. He was just busted for antagonizing the new algebra teacher."

My mouth parted in shock. "Melissa?"

Jeff nodded. "Apparently several students heard them arguing, and she says he threatened her after she found him stealing an answer guide for her test."

Good lord. Trent was troubled, but I never expected that. I shook my head. "Is she okay?"

"A little shaken, I think, but she seems to be handling it well enough."

After Jeff arranged for the spider to be removed from my desk I cautiously checked the rest of the room before taking a seat at my desk and immersing myself in my work. When the lunch bell rang, I made a quick decision to pop in to check on Melissa and see how she was holding up after the events of the morning. Her head snapped up when I knocked on the door jamb. "Hey, I just heard about Trent. You doing okay?"

"Hey, yeah. Come on in." She waved me inside.

"I'm good," she said as I propped a hip on the corner of her desk. "I ducked out for a second during my free period and when I came back in, he was right here by my desk, going through my paperwork. When I asked him to give it back, he lost it."

I shook my head. "I didn't realize it'd gotten that bad."

"Yeah." A tiny tremor ran through her body. "It was a little scary, but thankfully one of the other teachers intervened before it got out of control."

"Good." I could understand her fear. Trent was a big kid, solidly built, with a hair-trigger temper. "I'm glad you're okay."

She offered a little smile. "Thanks."

"Hey," I said before I could stop myself. "You're new to the area, right?"

Her head tipped slightly to one side, her eyes cloudy with wariness. "I am."

"Have you been to Mason's Tavern yet?"

She shook her head. "I've driven past a few times, but I always felt weird going in by myself."

"How about we hit up Mason's this weekend? Maybe Friday around seven?"

While everyone else was at the game, I would spend the

evening having some girl time with Melissa. Maybe then I wouldn't think about missing Gray so damn much.

"That would be great," she said, a huge smile creasing her face. "It's been awkward not knowing anyone. And, honestly, I'm not a huge fan of football."

I laughed. "They'll have you converted soon enough."

Melissa shook her head with a little grimace. "They're more than welcome to try, but I don't know the first thing about it."

I grinned back. "Hang around here long enough and you'll be an expert."

Eight

GRAY

A KNOCK ON THE DOOR JAMB DREW MY ATTENTION, and I lifted my gaze to Vaughn as he stepped inside my office. "What's up?"

His brows drew slightly together as he tipped his head toward the front of the station. "There's a young woman in the lobby. She's asking for you, specifically."

My heart jumped into my throat. Was it Claire? Had something happened? I was already out of my seat and moving toward the door before I knew what I was doing. As soon as I rounded the corner, the air left my lungs in a disappointed rush. The young woman seated just inside the doorway was most definitely not the one I'd been hoping to see.

Though Claire had never visited me at work before, it didn't stop me from wishing she'd show up. I was relieved she wasn't hurt, but I craved the sight of her. It had been four long days since I'd walked out of her house, and I hadn't heard a single word from her. I fucking hated the distance between us, hated the fact that I'd caused this. Even worse was the fact that when she'd pulled away, I'd let her go. I should have stayed and fought for her; should have told her right then exactly how I felt. Instead, I'd insulted her, then clammed up and let her run from me.

In truth, I was terrified to reach out to her. Ever since last weekend, all I could think about was what I'd do if she didn't reciprocate my feelings. Could I let her go? I wasn't sure. It would kill me not to have her in my life, but the idea of living like this forever, always on the periphery, bothered me just as much. And the thought of her dating another man made me physically ill. So I'd stayed quiet, hoping she'd come to me. I didn't want to consider what it meant that she hadn't.

Focusing my attention on the situation at hand I forced my feet to keep moving, and the woman's eyes lifted to mine. They were guarded, wary, and I halted several feet away, then tipped my head in greeting. "Ma'am. I'm Chief Thorne. What can I do for you?"

Those dark eyes of hers skittered away, and she bit her lip. "Is there somewhere we can talk in private?"

"Of course." I led the way to the interview room, making sure to keep plenty of distance between us as we wound our way through the crowded bullpen. Inside, I gestured to a seat on one side of the table. "Have a seat."

She sat gingerly on the edge of the chair, and I closed the door before seating myself across from her. Several seconds passed in silence, and the woman began to look more and more uncomfortable by the moment. Finally she spoke. "I... I don't know where to start."

"Wherever you feel comfortable," I said gently.

"My name's Kristi Holcomb." She bit her lip again and twisted the strap of her purse between her fingers. "You helped my grandfather last year. Lenny Holcomb."

I nodded. He'd been involved in a dispute with his neighbor but had been in the right. "I remember."

She shifted nervously. "I saw how you helped him—that's why I asked for you. I was hoping you could help me, too."

She studied my face, seeming to seek some kind of affirmation. I tipped my head. "I'll do my best."

"This might sound a little crazy, but..." She drew in a deep breath, then blew it out. "I was at Mason's last night. Had a couple drinks, played a round of pool." She drifted off and bit her lip. "After that, I don't remember anything. I'd made it home, but I don't know how I got there."

Every instinct went on alert as I studied her. The woman's shoulders were rounded inward, almost as if she were trying to close in on herself. I'd seen it before, that same defensive posture meant to protect oneself. I waited another moment for her to continue, but she stayed quiet, lost in thought.

I had a terrible feeling I already knew the answer, but I asked the question anyway. "What prompted you to come in this morning?" I asked quietly.

"When I woke up this morning, I was..." My stomach sank as she bit her lip, moisture glazing her eyes as they darted away. Her next word was barely a whisper. "Naked."

A knot formed in my gut, but I forced myself to keep my face expressionless despite the implication. "Do you ever sleep that way?"

"No." She gave an abbreviated shake of her head. "Never."

I took a measured breath through my nose as I studied her face. "And what do you believe happened?"

Kristi swallowed hard. "I think someone was there... in bed with me."

"What makes you think that?" Below the table my knee began to jump anxiously. I fucking hate cases like these.

She closed her eyes briefly, and her chin dropped toward her chest. "I know it sounds weird, but... I swear I can still feel him."

My muscles quivered under the tension of barely

restrained rage, and I forced myself to stay calm. The absolute last thing she needed right now was anger, especially from me. Even though I was furious on her behalf, she'd come to me for help and it was my duty to remain as clear headed as possible so I could help her. She'd already taken a huge risk coming here to talk to me; I didn't want to frighten her away.

Situations like this were always delicate, and I didn't want to push her too hard. At the same time, I needed as many details as possible. I kept my tone low and measured as I spoke. "Would you like to speak with one of the female officers instead?"

She shook her head. "N-no. I'll be fine."

I gauged her reaction. "I'd at least like to ask one of our detectives to join us, would that be okay? He's my younger brother, Drew."

Her teeth sank into her lower lip, and her gaze met mine for a second before flitting away again. Finally, she gave a tiny nod. I rose slowly from the table. "I'll be back in just a moment."

I left the interview room and weaved through the maze of desks until I reached Drew. He had his phone to his ear, head bent as he scratched something almost illegible into his notebook. He glanced up at me, a question in his eyes, and I tipped my head toward the interview room, indicating for him to join me. He fell into step next to me and wrapped up his conversation as we walked.

Once he'd signed off, he tucked his phone in his back pocket and lifted his chin my way. "What's up?"

"I've got Kristi Holcomb in here, and I'd like you to join me." I quickly briefed him on the few details she'd shared with me, and Drew swore.

"I hate rape cases."

So did I. "Let's see what she can tell us, then we can check in with Mason and see if he knows anything."

Drew followed me into the room, and Kristi's wide gaze bounced between the two of us as we settled across from her. "Kristi, this is my brother Drew. He's going to be handling your case, so I'd like for you to walk us through what happened last night. I know it's hard, but tell us as much as you can."

She gave a little nod, then began to speak. "Like I said, I stopped in after my shift at the Gas N Go. Tuesdays are wing nights, so I ate dinner, then had a drink while I played a round of pool."

"Just one drink?" my brother asked.

"Two," she clarified. "One with dinner, then another afterward."

Still not enough to incapacitate a normal person. Drew nodded for her to continue, and she took a deep breath. "I bummed a cigarette off one of the guys I'd been playing with, then headed out back for a smoke."

"Was anyone else with you?"

"There was another couple, a guy and a girl, but they went back inside before I was done. It was a nice night, so I wasn't in a huge hurry to finish and get home."

She paused for a second. "I thought I heard something behind the dumpster, so I grabbed my keys and started toward the parking lot."

I'd been to Mason's before, and I knew that the parking lot wound around the front and left sides of the building. There wasn't much out back aside from a few trees, but it would have been easy enough to cut around to her car from where she'd been standing. "What happened then?"

Her chest rose and fell on a deep breath. "I don't know. I vaguely remember being carried, then nothing until this morning."

I watched Drew tense out of the corner of my eye, an

almost imperceptible clench of his fist before he relaxed again. "Anything else you can think of?"

She shook her head. "I don't remember seeing him, only the feel of him. I..."

Her voice cracked, then trailed off. Kristi dipped her head, but I caught the glimmer of tears as they tracked down her cheeks. I shared a quick look with Drew, whose eyes flashed with fury. He grabbed a box of tissues from the table behind us, then silently slid them her way. She accepted them without a word and wiped the moisture from her face.

After she'd gathered herself, she fixed her stare on her hands, still clutching the tissue, and continued. "The other reason I think something happened is because I'm still... tender... down there."

"Have you showered?" I asked, praying to God she hadn't.

She gave a tiny shake of her head. "Not yet. I didn't want to, just in case..."

A relieved breath filtered from my nose. A lot of women in her situation would have washed immediately to remove the sensation. I was incredibly thankful and proud of her for having the courage to come in, as well as the foresight to preserve any evidence we might find on her. I picked up her train of thought. "You did exactly the right thing. I have to ask, then—would you be willing to have the hospital look you over?"

Her chin dipped in a nod. It was an incredibly intrusive process, but it was the only possible way we could catch this guy and make him pay for what he'd done.

Drew and I escorted Kristi to Cedar Springs General where they immediately pulled her into a room. A female nurse conducted the analysis, then came to us. She glanced my way. "We'll send this to the lab, but preliminaries definitely show evidence of sexual assault."

I ground my molars together. "We appreciate anything you can find for us. Just send it to the station when it's ready."

I turned to my brother. "Let's run down the people she was with, see if they remember seeing anything."

He nodded, his eyes dark. If the men Kristi was with were hiding something, I knew Drew would be the one to find it.

Nine

CLAIRE

GRAY'S LIPS FEATHERED OVER MINE, ACHINGLY *tender and sweet. I ran my hands over his biceps and shoulders, committing every hardened muscle to memory. The tiny flame of desire in my core roared to life, and liquid heat curled through my body as I melted against him. My brain was fuzzy, delirious with pleasure, and I could practically feel my blood oozing through my veins. My body felt both heavy and light at the same time, and my mind struggled to reconcile the myriad of sensations. All at once it was too much, yet not nearly enough.*

A tiny whimper escaped my lips, and Gray lifted away from me. "Shhh.... I've got you, sweetheart."

Sliding one hand along the curve of my hip, he pulled me closer, then lowered his head and dedicated himself to the task of kissing me deeper, more sensually. His tongue slid over mine as his hand explored my body, sliding lower to caress the outside of my thigh. I hitched my leg over his hip as his thumb slid along the crease between my torso and hip, igniting a spark low in my belly. His fingers trailed lower and lower until they slipped beneath the elastic of my panties then nudged the fabric aside.

One thick finger moved to the tiny nub at the apex of my thighs, and I bit my lip at the sharp bolt of pleasure that streaked through me. He teased the bundle of nerves before slipping inside. More surprised than anything, I gasped at the sensation of his finger filling me. My legs fell open, and my breath came in pants as he dipped in and out, sliding a second finger inside. He lubricated the folds with my arousal, gently rubbing my clit in a circular motion. I lifted my hips, moving with him, the friction pushing me closer to the edge with every stroke.

A soft cry ripped from my throat as he sank his fingers deep. "Come for me, sweetheart." He nipped my lower lip, then flicked his tongue over it. "I want to feel you squeezing my fingers."

His thumb pressed down on my clit, pushing me closer and closer to the edge. "Gray!"

I thrust my hips upward, seeking more. I was close.

So close...

Just a little more...

I jerked awake, lungs heaving on rough pants as my heart slammed against my ribcage. Sweat covered my body, drenching my clothes and sheets. My core throbbed with unrequited desire, but my bed remained cold and empty. Gray wasn't here. It was just a dream.

My hand was still trapped beneath the waistband of the underwear I'd worn to bed, and I snatched it away. Shame and humiliation raced over my nerve endings, making my skin flush hot then cold. Tears burned the backs of my eyes and over the bridge of my nose. I turned and buried my face in the pillow, my sobs muffled by the thick fabric. What the hell was wrong with me?

I bolted upright and moved to swing my legs over the edge of the bed. They tangled in the sheets, and I crashed to the floor with a jarring thud. "Damn it!"

The tears came harder as I thrashed wildly, almost incoherently in my need to extract myself from this damn bed. Every time I fell asleep, I dreamed of him. This was the first time, though, that I'd almost brought myself to orgasm over the specter of my best friend.

Finally free of the material, I gathered the sheet and pitched it to the side. It landed in a heap in the corner, and I stormed out of the room. I couldn't stand to be here anymore. I was getting less and less sleep each night, and I was on the edge of a breakdown. Five days had passed since Gray and I had spoken, and each had felt like a lifetime. I missed him so much it hurt. I wanted to reach out to him, but I was scared. I knew he'd caught me in a lie last weekend, on top of me acting like a lunatic after waking up next to him.

Wide awake now, I stomped off to the bathroom. I flipped the handle for the shower and stripped out of my sweat-dampened clothes, then stepped under the spray. I sucked in a breath as the cool water cascaded over me and quickly began to soap up. Shoving thoughts of Gray way down deep, I made a mental list of all the things I needed to do today.

After I finished my shower, I plodded back to my room to dress. I gathered my sheets, tossed them in the washer, then headed for the kitchen. I needed caffeine. And maybe an exorcist. I had to stop thinking about Gray naked one way or another.

The clock on the stove read just a few minutes after five, and it was still dark out. I took my time doctoring my coffee, then leaned against the counter and stared up at the giant full moon overhead. Maybe that's what was wrong with me. People always said crazy stuff happened during a full moon, right? Things had to go back to normal eventually. What I needed to do was face it head-on instead of hiding away.

Maybe by now he'd even forgotten all about it. Gray never

flat out ignored me, so I could only assume it was a combination of him being busy and trying to put the unease of last weekend behind us. Saturday was only two days away; surely by then we would be back to normal. We could fall right back into our routine and pretend it never happened. I could do it. I could bottle up all these unwanted emotions and shove them back down where they belonged. Because they obviously weren't welcomed by either of us.

Maybe I was making it worse by ignoring him. In retrospect, I should have played it cool, made him think it was no big deal. Except it was a huge freaking deal. I was in love with him. I wasn't sure I could look him in the eyes without him knowing.

God, I was so bad at this. I hadn't dated a man in years, and it showed. It was only natural that I fixate on Gray. He was a constant fixture in my life, the only man I'd been around since I'd graduated college. He was handsome and kind and... damn it.

The jolt my heart gave at the thought of him told me I was only lying to myself. Somehow I'd fallen completely head over heels for him without even realizing it. Damn it, I had to get control of myself. I knew what I needed to do. I needed to clear things up with Gray. I needed to push all my feelings to the back of my heart, shove them down deep, and try to move on. I needed to find another man to go out with, someone who could help take my mind off Gray.

The thought alone hurt, and I rubbed the space over my heart. But my pain wasn't important. I knew it was the right thing to do. I couldn't stand this rift between us, and I would do whatever I had to in order to keep him in my life. It wouldn't be easy, I knew that, but maybe if I had someone else to focus on it wouldn't be so bad. And maybe I'd even come to love someone else—almost as much as I loved Gray.

With a sigh, I pushed away from the counter and headed

back to my room to dress. I got to school early and threw myself into my work, avoiding the other staff as much as possible. I knew my emotions would be plastered all over my face, and I wasn't ready to talk to anyone about it just yet. Only Jane knew how I was feeling, but even she didn't know the extent of it. I wasn't sure I could talk to her about the turn my dreams had taken. They were too private, too... intense.

The first step moving forward was to put this thing between Gray and me behind us. I pulled out my phone several times over the course of the day, prepared to text him and ask about our standing breakfast. But each time I chickened out. I'd put my phone back into my desk where I wouldn't see the empty screen taunting me. By the end of the day, my nerves were fraught with tension, and I felt like crying. I scooted out of work without being noticed and made my way home. I needed a long, decadent bubble bath, and some time to think.

In the driveway I pulled to a stop, then tipped my head back and closed my eyes. It felt like a physical loss, not having Gray around. How was I going to manage this in the weeks and months going forward?

I sighed and turned off the ignition then gathered my things and headed inside. The house was quiet, and it felt emptier with each passing day. More often than not Gray was here for dinner, or he stopped by to watch a movie. Now his absence was profound. I heard every little sound from the hum of the refrigerator to the soft *tick tick tick* of the clock over the mantle.

I dropped my things on the table and had taken two steps toward the bedroom when my phone rang. My stupid heart lurched in my chest, and I grabbed for my phone. Disappointment lanced through me when the screen registered an unknown number. Biting back a sigh, I swiped to answer and held it to my ear.

"Hello?" Silence filled the other end, and I glanced at the screen to make sure the call had connected.

"Hello?" I waited several seconds, but no one responded. With a little growl of frustration, I hung up then tossed my phone down on the table.

In my room, I washed off my makeup and changed into a pair of comfy sweats. Dinner was quiet and lonely, and I went to bed early after trying and failing to watch one of my favorite shows. Despite my body being tired, I tossed and turned all night long. I dreamed again in the early predawn hour, thankfully only of the kiss this time. Finally I dragged myself from bed just as the sun crested the horizon and forced my feet toward the bathroom. After a shower I felt a little more human, and I poured coffee into a travel mug before heading to my car. I'd just stepped onto the porch when my phone rang. I juggled my mug as I rooted through my purse and pulled it out.

"Hello?" Just like last night, silence filled the line. A shiver rolled down my spine despite the heat of the morning, and goosebumps pricked the skin along my arms. It could be a complete coincidence, or...

I hung up, but within seconds it was ringing again. I cautiously held it to my ear. "Hello?"

There was a brief pause, and I thought the caller would remain silent. But this time they spoke, the voice tinny and warped. "I see you."

A gasp escaped my lips, and my heart lodged itself in my throat. I quickly ended the call and practically threw myself into my car, hands shaking as I shoved the keys into the ignition. Who the hell was calling me and what did they want? Could it be Trent? He'd looked so angry that last day...

The hairs on the back of my neck lifted as I glanced around at the houses that bordered mine. Someone could be watching me right now, lurking in the tree line or spying on me from behind one of those darkened windows...

Disturbed, I backed out of the drive and headed to school. Maybe it was Trent, just stirring up trouble. I could only hope that was the case, but my mind told me to proceed with caution.

Ten

GRAY

EVEN THOUGH IT WAS BARELY TWO O'CLOCK IN THE afternoon, a handful of cars were already lined up in front of Mason's Tavern when I pulled into the parking lot. While Drew was interviewing the group of people Kristi had been playing pool with Tuesday night, I'd offered to come take a look at the footage.

I climbed from the car and headed inside, my gaze sweeping over the dim interior. Five men were seated at the bar while another two played pool in the room tucked off to the right side of the bar.

I nodded to the bartender who leaned her elbows on the bar and threw a smile my way. "What can I get ya?"

I waved off her offer. "I'm on the clock, Liz, but thanks anyway. I'm here on business."

"Oh?" Her head tipped slightly to one side. "Usually I hear if things got out of control."

Mason's Tavern had seen its fair share of fights, but that wasn't why I was here today. "I was actually wondering if you remembered someone who was in here Tuesday evening."

Each night they offered different menu specials, but

Tuesday's wing nights were particularly busy. People flocked to the bar for their twenty-five-cent wings, the cheapest in three counties. I was hoping that, even with the crowd, someone would remember her.

I pulled the paper from my pocket and unfolded it on the bar between us. The image of Kristi had been pulled from her driver's license, and I watched Liz study it for a moment before nodding. "I think I remember her, yeah."

"Was she with anyone that you know of?"

Liz stared off into the distance for a second, seemingly lost in thought. "She came in alone, I remember that much, because she sat right there." Liz pointed to the stool nearest the hallway that led to the bathrooms. "Looked like she kinda wanted to keep to herself, ya know?"

I nodded a little as I folded up the photo and stowed it away again. "Was she drinking?"

"Beer, I think, but I can't remember which one. I could check the computer system."

I waved off her offer. "Did she seem intoxicated?"

Liz shook her head. "Not that I remember. I poured the first drink for her, and she nursed that while she ate. Mason got her a second draft a while later. It was busy, but I'm pretty sure she left soon after that."

I flicked a glance at the ceiling where a tiny red light flickered sporadically inside a domed camera. I pointed upward. "That thing work?"

I was almost positive that Mason wouldn't install a camera just for looks, but one never knew.

Liz followed my gaze then nodded, brows drawn slightly together. "You need to see the footage?"

"If you've got it." I didn't want to get my hopes up, but maybe there was something on there that could help us figure out who'd attacked Kristi.

"I'll need to check with Mason."

"Whatever you need to do."

Liz checked on her customers before ducking into the back room. Less than three minutes later she was back. "Mason is on his way in. He said he'll get the footage for you."

"No problem." I slid onto the stool next to me to cool my heels for a bit until Mason showed up. While I waited, I studied the interior of the bar. Although I'd been here before, I looked around with fresh eyes.

My thoughts were interrupted as Mason strode through the doorway that connected the kitchen into the bar.

"Chief."

I slid off the stool and tipped my chin to him. "Good to see you."

"Come on back." Mason waved me around, and I fell into step as he led the way through the kitchen to a small office. "Liz said you wanted to review the footage from earlier this week."

"That's right."

"Is there a specific time frame you're looking for?"

"Tuesday, between eight and ten." Mason closed the door behind us, then took a seat behind his desk while I sat opposite him. "Can you tell me if the camera above the register captures the entire bar?"

"Most of it," Mason replied. "Mind me asking exactly what you're looking for?"

"A young woman came in Tuesday night and sat at the end of the bar closest to the restrooms. She came into the station Wednesday morning, claiming she had no idea how she'd gotten home. We took her to the hospital, and the tox screen showed trace amounts of a substance similar to GHB." I left out the evidence of sexual assault, and instead allowed him to draw his own conclusions. "I'm trying to figure out how it was administered."

Mason's lips flattened into a thin line. "Brunette?"

I nodded. "Do you remember her?"

"Yep. Stayed for about an hour and a half or so. Liz poured her the first drink, and I got her a refill before a large party came in around ten."

"Just those two drinks?" I asked.

Mason nodded. "McGowan's, I think. I closed out the tab for her at the end of the night, right before she left."

Same story as Liz, then. "Did she seem intoxicated at all?"

Mason mulled it over for a second, then shook his head. "No, not unless she hid it really well."

"She said she played a round of pool, too. Do you have cameras back there?"

"One, up in the corner. Should be good enough to tell if anything happened, though."

"Would you mind if I took a look?"

"Sure thing."

Mason was silent for a moment as he fiddled with his computer monitor, then swiveled the screen toward me. The timestamp in the lower right corner showed it was 8:17. The camera was situated over the bar, and it had a decent view of the cash register and drink well, as well as several seats around the bar top. At 8:21, Kristi arrived and slid onto the stool in the far corner. Another two minutes passed before Liz slid the first beer in front of her. On the screen, Kristi alternated between watching the other patrons in the bar and playing on her phone until her food arrived. I carefully studied the people sitting next to her while she ate, but no one touched her drink. At 9:14, Mason delivered the second beer. I watched as he closed out the tab for her, then Kristi slid off the stool, taking the glass with her as she presumably made her way to the back room for a round of pool.

"Switch?" Mason tossed a look my way, and I nodded.

"Please." There'd been nothing of value on the first video, not that I'd expected much. She'd been surrounded by too many people who could have potentially witnessed it. Hopefully the next video would yield something for us.

Mason clicked around on the screen, rewinding back to yesterday evening. Around 9:20, Kristi moved into the room and watched for a moment as the game being played finished up. A man passed her a cue stick, and she set her glass on a high-top table in the corner. A handful of people milled around the room, but none came close to the glass on the table. The game finished and Kristi left the room, leaving the beer glass behind.

"Damn," I swore. I thought for sure the footage would've revealed something.

"Sorry," Mason apologized.

If no one had tampered with her drink, how had the man incapacitated her with no one noticing?

"Maybe she had another drink before she left," Mason offered.

My brows drew together. "Do you remember seeing her again after that?"

Mason shrugged. "No, but I can't rule it out. Maybe she went out the back door, met up with a friend or someone back there."

She did mention bumming a smoke off someone. I supposed it was possible she could have had another drink as well. "Mind if I take a look back there?"

"Sure." Mason splayed his hands on the desk and heaved himself out of the chair. "I'll walk you back."

Mason held the door for me as we stepped outside. The back of the property was bordered by woods, and I scanned it for anything that might prove useful. Several cigarette butts littered the ground, along with a couple of candy wrappers that had missed the dumpster sitting at the right rear corner of the building.

Had he drugged her back here? He could have followed

her when she stepped outside, then drugged her and carried her to her car. I doubted anyone would have said anything. More than likely, anyone watching would have assumed she was drunk and he was taking her home.

Anger burned in my gut, but I forced it down as I turned to Mason. "I don't suppose you have cameras back here, do you?"

"Sorry." A grimace pulled at his mouth as he shook his head.

I waved him off. "No problem. I appreciate your time."

"See ya 'round. Let me know if there's anything else I can help with."

"I will." With that, I rounded the building and headed for my car. As soon as I slid inside, I yanked off my tie and tossed it onto the passenger seat. For a moment I just sat there drumming my fingers on the steering wheel, lost in thought. Frustration coursed through every cell of my body. I wanted answers, damn it. I hated that he was going to get away with this.

After the day from hell all I wanted to do was go home and chill. No, that wasn't true. What I wanted—needed—was to see Claire. I was so fucking tired of this. One way or the other, I needed answers. Tonight I was going to tell her exactly how I felt and hope to hell she wanted the same thing.

I dug my phone from my pocket as I cranked the engine, then dialed up her favorite Chinese joint. Twenty-five minutes later I pulled into her driveway and parked next to her sedan. The front door was locked, so I grabbed the spare key from beneath the flowerpot in the corner of the porch, then let myself in. I dropped the key and bag of food on the kitchen counter and cocked my ear, listening for movement. I heard the soft scuffle of footsteps upstairs, so I assumed Claire had just gotten home and was changing into something comfy.

God, I couldn't wait to see her. Though it had only been six days, it felt like forever. "Claire? It's me."

There was a brief pause before she called back to me. "Hey! Hold on one sec, I'll be right out."

A sigh of relief filtered from my lips. It was so good to hear that sweet voice. I leaned a shoulder on the wall, a smile stretching my face at the happiness in her tone. Thank God. I was worried I'd fucked everything up last weekend.

Footsteps sounded on the stairs, and seconds later she rounded the corner. Claire's honey-colored eyes lit up when she saw me. "Hey."

My heart gave a hard thump as she came into view. I damn near swallowed my tongue at the sight of her dressed in a pair of tight jeans and a form-fitting black top. But the heels were the cherry on top. Bright red and spiky-heeled, my mind conjured a thousand dirty images of them digging into my lower back or pointing up to the sky while I sank deep inside her.

My synapses finally began to fire again, and I forced my gaze to hers. "Jesus. You look gorgeous."

"Thanks." She threw a huge grin my way as she stepped toward the hall table. "I was just getting ready to hit Mason's."

Wait. What?

Mason's was the popular place in town to get drinks—the place where couples met up for first dates. My mind spun, and I struggled to order my thoughts. I couldn't think straight, couldn't focus on anything but the woman standing just a few feet away. The only thing that mattered in that moment was that she was dressed to the nines, getting ready to go out for drinks. With someone else. I said the first thing that came to mind. "You don't drink."

She rolled her eyes as she palmed her keys. "No, but a girl's gotta eat, and I'm starving."

My stomach pitched violently, threatening to empty its contents right there on the floor. This couldn't be happening.

"You going?"

I blinked as her words cut through my meltdown. "What?"

"The game." She tipped her head to one side. "Cedar Springs has a home game tonight. You going?"

And see her there with her date? Fuck, no. My blood turned to ice as my heart pinched. Automatically I fell back a step, needing to get the hell out of there before I lost it. "Uh, no. I'm busy. But have fun."

Without waiting for a response, I turned on a heel and slammed out the front door. I dimly heard the sound of my name over the blood rushing in my ears, but I didn't stop. I couldn't. She'd thrown up a hundred red flags, but I'd ignored every single one. Fuck.

Disappointment weighed heavily on my shoulders as I trudged toward the car and climbed inside. My body felt heavy yet strangely numb at the same time. My brother had been right all along, and I'd been completely blind to the truth. She would never want me the way I wanted her.

Eleven

CLAIRE

I sipped at my tea, still pondering Gray's reaction from earlier. He'd run out of the house like his heels were on fire, no explanation. After the incident last weekend, I couldn't help the swirl of unease in my stomach. It wouldn't be the first time he'd dropped everything to go work, but before he'd always let me know, at least through text. This time though there was nothing.

Was he upset that I was going out with Melissa? I couldn't imagine, though Gray had been my only real friend here in Cedar Springs for the past two years. I'd been more than a little surprised when he showed up anyway. I thought after my freak out last Saturday that I'd scared him off for good. Why in the world had he stopped by only to run right back out again?

I checked my phone once more, but the screen remained infuriatingly blank. With a little sigh I flipped it over again and lay it face down on the table. I glanced around Mason's Tavern, looking for Melissa. We'd agreed to meet at six, and it was now almost ten after. Belatedly I realized I didn't have her number, so I couldn't even check with her to make sure everything was okay.

I knew I was being a little ridiculous. It was only ten minutes; people ran late all the time. But ever since my college boyfriend had died in a car accident our senior year, I'd developed a sort of neurotic obsession to check on people when they were running late.

My heart leaped as my phone rang, and I snatched it up, almost dropping it in the process. Half expecting it to be Gray, I answered without even glancing at the screen. "Hello?"

My pulse accelerated at the sound of the deep, even breaths. "Who is this?" I hissed.

The haunting chuckle started low, then grew in intensity, and goosebumps popped up along my arms. I ended the call, abruptly cutting off the hysterical laughter. Almost immediately it rang again, and I glanced with trepidation at the unknown number flashing on the screen. A combination of fear and anger gripped me as I tapped the button to ignore it. A shiver raced down my spine as I stared at the phone. Was it Trent? Or someone else?

The sight of the front door opening caught my attention, and relief flooded me as I watched Melissa walk inside. She glanced around, and I lifted a hand her way with a smile.

"Hey!" Melissa slid into the seat across from me, a bright smile on her face.

"Hey." I tossed my phone in my bag, determined to ignore it. "You find the place okay?"

She laughed. "Yeah, it's a pretty small town."

I grinned at the understatement. "True. It's hard to get lost in Cedar Springs."

Liz materialized next to the table to take Melissa's order. "What can I get you?"

"Coke for me, please."

I glanced across the table at Melissa once Liz had disappeared behind the bar. "Not drinking tonight?"

She shrugged one shoulder, a sheepish smile on her face. "Actually, I don't drink."

"Small world. Neither do I."

Melissa laughed. "I think we're in the wrong place."

"Guess so." I took a sip of my tea. "Actually, they have some of the best food around, so if you're hungry, this is the place to eat."

"Good to know." Melissa perused the menu for a minute before replacing it in the condiment rack.

She graced Liz with a smile when she set the Coke in front of her. "Thanks."

Liz pulled a notepad from her apron. "Would you like anything to eat?"

We both ordered burgers and fries, then I turned back to Melissa. "Big plans for the weekend?"

She shook her head. "I usually just chill, but I was thinking of heading to the beach tomorrow morning, stay there for the weekend."

"That sounds like fun."

I folded my arms on the table in front of me and regarded her. "So, I know you're not a fan of football. What else? Tell me about yourself."

"Not much to tell." She made a little face. "Right now I'm just working and trying to settle in."

I cocked my head to one side as I studied her. "How are you adjusting to Cedar Springs?"

"It's been... interesting," she said with a little laugh. "Kind of a culture shock sometimes."

"Do you have family around here?"

Melissa took a drink, then shook her head. "No, it's just me."

I felt a little twinge of sympathy. "How did you end up in Cedar Springs?"

"It's kind of a long story."

She eyed me, and I gestured for her to continue. "Go ahead, I've got all night."

"Well, I used to live with my parents up north. They got sick a couple years ago, so I spent most of my time taking care of them. I technically should have graduated a year ago, but I took some time off to spend it with them."

She took a sip of her drink before continuing. "I finished my degree a little at a time, hoping something would come up near where I lived. I'd always wanted to come south, but I kind of felt obligated to stay with them, you know?"

I couldn't begin to imagine how hard that had been on her. I nodded. "Of course."

"Anyway." She let out a sad sigh. "My parents passed away last year, so there was nothing holding me back anymore."

"I'm sorry," I said softly. "I didn't know." My stomach did a little flip, and my appetite disappeared. I didn't deal well with death and loss. Guilt and unease hung heavily around my neck, weighing me down.

She waved one hand in the air. "It's okay. They weren't well for a long time, so it wasn't unexpected. I actually feel more relieved than anything now that they're not in pain anymore."

"I can understand that. I really admire what you did," I offered. "I'm sure it wasn't easy for you."

"It was hard, but..." She lifted one shoulder. "I did what I had to do. I still miss them, though. The pain never really goes away, I don't think," she replied, looking lost in thought.

"No," I agreed, "it doesn't. I think over time you just become accustomed to living with it and it becomes second nature."

Melissa offered a tight smile. "What about you? Have you always lived here?"

"No." I shook my head with a little laugh, glad at the change of topic. "I don't see my parents very often."

She tipped her head. "They live far away?"

"Opposite ends of the country—literally. We grew up in Oklahoma but my parents split when I was twelve. Mom took me, dad took my sister."

"That's rough." She made a face. "You have a sister?"

"Yep. One older sister, Jane."

"Do you ever see her?"

"Actually, yes." I nodded. "She lives about forty minutes northwest, so we try to get together once a month or so."

"That's nice." Melissa looked wistful. "At least you have someone here."

"Things will be better once you settle in and people get used to you."

She grinned. "Yeah, I'm not sure I'll ever get used to small town life. Everyone staring at me walking down the street makes me want to hide."

I laughed. "My first six months were like that. But Gray and his friends helped smooth the way, and they welcomed me in pretty quickly."

"Is that your boyfriend?"

I felt my cheeks heat as thoughts of Gray flooded my brain. Damn those dreams. "He's just a friend."

"Uh huh..."

I lifted my head at her skeptical tone and found a speculative gaze on her face. "But there is a guy."

I bit my lip. I had no idea what was going on between Gray and me, especially after last weekend. Not to mention the strange way he'd rushed out of the house earlier while I'd been getting ready. "Kind of," I admitted. "I just... I'm not sure it's going to turn into anything, so..." I shrugged, and Melissa nodded.

"I understand. How long have you known him?"

I shifted awkwardly. "Almost two years."

She seemed to process that for a second. "That's a long

time to hold on to just a crush. He must be important to you."

"He is. It's just... complicated," I finished lamely.

"You care about him?"

Such an insignificant word for the way I felt about Gray. There was no way I could tell Melissa about the dreams I'd been having, but I did need a little advice. "I think I'm in love with him. The problem is... I don't think he's interested in me like that."

"Why not?"

I pressed my lips together. "We've known each other for two years. I think if he wanted to date me he would have said something a long time ago."

Her nose crinkled. "I'm sorry."

Yeah, so was I. Feigning indifference, I forced my lips into a smile and shrugged. "It's no big deal. We're probably better off as friends anyway."

She studied me. "You obviously want to be with him. I say tell him how you feel."

My lips twisted into a self-deprecating smile at the memory of last weekend. "That might be easier said than done."

I wasn't entirely sure why, but I found myself telling her about Gray—how we'd met, how things had evolved over the last several months. Liz delivered our food, and Melissa listened as she ate. "I think all you can do is ask. I know it'll suck if he shoots you down, but at least then you'll know."

Sadness pressed in on me at the thought. "Yeah, that's true."

"And if he does, there are plenty of men who I'm sure would love to date you." Using a french fry, she gestured around the bar. "You just can't have the blond sitting at the corner of the bar. I've got my eye on him," she joked.

Even in street clothes I recognized him as one of the

patrolmen who worked under Gray. "That's Scott Mackenzie —Mac to anyone who knows him. He's an officer for Cedar Springs."

"Mmm..." Melissa licked her lips. "Love a man in a uniform."

How true that was. I couldn't help but laugh at her attempt to make me feel better. "Thank you. For the advice, and for coming out with me tonight."

Liz brought our bill, and we both cashed out, then continued to chat. Melissa's gaze drifted toward Mac again, and I smiled. "Come on." I tipped my head in the direction of the bar. "I'll introduce you."

"Are you sure? I..." She trailed off as I slipped from the stool and slung my purse over my shoulder.

Mac caught my gaze and I lifted a hand in greeting. "Hey, Claire. How's it goin'?"

"Good. You staying busy?"

"Can't complain." His gaze slid over my shoulder and his eyes widened appreciatively when they landed on Melissa. I bit back a smile. I knew he wouldn't be able to resist the pretty blue-eyed blonde.

I turned toward her and held out one hand. "Melissa, this is Scott Mackenzie. Most everyone calls him Mac. Mac, this is Melissa. She's subbing at the high school and is new to town."

He held out a hand and Melissa slipped her palm into it. "Good to meet you.

"You, too."

I hovered for a moment as they made small talk, then made a show of looking at my phone. "Hey, I've got to run. Melissa, I'll see you Monday." I waved to Mac. "See ya 'round."

I couldn't help but grin as I made my way out of the bar and climbed into my car. At home, I flipped on the kitchen light and dropped my purse and keys on the counter. I froze when I saw the white takeout bag sitting off to one side, and I cautiously peeled it open. A twinge moved through my heart when I found containers from my favorite restaurant. Gray must have brought them earlier, but why hadn't he said anything? Next to the bags lay the spare key I kept under the pot on the front porch. I picked it up and twirled it between my fingers.

Gray had looked devastated when he left. I pondered his reaction again, and a giant pit opened up in my stomach as I mentally replayed our conversation from earlier. I'd been vague about going to Mason's, but not intentionally. Did he think I'd had a date?

Damn. Guilt assailed me. He'd brought food as a peace offering, and I'd completely ruined it.

Twelve

GRAY

I TAPPED THE KEYBOARD A LITTLE HARDER THAN necessary, like me prompting it a dozen times would somehow make the system work faster. *Fucking computer.*

I let out a little growl and threw myself back in my seat. Finally the results populated on the screen, and I practically leaped for the mouse. I scrolled to the part of the report I was looking for and scowled.

Goddamn it. We'd printed and examined every damn inch of Kristi's space, but the asshole hadn't left a single shred of DNA anywhere. The car was clean, her bedroom was clean, and we didn't have a single piece of evidence to point to whoever had taken advantage of her. Even the report from the hospital showed no bodily fluids, which meant the fucker had at least used a condom. Unfortunately, he'd either taken it with him or flushed it. Which still left us without a single damn lead.

The tox screen they'd run showed traces of a substance in her system that, on a molecular level, was incredibly similar to the popular date-rape drug GHB. It wasn't unheard of to find generic versions of the drug on the street, so Drew was in the process of following up with Kristi to see if she remembered anything else from that night. If nothing else turned up, there was a very real possibility that this asshole would get away with it. Fuck.

Why could nothing go my way? It seemed like everything was slipping out of my control. I grabbed my phone lying on the corner of my desk and checked the screen. The messaging app still showed a tiny red badge with a glaring number 2—the number of messages I'd received from Claire. And had been ignoring at all costs. I didn't want to read them. I didn't want to hear about her date Friday night, or how amazing it was. I wanted to throw up just thinking about it. Those two unread messages had taunted me incessantly over the past few days, but I wasn't ready to deal with it yet. I wasn't sure I'd ever be ready.

The thought of her with someone else still had the power to bring me to my knees. My heart felt shredded. Over the past six days I'd ignored those texts, throwing myself instead into all the open cases we had. I worked eighteen-hour days, fell into bed, then did it all over again the next day. I wished I could just erase them without ever looking at them, but I knew I wasn't strong enough for that, either. Eventually I'd need to see what she'd said. Just... not yet. I tossed the phone back on my desk, face down.

Fucking phone. Fucking—

"What the hell's going on with you?" My brother demanded as he stepped inside my office and closed the door.

—Nosy ass brothers.

Keeping my gaze fixed on the computer in front of me, I ignored him completely. I didn't want to talk about it, especially not with him. I couldn't fucking stand to hear him say *I told you so.*

My brother stomped across the room and slapped his palms down on my desk. "Seriously, Gray, what the fuck?"

"What do you want from me?" I exploded, fury propelling me from my chair. "Can't you just leave me the hell alone?"

"No," he snapped. "I've never seen you like this before. What the hell is going on?"

"Nothing."

"Bullshit." He pointed at me. "You've been a dick all week, and I'm fucking tired of it. You need to deal with whatever the hell crawled up your ass and died, because you're taking it out on everyone else."

Fuck. I scrubbed my hands over my face before locking my fingers together behind my head and staring at the ceiling. A thousand emotions brewed violently inside me, but guilt bubbled to the surface. "I'm sorry."

Drew waited a beat, absorbing my quiet apology. "Seriously, man. What's going on?"

I dropped into my chair and regarded him across the desk. "You were right."

His brows drew together. "About what?"

"All of it." I waved my hand. "Claire doesn't want me." The words threatened to choke me, but I forced them out. "She's seeing someone."

Surprise flashed across his features, and he sank into the chair. Several seconds passed in stunned silence before he spoke. "Shit, man, I'm sorry. I had no idea."

"Yeah." I swallowed hard and tried to shove down the hurt. "I showed up last Friday, brought her dinner, but she was getting ready to go out with someone else."

"Who?"

"I don't know." I shrugged and snorted out a mirthless laugh. "Does it matter?"

He studied me for several seconds. "You sure?"

"Yeah, I'm fucking sure. Saw her with my own two eyes."

"I mean, did you ask her?" Drew looked contemplative.

"That doesn't seem like Claire. Y'all talk about everything. I can't believe she never mentioned it."

"Whatever." I feigned indifference. "She's free to go out with whoever she wants."

Even if it fucking killed me, I wanted to see her happy.

Drew was quiet for a minute. "Just... hear me out. You're sure it was a guy?"

I threw a bewildered look his way, and he waved me off. "Not like that. I mean, Mac mentioned seeing her at Mason's last week with a teacher from the school. Claire introduced him to the teacher, and they're apparently going out."

"Fucking awesome for him," I grumbled.

"Listen to me, you stupid shit," Drew snapped. "What I'm saying is, maybe she was just out with a friend."

A wave of relief rolled over me, and I stared at my brother. "You think?"

"I can't say for sure, but yeah." He lifted one shoulder. "Ask Mac what day it was and you'll know for sure."

I blew out a breath. God, I couldn't begin to explain how much better I felt hearing that. "Thanks, man."

He rolled his eyes. "You know, you could have saved us all a hell of a lot of trouble by just talking to her."

Heat climbed up the back of my neck. He wasn't wrong, though I hated to admit it. "Whatever, asshole."

"Next time I'm going to let your dumb ass figure it out on your own. Christ." His features creased with disgust. "I don't get paid enough for this. You two need to figure your shit out already. Just fucking tell her you love her so we can all move on with our lives."

I flipped him off as he moved toward the door, but I couldn't help the smile that curled the corners of my mouth. So he might be right. I hated feeling this way, being in limbo. No matter what happened, I wanted to get this off my chest once and for all. As the door clicked closed behind my brother, I reached for my phone and pulled up the messages I'd been ignoring for the past week.

Holding my breath, I read through the text she'd sent last Saturday.

Thanks for bringing dinner. Sorry you had to run. See you soon.

She'd tacked a smiley face emoji at the end of that one. Then, two days later, a second one had come through. **Hope everything's okay with work.**

Neither mentioned another man, and I couldn't help the relief that billowed through me. Before I could think better of it, I tapped out a message to Claire. **Sorry, didn't mean to ignore you. Things have been hectic. Breakfast Saturday?**

Three little dots appeared in the lower corner, and Claire's reply came almost instantly. **Sounds good to me.**

I wondered with a tiny smile if she'd been watching her phone the way I'd been staring at mine. I set the phone down and drew in a deep breath. I had no idea what I was going to say to her... but I had two days to figure out exactly how to tell her I was in love with her.

Thirteen

~~

CLAIRE

As soon as the final bell rang, I waited for the students to disperse from the hallway, then I headed to the main office at the front of the campus. Mrs. Knowles waved at me. "Hey, Claire."

"Hey." I smiled. "Is Jeff in?"

"I believe so," she acknowledged with a small nod. "I'm surprised you're still here," she joked. "No big plans for the weekend?"

The team had another away game, and I still had no idea whether Gray planned to come over tonight or not. A few weeks ago, I would have considered it a given. Now I felt like I was walking on eggshells. Although he'd texted to ask me about breakfast tomorrow, he'd said nothing else. I still hadn't decided whether that was a good thing or not. Didn't men typically take women out to a public place to break things off? Even though we weren't technically together, this could be his version of putting distance between us.

Pasting on a small smile, I shrugged one shoulder. "You know me. I'm pretty much a homebody."

Mrs. Knowles grinned as she shut down her computer and gathered her things. "Nothing wrong with that."

"Have a good weekend." I waved, then headed down the hallway to the principal's office.

Jeff was on the phone when I paused in the doorway, and he gestured for me to enter. I took a seat across from him and waited for him to finish up his conversation. Once he hung up, he turned a smile my way. "Claire, what can I do for you?"

"Just checking in to see if we'd heard anything on Trent Jones."

He tipped his head to one side. "Impeccable timing. I just got a notification about half an hour ago that he tested out." He riffled through some pages on his desk before handing a paper to me. "Looks like we won't be seeing Mr. Jones again."

I skimmed the paper in my hands detailing Trent's scores as he was awarded a GED and released from the school system. I was both relieved and disappointed. I knew it was exactly what I told him to do, and it was undoubtedly in his best interest. Still, I couldn't help but worry for him. I passed the paper back to Jeff. "What will he do now?"

He laid it aside and laced his fingers over his stomach as he leaned back in the chair and regarded me. "That's not really our concern."

"But you know how his home life is," I pushed. "What is he—"

"Look, Claire." Jeff cut me off with an abrupt shake of his head. "I know you're worried about him, but Trent Jones is no longer enrolled at Cedar Springs. Your job is to help kids within the district, not every stray from a broken home."

His words stung, though I recognized the truth behind them. They weren't going to pay me to chase down a kid who wanted nothing to do with receiving help or advice, no matter how badly I thought he needed it. I swallowed back the emotion clogging my throat. "I understand."

Jeff seemed to sense the conflict brewing inside me, and he sighed. "I feel bad, too, and I know you just want to help. But it's out of our control."

I nodded. "Thanks for letting me know."

"Hopefully we can enjoy some peace and quiet around here now." He smiled wryly, and I forced myself to return it as I stood.

"Well, that was all I wanted." I shot him a half-hearted wave. "Have a good weekend."

"You, too."

I headed back to my office, a strange sensation welling in my chest. I wasn't entirely sure what was bothering me, exactly. Maybe it was because I wanted to see Trent face-to-face and ask him about the phone calls. A deeper part of me recognized that I wanted to make sure he was okay.

I waved to a few teachers gathered in the hall gossiping, then ducked into my office. I still had some grant paperwork to finish up, and it wasn't like I needed to rush home for anything, so I settled back at my desk for another half-hour. Once I was done, I grabbed my things then locked up and headed out to the parking lot.

The situation with Trent weighed heavily on my heart and mind. The phone calls had continued to plague me sporadically for the past week, but even those weren't as terrifying as they'd been. Often the caller remained silent on the other end; sometimes it was the maniacal laugh I'd heard last week. But nothing else had happened, and I assumed it was more a scare tactic than anything else. At this point, I was positive it was Trent. Why he'd chosen me, I wasn't quite sure, but it was nothing I couldn't handle. He'd need an outlet to vent his rage and injustice at the world, and until he'd come to terms with it, I had to stay calm.

Just yesterday he'd called as I was getting out of the shower. I'd heard the familiar heavy breathing and decided it was time to address it head on. I'd called him by name, offered to let him talk to me. His only response was to slam the phone down in my ear. As unsettling as it was, I was still worried for him. I felt like we made progress at our last meeting, and I wished we'd had more of an opportunity to discuss it further. But as Jeff had said, Trent was no longer my concern. Unless something else happened, I was just going to leave it alone.

I probably should have told Gray about the phone calls and the recent issues with Trent, but something had stopped me. And not only because things were so tumultuous between us right now, but because I knew Gray would flip his shit if he found out Trent had been harassing me. It was dumb to protect him, but I couldn't help it. He wasn't hurting anyone, and if a few phone calls were the worst that happened, then so be it. He'd eventually move on and everything would go back to normal.

That didn't fix my issue with Gray, though. Tomorrow was Saturday, and I had no idea what I was going to say to him. I'd conjured a thousand different scenarios in my mind over the past two weeks, but I hadn't settled on a single one. Should I tell him how I felt, or was it better to play it cool and pretend everything was fine? I hadn't expected him to reach out to me after last weekend, and I wasn't at all sure where we stood. Maybe it was better not to get my hopes up and feel my way through it before I made any rash decisions.

Lost in thought, I opened the back door of my car and dumped my bags on the back seat, then climbed into the front and headed home. I'd just passed the Beaumont's farm when a strange sound drew my attention. Ears on alert, I turned the radio down a couple of notches to hear better. A soft hissing noise filled the cab, and I eased off the gas, trying to decipher whether the sound was coming from the engine compartment or inside the cab. Several seconds passed with no suspicious sounds, and I fiddled with the controls for my heat and air conditioning before I finally heard it again—that same soft hiss, like air escaping a hose.

A tickling sensation feathered across my ankle, and I automatically reached down to scratch it before my eyes were drawn to the floorboard. Something dark occupied the space next to my feet, and my heart jumped into my throat as I recognized the scaly pattern on the snake's back. A scream suspended itself in my throat as I yanked my feet up to my seat. Dimly, I was aware of the car weaving wildly, and I clenched the wheel to bring it back under control.

Reluctant to put my feet back down, I shifted into a crouch instead and allowed the car to coast for a minute, all the while keeping one eye on the snake just a few feet away. I couldn't tell if it was venomous—not that it mattered. A snake was a damn snake.

Eager to get away from the snake, I shifted the car into neutral. The tires bumped along the berm as it began to slow, and I whimpered as the snake tensed and coiled. No longer caring about what happened to the car, I tossed a quick look in the rearview mirror. The road around me was empty, and I made a split-second decision. The car had slowed significantly thanks to the terrain, so I took a deep breath and braced myself before throwing the door open and clambering out.

The momentum carried me forward, and I crashed to the pavement. Instinct kicked in, and I tucked my arms in close to my body as I tumbled awkwardly before coming to a stop. Shaking off my fear, I climbed to my feet and took quick stock of my body. Despite the fall, nothing hurt too badly. My palms were a little sore from catching myself on the pavement, and I wiped them on my pants to remove the tiny rocks and debris that had embedded itself in my skin. Everything else seemed to be okay.

My entire body trembled wildly as I turned my attention back to the car and watched as it slowly rolled to a stop a hundred feet away. God, I hated snakes. The door had closed behind me, thank goodness, so the snake was at least contained inside. Another shiver racked my body as I approached, then peered in through the driver side window. How had the snake gotten in there? Better yet, how the hell was I going to get rid of it?

I threw a glance around the empty road and bit my lip. Was there some kind of animal control for this? I remembered Gray telling me that the police often showed up first, then contacted whoever was necessary to remove them. That was all well and good, but my damn phone was in the car. With the snake.

At the moment it was curled up on the floorboard near the pedals, and I watched for several seconds. So far the snake had stayed in place, so it was now or never. I rounded the car and cautiously opened the back door on the passenger side, half-expecting another one to be inside. I swept my gaze over the back seat and floorboards, but everything seemed to be clear. The snake still hadn't moved.

Keeping it in my line of sight, I reached inside. With one eye on the wretched animal, I felt around the back seat until my fingers found the strap of my purse. I quickly yanked it out, then breathed a sigh of relief as I closed the door again. Overly cautious, I used my fingertips to open my bag, half expecting something to jump out at me. I couldn't help the hysterical laughter that bubbled up when I found my purse empty of critters, and I pulled out my phone to dial Cedar Springs Police department.

"Mackenzie," one of the men answered on the third ring.

"Hey, Mac." My voice shook, and I fought to bring it under control. "It's Claire Gates."

I briefly explained what had happened, and he promised to send someone out within a couple of minutes. True to his word, less than ten minutes later a cruiser pulled up, followed immediately by an unmarked black car.

Andrew Thorne unfolded from the driver seat and cast a concerned glance my way. "Claire? Is everything okay?"

"Um..." I bit my lip. "I'm not entirely sure."

I gave him a brief rundown of the debacle with the snake, and he eyed me shrewdly. "I think maybe you should come into the station and tell me everything."

I sighed, my stomach twisting into a knot as I imagined Grayson's disappointment. "I was afraid you would say that."

Fourteen

≈

GRAY

SHOCK ROOTED MY FEET TO THE FLOOR, MY BODY numb with disbelief. What the fuck was going on?

"Don't freak out," Drew murmured next to me.

I wasn't quite sure when he'd appeared by my side; I'd been too preoccupied watching Claire be marched into my station. His warning didn't help. I whirled on him. "What the hell happened?"

I stared after her, still not quite believing my eyes. Why in Christ's name hadn't Claire called me if she needed help?

"She's fine," my brother reassured me. "She just had a little trouble today, is all."

I tensed, and fury seethed into my voice. Whatever it was, whoever it was, they'd have to answer to me. "What kind of trouble?"

"We're still figuring everything out."

I was pissed that he knew more than I did, not to mention a little betrayed. I was closer to Claire than anyone. Or so I thought. She avoided my gaze as Mac led her into the small interview room off the bullpen, and it served only to increase my ire. I was moving before I realized it, and a firm hand on my shoulder halted my steps.

"Relax," Drew ordered. "You can't go in there like this. You really shouldn't be in there at all."

I opened my mouth to blast him, but he shook his head. "Come on, you know how this works, even here. You're too close to her; it's a conflict of interest."

I knew that, and yet... I had to know. "I'm not leaving her in there alone."

Drew studied me. "Fine. But let us handle it."

I nodded once, unable to form words. My head still spun as I followed him into the room and took up residence in the corner. Acutely aware of my presence, Claire turned slightly. She bit her lip as she glanced at me beneath her long, dark lashes, her eyes filled with guilt. It was like a stab to the chest, and all of my doubts from the past week came rushing back. What the hell was she hiding from me, and why?

My brother seated himself opposite her. "Claire, can you please explain what happened today?"

My fists clenched as she tossed another surreptitious look my way before speaking, her voice trembling. "I... I stayed late to catch up on some work, then left school about an hour after my normal time—"

"That's where you work, right?" my brother prompted her.

She gave him a blank look. Of course he knew that, but she seemed to understand that he was gathering as many details for the report as possible, so she clarified. "Yes. Sorry. I'm the guidance counselor at Cedar Springs High School. I was on my way home and—"

"What time did you leave?" Mac interrupted.

"I..." Her lashes fluttered, and she stammered over her words, flustered.

I tensed and started to step forward to stop this charade,

but my brother held one hand low in my direction. I forced myself to bite back a growl as I returned to my corner like a fucking dog on a leash.

Claire flicked a glance my way, then immediately dropped her eyes back to the table in front of her, a red flush sweeping up her neck and into her face. "I think right around 4:00, I can check."

Drew nodded and waved off her offer to check. "That's fine."

Claire took a deep breath. "Anyway, I was driving home when I thought I heard something. I wasn't sure what it was. I remember turning down the radio, thinking it was maybe my engine or something. I..."

She paused and licked her lips, seemingly lost in thought. "Nothing seemed out of the ordinary so I kept going. Then I felt it. It brushed my foot and I—"

My entire body went rigid as she broke off, her face pale with fear.

"What was it?" my brother asked softly.

She swallowed hard. "A s-snake."

My molars snapped together in fury as Claire wrapped her arms around her waist. "I... I don't remember exactly what happened next. I kind of freaked out when I saw it. I jumped out of the car and slammed the door."

"How did you contact the police?" Mac asked.

Claire rubbed a shaking hand over her temple. "I... I always keep my purse in the back seat. I saw the snake was still in the front so I went around the car and opened up the back door, then grabbed my purse."

Inwardly I seethed. She was fucking lucky she hadn't wrecked trying to get away from it. I knew how terrified she was of snakes.

"Any idea how it may have gotten there, or who might have put it there?"

Claire's honeyed eyes flicked my way, and a chill ran down my spine as she slowly shook her head. "No. I'm not sure."

She was lying. Panic and something else clutched at my throat as I stared at her. What the hell was going on?

Drew didn't seem to notice because he continued to speak. "Sometimes they get in all by themselves, but we'll keep your car overnight and take a look just in case."

Claire nodded, looking lost. "Okay."

My brother glanced up at me before voicing his next statement. "We'll give you a ride home."

She blinked. "That's okay. I'll call—"

"I'll take care of it," I cut in.

Her gaze snapped to mine, then quickly slid away again. No fucking way was I letting her walk out of here without an explanation. One way or another, I was going to figure out what the hell was going on.

Dread etched into every line of her body, Claire stood slowly, still doing her best to avoid me. I held the door, and she paused before brushing past me.

"Be careful," my brother warned low in my ear. "Don't do anything stupid."

I suspected he hadn't been ignorant of her lie, either—he'd chosen to let me handle it instead. I nodded but didn't say a word as I left the station, Claire trailing a step behind me. I didn't touch her. I couldn't. I was terrified that if I touched her I'd be tempted to shake some sense into her, demand she explain why the hell she hadn't said a word to me. Either that or pull her close, wrap my arms around her and never let her go.

She followed me out to the car where I held the door for her as she climbed inside. I slammed it harder than necessary and caught her flinch through the passenger window. Good. She needed to know I was pissed at her. I rounded the car and slid inside, then cranked the engine. We'd just pulled onto the main drag when she finally broke the silence.

"Gray—"

I held up one hand with a shake of my head. Wrapping my hands around the wheel I stared straight ahead, concentrating on the road instead of the woman at my side. I felt her open her mouth as I turned down the road that would take us to my house instead of hers. I threw a look across my shoulder at her, and she immediately snapped it closed again. Her eyes dropped to her lap, her fingers nervously twisting the hem of her shirt.

I still wasn't sure why she hadn't said anything to me, but one thing was for damn certain. I wasn't letting another day go by without telling her exactly how I felt. If that was the end of us, then so be it, but I couldn't stand it anymore. And when I told her, I wanted to be on my turf.

A few minutes later I pulled into the garage and parked. We climbed from the car in silence, the only sound the whine of the garage door opener above our heads. Fury coursed through my body as I led the way into the house. I was still so fucking angry with her. But more than that, I was disappointed she hadn't come to me. Was she protecting someone? And if so, who? Why would she lie about this, especially when it was something that had obviously terrified her?

I was trying so hard not to blow it out of proportion. I felt ultra-protective of Claire, and I wanted to care for her. I wanted her to depend on me, but I couldn't do that if she continued to withhold information from me. She knew I would've jumped at the chance to help her. Would she really rather shoulder that burden than come to me?

The question escaped my mouth before I could stop it, and tears welled up in her whiskey eyes, stabbing into me like a knife. "I didn't want to bother you. And, honestly..." She bit her lip, her gaze sliding away for a moment. "I didn't want you to know."

I stared at her, baffled. Anger bubbled in my veins. "Why the hell not?"

"Because." She licked her lips and shifted uncomfortably. "You'd charge in and take over."

A scowl pulled at my mouth. "What's wrong with that?"

"I can't let you do that forever." She gestured wildly with her hands. "What happens when you aren't around one day?"

I shook my head. "Won't happen."

"How can you be so certain?" Her eyes, huge and liquid in her pretty face, pleaded with me to understand. "Things have felt so different between us recently, and..." She broke off and bit her lip like she'd said too much.

The way she'd looked at me, eyes full of guilt and... Desire? Need? Was it possible she felt the same way I did? My heart kicked up in my chest.

"Claire." I closed the distance between us and smoothed one thumb over her cheek. "Let's get one thing straight. I will always be here for you."

She blinked up at me and swallowed hard. "B-but..."

Sliding my hand backward, I threaded my fingers through her hair and cupped the back of her head. "Always."

Her breath came in stilted pants, her chest lightly brushing mine each time it rose and fell. Desire overrode common sense, and I saw myself moving in slow motion as I leaned in. Unable to stop myself, I brushed my lips across hers. I pulled back a second later, studying her face.

Her eyes were wide, her mouth slack as she stared at me. "You kissed me."

Was that an accusation? I couldn't tell. "Yeah. I did."

She blinked once. Twice. "Why?"

"Because I've been waiting two years to do that." I tightened my hold on her hair, and she swayed slightly toward me. Eyes locked, I stared down at her. "You have five seconds to tell me no, that you don't want this, too."

I could practically see the dozens of questions flickering behind her eyes. Her lips parted, then snapped shut again.

Three...

Her eyelashes fluttered, her chest rising and falling as she inhaled deeply, a tiny shudder rolling through her body.

Two...

My heart raced in my chest as she blinked up at me from beneath those long lashes, her gaze hooded.

One...

I curled my fingers into her hair and angled her head up to meet mine. "Time's up."

Fifteen

CLAIRE

His mouth descended on mine, stealing the breath from my lungs. The first kiss had been soft. Tentative. Sweet. This kiss was wild and raw, his mouth claiming mine. I opened to him as he slanted his lips over mine, and his tongue swept inside. My legs felt weak, and my brain buzzed as everything around me dulled and fell out of focus. Gray was all I could see, all I could taste. He consumed me, his tongue exploring every inch of my mouth as he locked an arm around my waist and pulled me even closer.

He felt so damn good. It was just like my dream—only better. I lifted one leg and his huge hand wrapped around my thigh, angling me upward so his erection pressed the soft spot between my legs. A groan escaped my mouth at the feel of him, and Gray's fingers curled into my flesh as he let out a growl. "Christ."

Suddenly, I found myself being lifted into his arms, his hands curled around my upper thighs as he moved toward his bedroom. I wrapped my arms around his neck and sought his lips again, drunk on his kisses and needing more. His hold shifted to my bottom and tightened, and he nipped my lower lip. I let out a little mewl of pleasure and curled further into him, locking my ankles together at the base of his back.

I loved this feeling. The way he carried me so effortlessly made me feel small and protected, yet powerful at the same time. Raking my fingers through the short strands of hair at the back of his neck, I rubbed my core against his erection pressing firmly into my belly. I couldn't slow down; I didn't want to. I was terrified that at any moment he'd pull away and come to his senses. I wanted every second with him that I could get.

Swept away by a desire I'd never experienced before, I swooped in for another kiss. His tongue swept inside my mouth, tangling with my own, and heat spiraled through me. Everything around me disappeared until it was only the two of us. Every cell of my body was on fire, tingling at the sensation of Gray's strong fingers pressing into my flesh, the flavor of him bursting across my tongue. The hardness of his muscles. The heat emanating from his skin. The way my nipples tightened with need as they scraped against the fabric of his shirt. There were so many tiny details to catalog that my brain couldn't process them all.

Gray never paused as he shouldered his way through the door to his room, then strode to the bed. We tumbled to the mattress in a tangle of limbs, our heaving pants the only sound filling the room.

"God, you're so beautiful." His words came out low and throaty, and heat pooled in my core. "I can't tell you how long I've waited for this."

Lowering his head, he trailed kisses over my cheek and chin before covering my mouth again, and I fell headlong into the kiss. It was fierce and needy, and his tongue stroked over mine, dipping, tasting, teasing. I moved my hand under his shirt, sliding my fingers over his scorching flesh. He was so hot and hard everywhere; I couldn't wait to feel him against me.

His hand dropped to cup my bottom and I pressed further into him with a little moan.

Gray propped himself on an elbow and stared down at me, eyes sparkling with desire. My breath caught in my chest and my tongue tied, rendered speechless at the sheer need I saw there.

"Gray...?" I bit my lip. There were so many things I wanted to ask him. What would happen next? What if we hated it? What if this changed everything?

Seeming to sense the insecurity swirling in my stomach, Gray lifted one hand and framed my face. All the words that had sprung to the tip of my tongue dissolved away as I stared into those gorgeous eyes of his. For a long moment, he remained silent, and I held my breath as he lightly traced the arc of my cheekbone with his thumb.

"I want you." His eyes burned into mine, clear and true. "You are the only woman I want—the only woman I'll ever want."

Ruthlessly his mouth met mine again, stealing the words from my lips. His hands roamed over my torso, sliding along the curve of my hip and up to my breast. His long, strong fingers delved into the cup of my bra and found the tight peak of my nipple. Already over-sensitized, I almost came off the bed when he tweaked it between his thumb and finger.

Gray chuckled, the raspy sound sending an erotic vibration through my body and straight to my core. He rolled the taut tip once more before abandoning it, and a tiny mewl of protest bubbled up my throat.

"I've got you, sweetheart."

Lips never leaving my own, his hands coasted down my body to the button on my jeans and popped it free of its hole. My chest jerked as I sucked in a breath. Gray soothed away my worries as he caressed my belly, each sweep of his thumb taking him closer and closer to where I really needed him.

Finally—*finally*—he dipped beneath the fabric of my panties. One finger found my folds, and the world around me dimmed as I clutched at him. Even with that tiny touch, my body wanted to fly apart.

Gray circled and stroked along my slit but never breached my entrance. Frustration and desire pulled at me, and I lifted my hips. I needed more. I needed him deep inside me. I needed this to never end.

At the same moment, his control finally snapped. Gray broke the kiss only long enough to pull my shirt over my head, immediately followed by his own. I wrapped my arms around his neck, holding him close as his tongue delved into my mouth once more. He didn't give me the opportunity to speak again, his kiss leaching every bit of sense from my brain. It was the only thing I could focus on—the only thing I wanted to acknowledge. It was better than anything I'd ever experienced. Maybe it was because I wanted it so badly. Maybe it was because Gray knew me so well, seemed to know exactly what I needed. But deep down, I knew there was more to it. Because I was absolutely, one-hundred-percent head over heels in love with him.

Hooking his fingers inside the waistband of my jeans, he shimmied them down my legs, taking my underwear with them. I pulled one foot free, then the other. He dropped them to the floor and I felt his body lift away from mine as he used one hand to unsnap his own pants and shove them off.

Gray settled his huge body over me and finally lifted his head from my mouth. His male hardness brushed the inside of my leg and I sucked in a breath. One hand swept over my hair, then cupped the side of my face. "God, baby, you're so beautiful."

His eyes left my face and traveled down to my breasts. I should have been embarrassed that I was completely naked in front of him—but I couldn't dredge up the effort to care. He lifted a hand and reverently brushed the pad of his thumb over my nipple, sending a shockwave of awareness humming through my body. I curled my hands into his shoulders, my nails digging into the sensitive flesh. I knew it had to hurt him, but I couldn't let go. I felt like if I did, he would slip right through my fingers and disappear. I wanted this to be real, wanted him so much that every cell of my body ached with longing.

"I can't tell you how long I've been waiting for this. I want you so bad I can't stand it." Gray kissed the slope of my breast, and I shifted my hips beneath him, trying to urge him on. The head of his cock brushed my folds, and we both froze.

A low growl rumbled from his chest, and a blast of cool air hit me as he abruptly sat up. Reaching into the nightstand, he withdrew a condom, then quickly rolled it on. In seconds he was covering me again, fitting his mouth to mine. As his tongue danced with mine, he mimicked the motion with his hips, swirling them so his arousal bumped my sensitive folds again. A sticky moisture coated the space between my legs, and I knew there would be little resistance. Wrapping my legs around his waist, I silently encouraged him.

Lining himself up with my entrance, he pushed gently. I was so wet that the broad head breached my core, and my muscles clung to him, urging him deeper. Gray rolled his hips and surged forward, seating himself fully inside me with a deep thrust. Simultaneously we hissed in a breath. He filled every inch of me, and it felt absolutely delicious. Better than I ever imagined. My inner walls contracted, eagerly accepting him, holding him tight.

"Goddamn, Claire. I can't..." He looked down at me almost regretfully, his voice full of urgency. "I need you. *Now.*"

"Please, yes," I begged. I wanted anything, everything he'd give me. I tugged his head back down for a kiss just as he pulled out a fraction and shoved back in. The tip of his cock hit my cervix and he swallowed the low moan that ripped from my throat. He repeated the action, each slow grind pushing me closer and closer to the edge. I felt the stir of fire low in my belly and on the fourth long, hard stroke I shattered in his arms with a scream. Black spots danced before my eyes as I flew apart, heat rolling through my body.

Sixteen

GRAY

THIS WOMAN WAS GOING TO BE THE DEATH OF ME. Every muscle in my body was pulled taut, and fire lapped at my nerve endings. I thrust into her hard and fast, and little gasps left her mouth every time the tip of my cock bottomed out. I rolled my hips and she let out a little moan as my pubic bone brushed her clit. I felt her inner walls pulse with the remnants of her orgasm, and her fingers curled into my lower back, urging me on. Fuck, I loved this feeling. I loved *her*.

It took everything in me not to spill inside her the second the words flitted across my brain. I wanted to make our first time good for her, even if it killed me. Claire whimpered as I pulled out, and I gritted my teeth against the sensation of loss that hit me like a punch to the gut. I forced myself to take a deep breath, focusing on anything other than the blood pulsing in my groin, my cock practically begging not to stop.

Locking my arms and steeling my resolve, I leaned down and brushed my lips over hers. Claire's hands roamed up and down my back, her fingers pressing into my flesh at intervals, urging me to come back to her. One knee lifted to bracket my hips, and I cupped her ass, holding her away from me. If I let the heat of her wrap around me, it would be over.

Sliding my palm up her thigh I leaned back and pressed a kiss to the inside of her knee. She wriggled restlessly, her lips pressing together as if biting back her pleas to stop teasing her already. Teasing wasn't my intention; I was trying to prolong the moment, but it was fucking torture the way her heat and scent wrapped around me, swamping my senses. She was so damn soft and warm, I wanted to melt into her. I lowered her leg back to the bed then pressed a kiss to her belly. Her muscles retracted at the sensation and she shivered as a thousand tiny goosebumps sprouted over her pale flesh.

I loved that I could elicit that kind of reaction from her. She may have been able to withhold her feelings for me, but her body didn't lie. I noticed every tremor, every hitch of her lungs, the rapid tempo of her pulse beating at the base of her throat. Each increased the powerful possessiveness flowing through my body until I felt ten feet tall. I wanted to draw her into me, keep her there forever, imprint her on my soul.

Dragging my lips across her body, I kissed my way over each rib then up to the curve of her breast. I flicked my tongue over the tight bud, and Claire arched, her hands sinking into my hair. I licked and sucked and nipped at her, the fire in my groin coiling and leaping until it raged into a full-fledged inferno. My cock instinctively found her entrance, and I slid inside on a deep, hard thrust.

Her teeth sank into my shoulder, and I hissed at the sudden bolt of pain that shot through my body. It immediately melted away and turned to pleasure, and my cock swelled. "Fucking hell!"

I drove deeper, harder, plunging into her so fiercely the headboard slammed into the wall. Claire's chest heaved on breathless pants and she dug her head into the pillow, her face screwed up in an expression of tortured pleasure. I sank into her willing body over and over until her mouth opened on a silent scream, her sheath convulsing around me as she came.

"Fuck!" Curling my hand into her waist, I pistoned hard until my internal thermometer reached fever pitch. Fire licked over my nerve endings in a wave of heat and lust, and I let go, allowing it to consume me. A groan welled up my throat and I came harder than I ever had before.

Another tremor racked my exhausted muscles, and I dropped my head to the crook of her neck. My body vibrated with remnants of desire, and sweat slicked our flesh. Sealed together, our hearts raced and our lungs heaved as the world around us slowly began to return to focus.

Before I met Claire, emotion wasn't something I associated with sex. It was enjoyable, yes, and I cared for the women I'd dated in the past. But not like Claire. There was a distinct difference between having sex and making love, and what we'd just done definitely fell into the latter category. It was never like this with another woman and I knew it never would be. I didn't ever want to sleep with another woman again. Deep down, I knew none of them would compare to the woman in my arms. I loved her so fucking much it hurt.

I rolled slowly to my back, pulling Claire with me until she was settled against my side, her head nestled on my shoulder. One hand rested on my chest, and I lightly rubbed my thumb across her knuckles as we lay there in the silent, dim light of the early evening. With each minute that passed, I felt the tension in Claire's muscles increase. I wasn't sure where her head was at, but the absolute last thing I wanted was for her to pull away from me. I was tired of secrets, tired of hiding my feelings from her.

I bent forward slightly and kissed the top of her head. "Are you okay?"

She nodded but didn't speak. I wasn't sure if that was a good thing or not. Silence fell for a moment as I gathered the courage to continue. "These past two weeks have been the worst of my life."

I could tell from Claire's stillness that I'd gotten her attention. "Not being able to see you. Hold you. All I've wanted to do is tell you how I feel, how I've felt ever since we met."

Ever so slowly her head tipped up to mine. "Really?"

Her eyes fluttered closed as I dropped a kiss on her forehead. "Of course. I've always wanted you. I was just waiting for you to feel the same."

Those soft whiskey eyes blinked open and stared up at me. "I had no idea. You never said..."

She trailed off, and I squeezed her fingers. "I wanted to give you space. If being friends was all you'd wanted, I would have done it for you."

She nodded a little, her gaze fixing on a space off to my left. "I... I didn't know how to tell you," she admitted quietly. "After that morning, it just kind of hit me all and once, and..."

She bit her lip, stalling the flow of words, and I lightly coasted my fingers up her arm as I pulled her closer. "I was stupid jealous when I saw you all dressed up to go out last week."

Her eyes flicked to mine. "I'm sorry, I—"

I swept my thumb over her bottom lip, halting her words. "It wasn't your fault. My mind automatically jumped to the worst-case scenario, and I lost my shit. Those first couple of days were rough." A mirthless laugh escaped my throat. "Drew finally told me to pull my head out of my ass and just tell you how I feel."

"I'm glad you did," she whispered.

I stared down at her, and the urge to tell her just how much she meant to me hovered on my tongue. But Claire was still adjusting to this new facet of our relationship, and I didn't want to add any more strain. One day soon I'd tell her that I'd loved her for years. But for now I just cuddled her close, loving the feel of her next to me.

"Me, too."

Seventeen

CLAIRE

I FELT THE WARM PRESS OF LIPS AGAINST THE BACK of my neck, the heat and smell of Gray wrapping around me like a cocoon of comfort. Except this time it wasn't a dream. Gray's lips slid along the shell of my ear. "I've been waiting forever for you to wake up."

Drifting between wakefulness and sleep, I curled into him, loving the way he enveloped me so fully. A little sigh of contentment fell from my lips as I snuggled closer to Gray. One huge hand left its place on my bottom and skimmed along the curve of my hip then higher to cup my breast. He kneaded the soft globe, his thumb and forefinger finding my nipple and rolling it into a tight peak. I arched into his touch, a tiny moan filtering from my mouth as an electrical current shot straight to my core.

His knee pressed into the back of my leg, urging it forward so I was open to him. His hand skated downward, along the curve of my hip then over my bottom. I sucked in a breath as his fingers ventured even lower and skimmed over my slit. I could feel the moisture pooling there already, and Gray's appreciative hum confirmed it. He teased me with light, small circles until I was writhing with need. His teeth nipped my shoulder, and I jerked as he sank his fingers deep inside me. A shriek hovered on my tongue, and I buried my face in my pillow to stifle it.

His hot skin slid over mine as he maneuvered over me, his lips moving in a tortuously sensual path over the back of my neck. The bristle of his five o'clock shadow ignited tingles of desire that zipped down my spine, and I shivered at the sensation. The hard shaft of his cock slid between the cleft of my bottom, and I sucked in a breath, hips arching of their own volition to get closer. His heavy weight smashed me into the mattress, his heat consuming me. The sheets rasped against my sensitive nipples, and I bit my lip as the head of his erection brushed the folds of my entrance.

I whimpered softly, and Gray chuckled. "I'm going to like waking you up this way every morning."

A thrill of pleasure sparked through me. "Every morning?"

"Every morning," he confirmed.

It took my sleep deprived brain a moment to realize I'd spoken out loud. "But..."

I gasped as Gray bit my ear, and he sank an inch inside as my hips bucked upward.

"Are you on the pill?"

I nodded, all the words I wanted to say lodging in my throat. There was a brief pause, and I thought I heard him mutter "damn." But I didn't have time to process it as he slid the head of his cock along my folds. Our groans mingled as Gray's hands fisted in the sheet next to my head seconds before he thrust hard and deep. The stroke took my breath away, and I shifted beneath him, urging him on. He set a sensually slow pace, and heat licked along my skin. He felt so hot and hard and heavy pressed against my back, giving me no space, controlling every movement. My nipples brushed the sheet with every thrust, and the simmering fire in my belly grew until I could barely stand it.

"Please," I begged. "Oh, God, Gray..."

"What do you want, sweet girl?"

"I need..." I sucked in a breath as he slid particularly deep. "I'm so close." I whimpered. "Please..."

"Huh uh," he taunted, never breaking stride. "I've got a lot of time to make up for. You might never leave this bed." He nipped my ear again. "I'm going to fuck you for hours."

"Yes," I pleaded. "Oh, God, yes. Fuck me, Gray."

My words came in pants, his huge body restricting my breathing. "I need to come. Please!"

His left hand curled under my chin and turned my face to meet his. His mouth closed over mine with brutal force, his tongue stroking and sweeping over mine. His other hand slid around my hip and between my legs. A broken mewl welled up as his fingers brushed over the sensitive bundle of nerves. His cock hit a place deep inside me just as his fingers pinched my clit, and I couldn't help the scream that left my throat. My inner muscles clamped down on him and Gray moaned as he picked up the pace, thrusting harder and deeper. On the fourth pass, he growled and came hard.

Braced on his elbows over me, his rising chest brushing my back with every deep, panting breath, I couldn't move. Couldn't think. But I'd never felt better in my entire life. I grinned, turning my face into the pillow to hide it. But Gray didn't miss a thing. He never did. One huge hand swept my hair over my shoulder and he gently turned my face to his. "Good?"

"Very."

His lips grazed my temple as he withdrew, then rolled me to my back. A tiny smile quirked his mouth. "Damn, babe. It wasn't supposed to be over that fast."

"I didn't mind." I slid my fingers into the hair at the nape of his neck, gently massaging his scalp. Somehow, I was both wide awake and exhausted, and I wished we could just lie here and live in this moment forever. The weight of Gray's body suspended over me felt delicious as it pressed me into the mattress. It made me feel protected, claimed in a way, and I never wanted to give that up. I wished I could stay right here, with him, forever.

Gray's smile slid away as he stared down at me. His fingers sifted through my hair as he studied me, and suddenly I felt incredibly self-conscious. He must have sensed it because his hand cupped my face and he met my gaze. "Christ, you're so beautiful."

The sentiment took my breath away, and I barely had time to process his words before his head lowered and his lips brushed over mine. This time the kiss was slow and sweet, absolute perfection as he made love to my mouth, seducing me with brushes of skin on skin.

Eighteen

GRAY

A SHEEN OF SWEAT COVERED MY BODY, AND HEAT rolled off of us in waves as I cuddled Claire close. I kissed her temple, stroking one hand up and down her arm, wishing we could stay here forever.

Claire's stomach rumbled, and I smiled as I glanced at the clock. Just in time for our weekly breakfast. I dropped a kiss on her spine, loving the way she curled into me. "Come on, pretty girl. Let's get you fed."

Besides, we had a lot to talk about, and if I kept her in bed I might never get around to it. As it was, it took nearly half an hour to get ready, but that was mostly because I couldn't keep my hands off her. Any time Claire was even remotely near I was overcome with the urge to touch her, to pull her in for a kiss. I loved her more than I thought possible, and I wondered how much longer I could wait to say those words. She knew, she had to. Those three little words hovered between us, just waiting to be said.

Once we finally made it to the café I held the door for Claire, then settled a hand low on her back as we stepped inside. Her muscles bunched beneath my fingers, and I swept my thumb along her spine in a comforting motion before dropping it away. We hadn't discussed the evolution of our relationship yet this morning—hadn't discussed much of anything that didn't include the words *more, harder,* or *don't stop.*

I knew she was still adjusting to everything, but I wasn't going to act like nothing had changed between us. Because everything had changed. I couldn't get enough of her, especially not after last night. A huge part of me wanted to lift her right off her feet, toss her over my shoulder, and carry her back to bed. I wanted to drown in that skin-to-skin connection between us. She was everything I'd dreamed of and more.

That train of thought brought to mind something that had been buzzing at the back of my brain for the past several days. I still wondered about her dream, the one she had before fleeing from me. The events of that morning had driven us apart, and I couldn't help but wonder if the dream had been the catalyst. While I'd blamed myself, it seemed she'd been doing the same. Did she feel guilty about the dream? Is that why she'd stayed away?

Making a mental note to ask her, I led the way to our favorite booth—the one with the movie poster from *The Wizard of Oz*, Claire's favorite movie—then urged her in. Once she was settled, I slid in next to her. Claire glanced over at me, her eyes wide with shock and surprise. I'd always sat across from her. But that was before. Now that I had her where I wanted her, I wasn't letting her go.

I glanced up as Emery headed toward us, drinks in hand. We were that predictable couple—the ones who ordered the same thing each weekend. And just as we always ordered the same thing, we'd always kept our distance as the bounds of friendship dictated.

Emery's eyes widened slightly, her smile growing as it

dawned on her that I was seated beside Claire today. Undoubtedly she could sense the shift between us; she'd been waiting on us for the past year and a half she'd been working here. Emery was also Izzy's best friend in the whole world, and I knew that she'd be reporting back to my baby sister the first chance she got. I flashed her a quick look, silently conveying not to say anything to embarrass Claire.

She set Claire's sweet tea in front of her with a bright smile, then delivered my chocolate milk and water. "The usual for both of you?"

"Yes, please."

She tipped her head. "You got it."

Once she was gone, Claire eyed my chocolate milk with mock disdain. "I still can't believe you drink that stuff."

"What's wrong with chocolate milk?" I defended as I lifted it to my lips and took a sip.

She shook her head, lips turned down in dismay. "The big bad chief of police drinks chocolate milk. How masculine."

I snorted. It had been a running joke between us since we'd known each other. Each week I ordered chocolate milk, and each week she teased me that it was the least manly drink ever. I set the glass down with a clink. "Milk is good for you. Lots of protein. Besides, I need to replenish after last night."

I slid my hand along the inside of her thigh, and Claire jumped. Her breast brushed my arm, turning my blood to fire. I remembered exactly the way she felt and tasted as I'd run my tongue over every inch of her, and I couldn't wait to do it all over again.

I traced tiny circles along the inside of her knee, her skin silky soft under my fingertips.

"What are you doing?" Claire grabbed at my hand, but I refused to let go.

"What?" I feigned innocence as I kicked my feet up on the

booth across from me and settled in. "Not like anyone can see anyway."

She bit her lip but stayed silent, and I studied her from the corner of my eye. Last night things had been perfect between us. But the moment we'd stepped into public, everything had changed. She'd withdrawn, pulled away from me, and I hated it. It occurred to me that maybe she was afraid of her feelings, afraid of our relationship changing. The more I thought about it, the more it made sense. I'd never been particularly good at beating around the bush, so the words came out before I'd even thought about what I was going to say.

"Tell me about your dream."

Claire froze, eyes glued to the faux wood grain of the tabletop. "What?"

Her voice was tight, her tone wary, and I knew I'd hit a sore spot. I bit the inside of my cheek to keep from smiling. "Remember a couple weekends ago when we woke up together?"

Her gaze flitted around the room, on the lookout for anyone who might be listening in. "Mhmm... What about it?"

"You seemed restless. I thought you might be dreaming."

Her fingers twitched nervously, but she lifted one shoulder in a casual shrug. "If I was, I don't remember it."

Liar. "Huh. Because I could have sworn you moaned my name, then—"

"Yes." Her voice rose several octaves as she cut me off. She glanced around, checking to see if anyone had noticed her outburst before clearing her throat and continuing, this time much more quietly. "Yes. I might have been... dreaming."

I bit back a smile. "About me?"

She glared up at me, eyes flashing with fire. "Dreaming about smacking some manners into you, maybe."

I couldn't hold back my grin this time. I loved when she

got all fired up. "You sure? Because I thought when you started groping me, you said—"

"Shhh!" She hissed at me like a rabid raccoon, her mouth set in an angry scowl. "Fine! You win." She threw her shoulders back defiantly. "I may or may not have dreamed about us... kissing."

I waited a beat. "And?"

Her cheeks flushed bright red. "And... other stuff."

Interesting. I dipped my head close to her ear and I skated my fingers along the inside of her thigh until I reached the hem of her shorts. "Like maybe some of the stuff we did last night?"

Her breath hitched as she shifted, and she licked her lips. "Maybe."

"Hmm..." I studied her for a second, debating just how far to push her. "What would you do if I kissed you right here in front of everyone?"

Her eyes widened, then darted around the room before returning to mine. "You wouldn't."

"Why not?" I tipped my head to one side. "Because it would bother you?"

"N-no," she stuttered. "It's just, I mean, everyone would think..."

She trailed off, looking conflicted, and disappointment flared to life deep in my chest. Was she embarrassed to admit we were together? Or was it something that ran deeper, tied to her past and her reasons for not wanting to date? One of these days I'd get that out of her, too.

"You're worried about what everyone will say when they find out we're dating?"

"No," she said stoutly. But the line between her brows belied her words.

"You think they don't already know I'm crazy about you?" Her eyes lifted to mine. "You think they haven't been watching me like a hawk every step of the way, waiting to see if we'd finally get together?"

Her mouth parted but no words came out.

"Because I guarantee you they have. They're watching us right now." I didn't tear my gaze from hers, didn't bother to look around the room. I could feel their gazes on us when they thought we weren't watching, the way they did each time Claire and I went somewhere together.

Her teeth sank into her bottom lip, and her cheeks flared red as her gaze skimmed the room. Claire swallowed hard and pulled the small container of sugars close. She riffled nervously through the packets, ordering them by color.

I laid a hand over hers, stilling her movements. "What are you so afraid of?" I asked softly.

Claire's eyes were haunted when she glanced up at me. "I keep waiting for you to come to your senses." Her gaze dropped to our hands. "I don't want to disappoint them when..."

"Sweetheart." I turned toward Claire and cupped her chin, then waited until she lifted her eyes to mine. "Forget about them. And forget whatever ridiculous thoughts are going through that pretty head of yours. I've already come to my senses. I told you how I feel—how I'll always feel about you.

"The second I laid eyes on you, I knew you were special. You were standing there in that blue sundress, and the first thing that caught my eye was that smile of yours. It lit up your entire face, made everyone around you smile, too. That was all it took; I couldn't stay away from you. I had to meet you."

I swept my thumb over her cheek, then continued. "Then we got to talking, and I found out that you were just as beautiful on the inside as you were on the outside."

A watery smile lifted Claire's lips, and I wrapped one hand

around the back of her neck. "I just want you, Claire. Always. I don't care about anyone else."

I pressed my lips to her forehead, and my heart swelled when Claire melted into me. I held her there a second longer than necessary before breaking contact. Progress was progress, even if it was one baby step at a time.

The moment was broken when the sound of approaching footsteps reached my ears, and Emery delivered the food to our table. "Can I get y'all anything else?"

"No, thanks." I offered a little smile. "I think we're good."

Claire kept her head down, gaze focused on her plate, and we ate in silence for several moments. I couldn't delay the inevitable though, and when she finally pushed her plate away ten minutes later, I turned toward her. It still bothered me immensely that she hadn't told me she was having troubles, and I needed to get to the bottom of it sooner rather than later. "I need you to tell me what's going on."

Claire sighed like she'd just been waiting for me to ask. "I'm not entirely sure. I've been getting phone calls, but—"

The hair of the back of my neck stood on end. "Phone calls? From who?"

Claire picked up two packets of sugar and built a tiny tent. Almost immediately, they fell over and she repositioned them. "Trent, I think."

"Trent?" Red crept into my vision. Who the hell was Trent?

The sugar packet tent collapsed a second time and Claire lifted her face to mine. "He's a student—was a student," she clarified. "He got kicked out a couple weeks ago, but..."

"You think he has something to do with this," I surmised.

"Maybe. I don't want to think the worst of him, but... he's troubled."

"Explain." My tone was harsh, and I looped an arm around her shoulder when she flinched.

"His parents are going through a pretty bad divorce. He's been lashing out, getting into fights... One of the teachers—Melissa—she's the one I met at Mason's last week, remember?" She tipped her head up to me for confirmation, and I nodded. "She says he threatened her. That was two Mondays ago."

She paused and bit her lip for a second, her gaze sliding away. I hated that look. It meant there was more to the story, and whatever the hell it was, it wasn't going to be good. "What happened?"

"He got expelled that very morning. I thought it would straighten him out, but..."

An almost unholy rage started low in my gut and began to grow. "Tell me about the phone calls."

"They started last week." She bit her lip. "I think Thursday. At first, I just thought it was a wrong number. But then Friday morning I was getting ready to leave for work, and..."

A delicate shudder racked her body, and I tightened my hold on her the tiniest fraction. "What happened?" I asked softly.

"I had just stepped outside when my phone rang. I didn't think anything of it, I just answered. The other end was quiet for a second, then he said, 'I see you.'"

My throat tightened, and I balled one hand into a fist. He'd been watching her, knew where she lived. It didn't come as a real surprise, considering it was a small town and her address was listed, but it bothered the hell out of me anyway.

"And the snake?"

She turned a guilty gaze on me. "So, here's the thing..."

Claire explained all about the photograph missing from her office, the tarantula that had been left in her desk, and the snake from yesterday. By the time she finished, my blood was practically boiling. I swore to God, if I ever got a hold of Trent Jones, I was going to throttle him.

Claire laid one hand on my thigh and threw a beseeching gaze my way. "He's just acting out."

"That's way past acting out," I seethed. "He's technically a fucking adult, and he knows better."

"Go easy on him. Please," she insisted, giving me that look she knew I couldn't resist. "Nothing has been outright harmful. He's just seeking attention."

I breathed deeply, willing myself to calm. She was partially correct. The snake that had been dropped into her car yesterday was nothing but a harmless black snake. Still. I was going to nail his ass to the wall if—*when*—I found him. And until I did, Claire would be safer with me.

"Come on." I nudged her shoulder with mine. "Let's go home."

I slid from the booth, then helped Claire out and settled one hand on her hip. I wasn't sure how Claire would handle the display of affection, but she hadn't objected yet so I was taking that as a good sign. I waved to the café's owner, Irene, as we headed for the front door.

Irene graced us with a smile. "See y'all later."

Her gaze dropped to my hand on Claire's hip, and a broad smile stretched her face. I pressed my lips together to contain my own grin, because *damn*, it felt good to be able to touch my girl in public. I wanted everyone to know she was mine, that she would never belong with anyone but me.

Nineteen

CLAIRE

I SHIFTED NERVOUSLY, MY HEART THUNDERING IN MY chest, the steel door in front of me looking like a portal to the gallows. It didn't matter that I'd been here dozens of times before; this was the first time I'd been at the Thornes' house since I'd slept with their oldest son. My face gave everything away; they would take one look at me and know. Oh, God. My stomach twisted, and bile rose up the back of my throat. I couldn't do this.

"You can do this." Gray's voice floated over my shoulder, seeming to read my thoughts. The tips of his fingers pressed ever so gently into my lower back, silently urging me forward.

"What if they freak out?" I whirled toward Gray and searched his gaze. "You know how bad I am at keeping secrets. Your mom is going to take one look at me and..." I trailed off, the words jamming in my throat.

His thumb swept along the curve of my waist, a silent reassurance. "Baby, it's going to be fine."

My heart pattered rapidly at the endearment. In all the time we'd been friends he'd never once called me by anything other than my name. But Gray had slid so easily into this new role, calling me baby or sweetheart, and it sent my head spinning. It didn't seem real. Sometimes I wondered if I pinched myself if I'd wake up to find this all a dream. I wanted so badly for this to be real, for him to love me the way I loved him, and I was terrified that he'd change his mind. He would see that we were better off as friends. Because family meant everything to Gray.

I already knew Drew was wary of me; I could see it in his eyes every time he thought I wasn't looking. And if the rest of his family didn't approve of us dating, I had no idea where that would leave us.

My stomach clenched again and my expression must have reflected my thoughts, because Gray lifted one hand to frame my face. "This is no different than the other times you've been here. It's just lunch, just my family."

I lifted a brow. "Except now we're sleeping together."

"There is that." Gray grinned, his fingers sliding through my hair so he could massage the base of my scalp. My eyes fluttered at the sensation. I loved when he did that. He was so strong, but his touch was so gentle, so reverent. "Trust me," he urged quietly. "They love you. Nothing will change that."

I drew in a deep breath, then slowly blew it out as I met his gaze. He was right. I couldn't change it; if they didn't approve then I would just have to deal with it as it happened. I nodded. "Okay."

He winked and gave my neck a little squeeze before dropping his hand away to open the door. I braced myself as he turned the knob and called out, "We're here!"

Chatter came from inside, and I seemed hyperaware of everything around me as we moved deeper into the house. His mom and sister bustled around the kitchen, and I tensed as their gazes flitted to mine.

"Hey!" Izzy offered a quick grin before turning her attention back to the pie crust she was preparing.

"Hi, honey." Gray's mother, Vera, tilted her cheek up for a kiss, and he obliged.

"Hey, ma."

She flashed a smile my way. "Hey, Claire! Glad you could make it this week."

I tensed, the smile freezing on my face. Before I had a chance to come up with an excuse to explain my absence for the past couple of weeks, she continued. "How's your sister? You should invite your family to lunch one of these days."

Some of the tension seeped from my muscles. The Thornes were loving and accepting, a stark contrast to the household I grew up in. "I'll check to see when Jane and Dex are both free."

"Do that." She nodded, then glanced at her son. "Gray, Aiden is here today. He and Drew are in the den."

Gray's hand slid surreptitiously along my waist, silently asking if I was okay. I met his gaze and gave a tiny nod, and he slipped away to go see his sergeant.

I turned to Vera. "Is there anything I can help with?"

She used her elbow to nudge the salad bowl my way. "If you could make the salad, that would be great. Thank you."

I gradually began to relax as she and Izzy made small talk, drawing me into their conversation about Izzy's school and the upcoming holidays and small-town drama. While they chatted, my thoughts drifted to Gray. I knew he desired me, knew he cared for me.... but was he thinking about forever the way I was?

Izzy popped the pie into the oven, then we gathered the food and carried it to the dining room.

"Come and eat!" Vera called.

She settled in her place opposite her husband, Wyatt, and everyone fell in around them. Izzy waited until Aiden slid into a seat across from me, then dropped into the chair next to him. "Hey, Aiden."

He nodded. "Hey."

"How's everything going?" she asked as she spooned a serving of green beans onto her plate.

"Fine."

He threw a suspicious look her way, and I pressed my lips together as I studied them. Typically they bickered like brother and sister, but there was a strange dynamic between Aiden and Izzy today. She was overly polite and sweet, and Aiden watched her throughout the meal with narrowed eyes.

The roast was almost completely gone before Izzy dropped her bomb. "I'm thinking about getting married."

A chorus of protests rose around the table, everyone clamoring at once to speak.

"How long have you even known this guy?" Drew practically yelled. "You just told us about him last weekend!"

Wyatt looked worried, her brothers looked positively murderous, but Vera barely batted an eyelash. "That's nice, honey. You should invite him for dinner next weekend if he plans to be part of the family."

"I think I will," Izzy said at the same time Luke and Drew both exploded.

"Ma! How can you say that?"

"She can't marry someone she just met!"

Izzy lifted one shoulder, looking completely unperturbed. "You can if it's the right person."

Beside Izzy, Aiden sat in stunned silence, a red flush sweeping over his neck and cheeks. I watched as his hand clenched into a tight fist before he pressed his lips into a flat line. Interesting.

Vera leveled a quelling look at her sons. "That's enough. Isabella is a smart young woman." She turned to Izzy. "I'm sure you've put a lot of thought into this."

"I have," Izzy replied cheerfully.

"Well, there you go," Vera replied, as if the entire matter

had been settled. "The heart wants what the heart wants."

"That's right." Izzy threw a dazzling smile at her mother, who remained unruffled, a placid smile on her face.

I had to give it to Vera—she was slick. While the men hadn't quite gotten the memo, Vera could read her daughter like a book. She knew that pushing back would only make Izzy want to disobey more, so she'd done the exact opposite and sided with her. Of course, that didn't change the fact that Aiden was practically apoplectic while Izzy just stared at her plate, a secret little smile playing along her lips.

Gray slid one hand under the table and settled it in my knee, a frown on his face as he studied his sister. I wondered if he saw what I saw; Izzy had a crush on the older man. And if I wasn't mistaken, the feeling was mutual. I was almost positive that marriage to this new man she spoke of was just a ploy to capture Aiden's attention—and he'd fallen for it hook, line, and sinker.

A tense silence fell, the only sound in the room the scrape of silverware against porcelain. Once everyone was done, we carried our plates into the kitchen. Aiden stormed out of the house, Drew and Luke hot on his heels, and Wyatt retreated to the living room.

"Guess no one wants pie today," Izzy said as she cut into it, a tiny smirk playing at the corners of her mouth.

I bit back a laugh. Even though she was the baby of the family, she wasn't naïve. She knew exactly what she wanted and how to get it. I almost felt bad for Aiden. He was in for a world of trouble with that one.

"At least one thing went well today," Vera commented wryly. She pressed a covered dish of pie into my hands, then pulled me in for a hug and spoke low next to my ear. "I'm happy for you two."

Stunned, I couldn't form words. I guess she'd noticed the change between Gray and me after all. She pulled back to study me, hands gently curling into my shoulders. With another smile she released me, and Gray settled a hand on my hip. "See ya, ma."

He guided me to the car, then we headed back to his place. The drive was silent, and Gray seemed a thousand miles away. When we were finally seated on the couch, I turned to him. "You okay?"

"I don't know." His brows drew together. "I'm worried about Izzy."

I considered my words before speaking. I believed that Izzy had a crush on Aiden—who happened to not only work under Gray, but was one of his best friends. "She has a good head on her shoulders. I'm sure she'll do whatever is best."

He pondered that for a second. "This whole marriage idea of hers is a sham."

When I opened my mouth to speak, he lifted a hand to stop me. "Last week she brought him up over dinner, but when she and I were talking afterward... I don't know. I got the feeling she was talking about someone else entirely."

"Oh?" I didn't have anything clever to say to that.

He nodded. "She said he was older and asked me if the age difference would be a problem."

Oh, jeez. That sounded a lot like Aiden. I bit my lip. "Maybe she's afraid of what everyone will say."

Gray met my gaze. "She's in love with him, isn't she?"

I froze, pinned in place by those intense hazel eyes of his. My heart raced. If I brought it up and was wrong, I could potentially burn a bridge with Izzy. If I was right... Well, I didn't want to think about what might happen between Gray and Aiden. I was between a rock and a hard place, and I had to make a decision quickly. Affecting my most naïve expression, I tipped my head to one side. "Who?"

One dark brow arched toward his hairline, and his lips flattened into a thin line as he regarded me. "You know I do this for a living right? That innocent little face of yours doesn't fool me."

I rolled my lips together, fighting the urge to smile, and Gray sighed. "I'd hoped I was wrong, but after seeing them together..."

So he *had* noticed. "How do you feel about that?" I asked quietly.

"Hell, I don't know." Gray shook his head. "Aiden's a great guy. But Izzy's... Damn. She's just so young."

"She is," I agreed. "But she's been trailing after all of you for years. She's used to your friends, and I think she genuinely likes Aiden."

"That's the problem," he said dryly as he dropped his head back against the couch. "She'll probably make his life hell."

I grinned. "I don't think he'd mind."

Gray rolled his head toward me. "What do you think?"

I leaned into him, and he looped his arm around my shoulders, pulling me close. "I think they need to figure it out on their own. They both seem to have their own reservations, so maybe they just need some time to work through it."

He smiled down at me. "Like you? Finally got tired of me chasing you?"

I couldn't help but grin. "It took a minute, but I finally caught up."

Gray cupped my chin and tilted my face up for a soft, sweet kiss. "I would have waited forever if that's what you needed."

"I'm glad it didn't come to that."

His hand slid down the column of my neck and gently wrapped around my throat. "Me, too."

His mouth fitted to mine, then pressed me backward as he maneuvered over me. Thoughts of Aiden and Izzy forgotten for the moment, Gray and I lost ourselves in a haze of pleasure, doing our best to make up for all the time we'd lost.

Twenty

GRAY

THE LITTLE SHIT HAD GONE TO GROUND. OVER THE past two days I'd checked every place Trent Jones typically frequented. I'd spoken with his parents, but both had denied seeing him for more than a week. Apparently Trent had lied to them and said he was staying with the other parent instead. Mr. Jones didn't seem to be too concerned; he was confident Trent would show up when he was good and ready.

Trent's mother was a different story. Once she'd finished crying, she'd screamed at me for no less than half an hour, demanding I find Trent and bring him home safely. It was incredibly ironic, considering she hadn't been concerned with his absence until I'd alerted her to the fact. People never ceased to amaze me.

I pressed my lips into a firm line as I retreated from the house and climbed into the cruiser. They were so wrapped up in their own drama that neither had bothered to check on their only child. I was beginning to understand Claire's perspective when she said that Trent was just misunderstood, a product of selfish, asshole parents.

I'd also checked his closest friends' homes, to no avail.

None of them had seen Trent since he'd been suspended almost two weeks prior. On a whim I'd stopped by his ex-girlfriend's house yesterday afternoon, but she denied hearing from him either. A growl of frustration bubbled up my throat as I cranked the engine and headed back toward the station. He was eighteen with no job; he had to show up sooner or later.

If the snake had been dropped into Claire's car during school hours, it was entirely possible that Trent had snuck onto school property to leave it for her. He fit in with the other kids, definitely fit the profile. Unless they knew he'd been suspended, no one would question seeing him there. Coupled with the missing photograph, the tarantula in her desk, and the creepy phone calls, it seemed pretty cut and dried. No wonder Trent had continued to lie low; he knew he was in deep shit.

I was two blocks from the station when my phone rang. Fishing it out of my cupholder, I glanced at my dispatcher's name lighting up the screen. No doubt it was something JoAnn didn't want to disclose over the radio. I swiped the screen and lifted it to my ear. "Thorne."

"Hey, Chief. We just got a call for a 1083 out on Vestra."

Damn. I grimaced. I hated deaths. "Details?"

"Landlord called it in and said the woman hadn't responded for several days. Went to check on her and found the door unlocked. She's inside."

"All right, I'm on my way. Have all available units meet me there, and please give the ME's office a call—see if Doc Davison's available."

"You got it." JoAnn hung up, and I released a sigh. Living in a small town like Cedar Springs our calls tended to be mostly domestic disputes or traffic citations. But death was unavoidable. I didn't bother with lights or sirens as I checked the mirror then whipped the car around and headed toward the west side of town. The landlord met me outside in the parking lot. If I hadn't recognized him at first, the sickly greenish hue tinging his skin would have been a dead giveaway.

"Hey, Lloyd." I knew most of my residents at least by sight, and Lloyd Alcott was a regular at The Village Café where Claire and I had our weekly breakfast. He tipped his head my way as I climbed from the cruiser and approached. He looked like he still might cast up the contents of his stomach, so I stayed several steps away. "You good?"

He nodded shakily. "Yeah, sorry. Just..." His gaze shifted away for a second. "First time seeing something like that."

I understood that completely. It was hard for first responders to experience death firsthand, let alone civilians. I'd always felt terrible for the people who found their family members dead, even if it was expected.

I pulled out the small notepad I kept with me. "Can you tell me what happened?"

He shrugged. "Jessica is a good tenant, always pays her rent on time. She was ten days late, so I went up to check if she was there."

I glanced at him. "You opened the door?"

Lloyd rubbed one hand over his face and nodded. "Yeah. Sometimes people skip out, so I check to make sure the place is clear."

"Whose name is on the apartment?"

"Jessica Cartwright."

"What do you know about her?"

Lloyd lifted one shoulder. "Like I said, she's a good tenant. Pays on time, don't hear much from her."

I nodded. "You see anyone around lately?"

"No one that stuck out." He shook his head. "She's had gentlemen over from time to time, but they've never caused a ruckus."

"That's helpful, thanks." I shut the notepad and stuck it in my pocket. "Where is she?"

"Upstairs." He pointed to the apartment in the corner. "Number 2F."

"Thanks." I tipped my head at him. "You touch anything?"

"Just the door handle. As soon as I opened it, there was this smell..."

He looked like he might gag, so I waved him off. "I'll take it from here. Send the others my way as soon as they get here."

Lloyd nodded gratefully then escaped back to his office. I popped the trunk and pulled on a pair of clean gloves from the box I kept inside. I gathered my kit, then climbed the stairs to the apartment. The stench hit me before I'd even reached the doorway, burning my nose and eyes. I paused to open my kit, and I applied a tiny bit of ointment to my upper lip in an attempt to block the smell.

Sweeping my gaze over the interior of the apartment, I paused to pull on shoe coverings, then stepped inside. There didn't appear to be any damage to the knob, but I was careful not to touch it anyway. I wanted to keep any potential prints as intact as possible. The apartment was a one-bedroom efficiency with a combined kitchen and living space. Dishes cluttered the countertop, and clothes and blankets cluttered the loveseat that sat beneath the window.

I cautiously made my way down the hall toward the bedroom, keeping an eye out for any potential evidence. The stench became stronger the farther I ventured into the apartment, almost overwhelming in its intensity. I paused in the doorway and braced myself for the grisly scene that I was sure lay ahead. I wasn't disappointed. My stomach twisted as I took in the woman lying naked on the bed, the purplish hue of her skin a stark contrast to the white bedspread beneath. Her eyes stared unblinking at the ceiling, and a trail of dried fluid clung to her jaw and pooled on the pillow under her head.

There was a portable air conditioning unit in the window, but it unfortunately wasn't running. The air inside the bedroom was hot and humid, and the woman's body was already in a severe stage of decomposition. The stench was almost stifling, and I fought the urge to gag.

The hum of engines rose in the air, and I gladly used the diversion to escape for a moment. Once everyone was gathered in the small apartment, I began to give directives. "We need to dust for prints—doors, windows, everything. Look for anything else. Fibers, hairs, lift anything you see."

They nodded my way, then dispersed to begin their collection. A new face in the doorway drew my attention, and I lifted a hand in greeting. "Hey, Doc."

Dr. Danielle Davison nodded my way. "Chief. What have we got this time?"

I apprised her of the details as she fell into step next to me. "Female, early- to mid-twenties. Landlord found her this morning and called it in."

We stopped in the doorway, and she took a moment to assess the scene. "Has anyone been in here?"

"Only me." I shook my head. "I haven't touched her, didn't even go near the bed."

"Thank you." She snapped on a pair of gloves, and I took that as my cue to step back and shut up so she could go about her work. She approached the bed carefully and perused the young woman for a moment. "Hard to pinpoint time of death considering the humidity, but I'd say she's been here a couple of weeks."

Damn. "What's your initial assessment?"

Davison made a little sound in the back of her throat. "I don't like to make any assumptions until I've fully examined the body, but..." She pointed to the fluid that had escaped the woman's mouth. "Combined with her state of undress, my guess would be overdose. I suspect we also might find evidence of sexual assault."

I grimaced. "I was afraid you might say that."

Her clear blue eyes met mine. "You had an incident involving sexual assault recently, yes?"

I nodded. "Unfortunately. Think they might be related?"

She shrugged. "Too early to tell. We'll run a tox screen and go from there."

I had a horrible feeling we'd just found our second victim. Or, depending on the condition of the woman's body, perhaps our first victim. We needed to get a positive ID and start running leads sooner rather than later. I didn't want the tiniest detail to slip through the cracks. If this was the same person, I wanted to nail his ass to the wall.

She removed forceps from her bag and lifted a hair from the woman's torso. A rap on the doorjamb drew my attention, and I found my brother's laser-like gaze focused on me. "Find anything?"

"Not yet." I shook my head as I approached. "Victim is Jessica Cartwright. Lloyd found her this morning and called it in. Said her rent was past due, and she wasn't responding."

He swore softly, then sighed. "I'll need to inform the family."

"Want me to go with you?"

"Nah." He waved off my offer. "You've got enough going on here. I'll take care of it."

He disappeared, and I turned back to the crime scene in front of me. It was going to be a long ass day.

Twenty-One

CLAIRE

GRAYSON HAD TEXTED EARLIER IN THE DAY TO LET me know that he would be tied up with work for most of the evening. He told me to head straight to his house after school, and he would meet me there once he was done. He'd seemed distracted and hadn't elaborated, and I hadn't asked.

Despite knowing Gray was busy, I checked my phone one last time just in case. There were still no notifications, no updates, and I repressed a sigh as I stowed it in my purse, then locked up my office and got ready to leave for the day. The students had long since vacated the premises, running for the hills as soon as the final bell had rung. A few teachers and staff lingered now, but even most of them had gone home, too. I put it off as long as possible, doing all the work that needed to be caught up on since I had no reason to rush home.

It was a little strange to think of Grayson's house as home, but I was becoming more comfortable with that every passing day. We were slowly merging our lives, and I had to admit it felt incredible. Some nights we stayed at his house, others we stayed at mine. It didn't matter where we were; Grayson was home for me.

I waved to one of the biology teachers as I pushed out the side door and headed toward my car, scanning the parking lot. My eyes immediately landed on the police cruiser a few spaces down from my sedan, and a tiny smile curled my lips. Though I tried to talk him out of it, Grayson had insisted on sending a patrol unit to watch over me until he got home. I thought it was a little excessive, but he insisted on ensuring my safety and keeping me protected at all times. He would always put my welfare ahead of anything else, including his own, and I couldn't even be mad about that.

Through the windshield of the cruiser, Vaughn caught my gaze and lifted a hand my way. I waved in greeting, and the driver side window rolled down as I approached. "Hey, Claire."

"Hey," I returned. "So you're the lucky one who gets stuck with me tonight?"

"You know I don't mind." He smiled. "You headed straight home?"

I briefly considered stopping at the grocery store, but the thought of having a police officer follow me around felt strange. I quickly dismissed the idea. "Yep. Gray asked me to meet him at his house."

"No problem." Vaughn started the engine and tipped his head my way. "You go first, and I'll be right behind you."

I stored my belongings in the back seat before starting my car and pulling out of the parking lot. The drive was short and uneventful, and fifteen minutes later I pulled into Grayson's garage. By the time I'd gathered my things, Vaughn had already backed into the driveway and was climbing from his car.

He tipped his head toward the house. "Just want to do a quick cursory check."

I barely refrained from rolling my eyes. Gray was so over the top sometimes. Personally, I didn't think anyone was stupid enough to try to break into a cop's house just to scare me, but my objections weren't going to stop either one of them. I gestured with one hand. "Be my guest."

I closed up the garage, then preceded Vaughn inside. I didn't bother to follow him around as he checked the windows and doors. Once he was done, he met me back in the kitchen. I wasn't entirely sure what time Gray would get home, but he'd told me to go ahead and have dinner without him.

I glanced at Vaughn. "Are you hungry? I'm going to make something to eat."

"No, thanks." He shook his head. "I'm good."

"Okay, just let me know if you need anything."

Vaughn disappeared, presumably to take up his post outside, and I locked up behind him. I took my time washing off my makeup and changing into shorts and a tank top before heading back downstairs to scrounge up something to eat. The next several hours slipped away as slow as molasses. The house felt too quiet, too still without his larger-than-life presence. It was a strange situation I found myself in. Even though we were closer than ever, it didn't sate my desire to see him and spend time with him. If anything, I wanted more. I ached to have him with me, wanted him there to eat with, laugh with... even just sit in the comfortable silence together.

All through dinner I listened with half an ear for his car to pull into the garage, but it never came. I flipped on my favorite home renovation show in an attempt to distract myself, but I couldn't help the niggle of worry and anticipation swirling in my stomach. I wanted to see Gray, wanted to make sure he was okay. I peeked out the window a couple of times, like in doing so I might magically conjure his presence. Once I'd even picked up my phone, tempted to text him. But the rational part of my brain had me putting my phone away. Vaughn would have told me if something was wrong, and I didn't want to bother Gray when he was busy.

Finally, I flipped off the TV with a sigh and curled up on the couch. No matter what time he got home, I'd be right here waiting for him.

Twenty-Two

GRAY

I PULLED INTO THE GARAGE AND PARKED, THEN scrubbed the tiredness from my eyes. Today had been long as hell, and all I wanted to do was go inside and wrap myself around Claire, lose myself in her for the next several hours before passing out. I rapped on the passenger side window, and Vaughn greeted me from inside.

"How'd everything go?"

I crossed my arms over my chest and leaned my hip against the door. "We'll know more once Doc Davison finishes up the autopsy, but preliminary findings suggest she was drugged and assaulted."

Vaughn swore. "Think it's the same guy?"

"Certainly looks that way." My lips pressed into a firm line. "I hope we find this asshole before any other women show up in my office."

Or dead, but I left that part unspoken. Vaughn seemed to understand because he nodded. "You good for the night?"

I nodded. "Anything happen while I was out?"

"Nope. Everything was still locked up when I got here, and it's been quiet ever since."

"Good." I stepped back and rapped my knuckles on the roof of the car. "Thanks for staying, I appreciate it."

"No problem, boss. See you in the morning."

Vaughn left, and I made sure the garage door was closed before entering the house. Everything was quiet and still inside, and I wondered if Claire had already gone to bed. I toed off my boots, prepared to head upstairs, but I froze in my tracks when I saw Claire curled up in the corner of the couch.

Unbidden, a smile lifted my lips as I studied her. She was the sweetest thing I'd ever seen, and I wanted to spend the rest of my life with her. Although we hadn't talked about anything permanent yet, I knew exactly what I wanted. Soon I would ask her to be my wife and the mother of my children. I didn't want to go another single day without her by my side.

She looked like an angel in the moonlight streaming through the sliding glass door, and I felt an almost unnatural pull to her. I silently approached the couch and dropped to a knee. One hand was tucked beneath her cheek, the other curled into a loose fist, her breath leaving her parted lips in deep, even sighs. A lock of hair had escaped her messy bun, and I used my index finger to draw it across her forehead and tuck it behind her ear. Claire's lashes fluttered and she stirred slightly at the gentle touch but didn't wake.

I both loved and hated that she was so naïvely innocent. My body was trained to be awake and alert at the slightest stirring of movement, yet Claire slumbered on even with me right next to her. Protectiveness came naturally to me, but I was acutely more possessive of Claire. I wanted to lock her away, keep her safe from all the evil in the world.

I brushed the pad of my thumb over her cheek, then dragged the backs of my knuckles down her jaw and across her shoulder. Claire shifted and let out a sleepy little sigh of protest that made me grin. "Wake up, beautiful."

Her eyes popped open, flitting around the room in

confusion for a moment before landing on me. "You're home."

The sound of that word on her lips sent tendrils of heat curling through me. I loved that she thought of me and my house as home. "Yeah, baby, I'm home. How was your night?"

Claire struggled to a sitting position, then smothered a yawn before speaking. "Quiet. Boring without you." Her eyes flicked to the front of the house before meeting my gaze again. "Did Vaughn already leave?"

I nodded. "I sent him home as soon as I got here."

"Oh, okay. I was going to offer him some leftovers earlier, but I fell asleep."

I maneuvered onto the couch, then lifted Claire into my lap and cuddled her close. She had the biggest heart of anyone I knew. "You don't have to feed my guys."

"I know," she assured me, "but I don't mind. I felt bad that he didn't get a chance to eat all evening. I invited him in for dinner, but he wouldn't hear of it."

A tiny flicker of jealousy flared to life low in my gut at the thought of Claire and Vaughn eating dinner together. No doubt that was precisely why he stayed in the cruiser. I couldn't stand the thought of my girlfriend and another man alone in the house together, despite the fact that he worked for me and I knew Claire would never stray. There wasn't a doubt in my mind that every person on the force knew exactly how I felt about her—they knew I would do anything for her.

Had Vaughn been alone inside with her for several hours, there almost certainly would've been streams of gossip tomorrow. Claire saw the world through rose-colored glasses, though, and I didn't have the heart to tell her that the more mean-spirited people wouldn't hesitate to rip her to shreds.

I traced tiny circles along her upper thigh, inching my way beneath the hem of her tiny pajama shorts. It was a damn good thing Vaughn hadn't stayed. I would have killed him if he'd gotten to look at her like this.

I closed my eyes for a second and breathed her in, allowing the heat and scent of her to calm me. The second I touched her, felt her skin next to mine, everything stopped. The world slowed until it was just her and me, the way it was meant to be.

Threading my fingers through her hair, I tipped Claire's face up to mine and took her lips in a hard kiss. It was rougher than normal, and she sucked in a breath as I curled my fingers into the flesh of her bottom. I was impossibly hard, my cock straining against the fabric of my dress slacks. The thin material was not at all forgiving, and I knew she could tell how ready I was for her. She shifted in my lap, rubbing against my erection, and I bit back a groan.

In a flash, I twisted so she was flat on her back staring up at me. Her eyes flared wide for a second before her tongue darted out and licked her lips. She looked unbearably sexy, and I couldn't wait another second to have her. I hooked my fingers in the waistband of her shorts and dragged them down her legs, taking her panties with them. She wrestled her shirt off and tossed it to the floor while I attacked my clothes and settled between her thighs. "You miss me?"

Her fingers curled into my biceps as she pulled me down to her. "You already know the answer to that."

I grinned. "Good."

I lined up the head of my cock with her folds, then plunged deep inside her. Claire arched under the sensation, her taut nipples brushing against my chest. "Fuck, baby..." I dipped my head and kissed her. "You feel so damn good."

Her eyes closed almost to slits, and her nails cut into my shoulders as she grasped at me. The horror of this afternoon still pressed in on me, and the slight bite of pain helped to ground me. Life was such a fragile thing. Things could change in the blink of an eye, and all I'd been able to think about all evening was Claire and how much she meant to me. Watching her stirred all the pent-up emotion deep inside me, and I couldn't hold it back anymore. I couldn't let one more second pass without telling her how I felt. I knew it was a fucking terrible time to say it, but...

"I love you."

Her eyes popped open, searching mine, and her lips formed a small 'O' of surprise. I continued to love her, thrusting in and out with slow, deep strokes as I watched her study me. "I've loved you since the second we met. I knew then that you were meant for me."

Her lashes fluttered and she bit her lip for a second before speaking. "And now?"

"Now I'm never letting you go."

I took her mouth in a hard kiss, and she returned it with equal fervor, tongue stroking over mine as she curled her body into mine, giving every bit of herself to me. I set a fast pace, unable to savor the moment. I stroked in and out, over and over, until she fell over the edge, my name a sharp cry on her lips. I came three deep thrusts later, spilling deep inside her. I could still feel the faint fluttering of her inner walls as her orgasm trailed off, and I glanced down to where she and I were connected. For just a second I allowed myself to imagine her all pretty and pregnant with our baby. The faster I could make her mine, the better.

A sense of contentment and something far more intense welled up inside me, and I took a moment to get myself back under control. I petted her hair away from her face and kissed her lips, this time lingering, keeping it slow and sweet. Her eyes were closed when I finally pulled back, her cheeks flushed, her lips curled into a tiny smile. The love I felt for her swelled until I felt like I might burst. "I missed you too, baby. Every single second I was away."

She ran a hand up the back of my neck and slid her fingers

through my hair. Her eyes turned soft and liquid as she stared up at me. "How did I get so lucky to find you?"

I wanted to soothe all of her fears but I knew it would just take time. She was still playing catch up and needed to adjust to the shift in our relationship. I'd give her some time to come to terms with it. Not a whole hell of a lot though, because I knew Claire better than she even knew herself. She was going to lose her mind when I asked her to marry me, but I wouldn't let her say no. She might fight me and tell me it's too soon, that I haven't fully thought it through. But what she didn't realize was that I made this decision a long time ago. I'd waited years for her. There was no way in hell I was letting her go now.

I shook my head. "I'm the lucky one."

She just smiled that sweet smile of hers, and I slowly pulled out of her, hating that lost connection. I slid my hands under her back, then shifted Claire into my arms and carried her to the bedroom. I climbed into bed and she automatically curled into me, tucking her head into my shoulder and throwing one leg over mine. Her hand rested over my heart, and I kissed the top of her head as I covered her hand with mine.

Claire shifted slightly, melding herself to me, and I could practically feel the contentment emanating from her. My body and mind finally began to relax with her by my side. All the bad shit could wait until tomorrow.

Her chest rose and fell on deep, even breaths, and I was half asleep myself before I heard her speak, so softly I almost missed it.

"I love you, Gray."

Twenty-Three

CLAIRE

THE VIBRATING OF MY PHONE DREW MY ATTENTION, and I pulled open the drawer to take a peek. Dread curdled in my stomach at the sight of the unknown number flashing across the screen. It had been nearly a week since I'd gotten one of these calls, and I'd hoped that Trent had given up. Apparently that wasn't the case.

Tapping the button to ignore the call, I made a mental note to tell Gray about it later. I wasn't sure what to do about him. I didn't want to file a restraining order, but at the same time, this whole thing was getting out of hand. I replaced the phone in my drawer and pulled out my lunch bag, then began to unpack it.

A soft knock on my door drew my attention, and I found Melissa peeking in, a sheepish smile on her face. "You busy?"

"Not at all." I set down the sandwich I had just unwrapped and waved her in. "I was just getting ready to eat."

She held her hands up in supplication, her own lunch bag swinging from her wrist. "It's okay, I don't want to bother you."

"No, really. Come on in."

Melissa came in, then sank into the chair across from me. "Sorry," she apologized again. "I don't know too many people yet, and the teachers' lounge is a little overwhelming."

I nodded empathetically. "I completely understand that. Sometimes it's nice to have a little peace and quiet." I made small talk as we dug into our sandwiches. "How's everything going so far?"

"Good." She grinned. "Mac and I went out again this weekend."

"That's awesome!" I hadn't spoken with her since the middle of last week, so I hadn't had a chance to catch up on all the gossip. "You seem happy."

"I am," she admitted. "He's really sweet, and we have a lot in common."

"I always kind of got that vibe from him," I said. "I'm really glad that worked out for you."

"Me, too." She opened a bag of chips, then popped one into her mouth and chewed before continuing. "I feel like I'm finally getting the hang of things around here, too. I—" She cut off abruptly when my phone vibrated again from inside my desk.

"Sorry." I quickly silenced it, then placed it face down beside my computer and gestured for her to continue.

"Oh, it's okay." She smiled. "I was just wondering how everything has been with you. You seem... different."

Was it that obvious? I felt heat sweep up my neck, and I cleared my throat. "Well... Remember that guy I told you about?"

"Chief Thorne, right?"

I couldn't help but laugh. "Yeah. That's him. We've started... dating."

I wasn't entirely sure that sleeping together constituted dating, but it was the best thing I could come up with at the moment.

"Yay!" Melissa clapped her hands together. "Mac said he's been crazy about you forever."

I should have known Mac and Melissa's pillow talk would bite me in the ass. Still, I couldn't help but smile. "I guess I just never noticed, or maybe I wasn't ready."

"Well, I'm glad things are going well."

"Me, too." I took another bite of my sandwich and chewed. "Any idea what you'll do for the spring semester yet? Did Kayla say if she's coming back?"

Melissa shrugged. "I haven't heard one way or the other, but I'm keeping my fingers crossed."

There was something in her tone I couldn't quite put my finger on. I peered over the desk at her. "Do you like it here?"

She opened her mouth, then closed it. Several seconds passed before she spoke. "I do like it here. I'm not used to the small-town vibe, but I think I could get used to that. It's just... I know it's weird, but I kind of feel like I'm always looking over my shoulder right now."

My brows drew together. "Why?"

"That episode with Trent was... unsettling."

She visibly shivered, and I affected a sympathetic expression. "I'm sure. I didn't see exactly what happened, but I've had my own issues with Trent."

She bit her lip. "I feel terrible admitting it, but now that Trent's gone, it's been a weight off my shoulders."

I dropped my gaze to the desk. I wished I could say the same. While I couldn't prove he was responsible for any of the recent upheaval, it was the only thing that made sense. Gray had even told me last night that Trent was nowhere to be found. He wasn't at his family or friends' houses, and no one had heard from him in more than a week. It was pretty damning, all things considered.

Almost on cue my phone rang, and my heart dropped to

my toes. Melissa's gaze dropped to my phone where it lay in front of me. "You can get that if you want."

"No, it's okay." I quickly silenced the call with a forced smile. "It's no big deal."

"You sure?" Her brows drew together. "It sounds like someone is—"

My phone immediately began to ring again, and I snatched it up, fury flowing through my veins. "What do you want?" I snarled into the phone.

There was a long pause, then—"Ms. Gates? I apologize if I'm calling at a bad time. This is Belinda from Dr. Burton's office calling to confirm your appointment for next Monday afternoon."

Heat flared in my cheeks, and across the table I watched Melissa's eyes widen with concern. I dropped my forehead into my hand, unable to help the embarrassed chuckle that fell from my lips. "Oh, my gosh, I am so sorry about that. I will definitely be there. Thanks for calling."

Without another word, I hung up and dropped my phone into my bag.

"Is everything okay?" Melissa began tentatively. "I mean, if you don't want to talk about it..."

"No. I mean, yes. It's okay." She'd had similar issues with Trent, so I knew she would understand. "I've been getting these weird phone calls. Ever since Trent got suspended..."

I knew the minute she connected the dots because her mouth dropped open. "You think he's stalking you."

"No." Her brows lifted in silent censure, and I bit my lip. "Maybe. I don't know."

"You need to be careful. Trust me," she added. "He's just a kid, but he can be scary when he loses his temper."

I nodded slowly. Maybe he really did blame me for not helping him more.

"Have you told the police yet?"

I nodded. "They know I've been having... issues." I didn't elaborate on exactly how far things had escalated. "The problem is, they don't have any proof that Trent's the one responsible. Right now there's not much they can do."

Melissa's mouth twisted. "Just... be careful, okay?"

"Thanks." I smiled. "I'm sure even if it is him, it's just some kind of scare tactic."

"I hope so."

I picked up my sandwich, but it turned to dust in my mouth. Trent needed to be stopped, and soon, because I wasn't sure how much more of this I could handle. We ate in silence for several minutes, and Melissa's gaze flitted around the room. She caught sight of the picture on the windowsill— that one thankfully hadn't been stolen—and she tipped her head to one side. "Is that your sister?"

I nodded and swallowed the bite I'd just taken before speaking. "Yep, that's Jane."

Melissa rose from her chair and crossed the small space, then bent down to take a better look. "I can definitely see the resemblance. She's older than you, right?"

"By five years." I leaned back in my chair and watched as Melissa studied the photo, a sad little smile on her face.

"I always wanted a sister. I begged my parents for years," she said on a chuckle, "but they weren't having it."

I couldn't begin to imagine what it was like to be an only child. Jane and I had fought occasionally, but no matter what happened, I still loved her. Our parents' divorce had been excruciating. I was devastated when my father took Jane and moved halfway across the country. In one fell swoop I'd lost not only my father but my sister and best friend. Despite the age gap between us, she'd let me sleep in her room when I was scared, and played dolls with me when I was bored. For a couple of years, the most interaction we got were phone calls once or twice a month. But as soon as we both graduated, we'd decided to settle in roughly the same area.

Just thinking of Jane made me want to call and talk to her, tell her everything about Gray. I'd been keeping that close to my chest so far, afraid to tell anyone for fear of jinxing it.

"Actually." I cleared my throat. "I used to have two pictures in here. There was another photo—one of Jane and me a few years ago. It was my favorite, but it was stolen a few weeks ago."

Melissa straightened and turned surprised eyes on me. "Someone took it?"

I nodded slowly. "Pretty sure it was Trent."

Her mouth dropped open in shock, then she bit her lip. "You know, that doesn't surprise me. He seemed like the type who enjoyed causing trouble."

"Yeah." I sighed. "I was hoping he would bring it back, but..." I shrugged.

"Sorry you lost your picture," she said as she took a seat across from me once more.

"That's nothing." I tapped my forefinger on the desk. "Remember the morning Trent was suspended? I found a tarantula in my drawer."

Her eyes widened. "I would have lost my mind." She shuddered dramatically. "I hate spiders."

"Me, too." Just the thought of its furry little body and blank beady eyes made my skin crawl. "Mr. Sutton had it returned to the biology lab. Apparently that's where he found it."

Melissa shook her head, and her eyes narrowed in concern. "A spider, and phone calls? It sounds like he has it out for you. You need to be careful."

I rubbed my forehead and let out a little half laugh. "Well, I haven't even mentioned the snake."

"Snake!" Melissa's mouth dropped open, and I found

myself telling her about finding the black snake in my car last week.

"Claire, that's ridiculous." Her face twisted with indignation. "You need to go to the police."

"I did." I gave a little shake of my head. "I hoped he would get it out of his system, but he just doesn't seem to know when to give up. The snake was the final straw, though. I told the detective everything that's happened, so they're looking for Trent right now."

She lifted a brow. "They can't find him?"

"Not yet." I lifted one shoulder. "I imagine he's hunkered down somewhere. Maybe he finally got a clue, because things have been pretty quiet the past couple of days."

Melissa made a little sound in the back of her throat. "Well, for your sake I hope he stays away."

Yeah, so did I.

Twenty-Four

GRAY

THE YOUNG WOMAN ACROSS FROM ME SNIFFED AND dabbed at her eyes with a crinkled tissue. "I'm sorry. I know it's a lot to process," I said softly.

Today I'd been tasked with interviewing the friend who'd been with Jessica the night she was last seen alive. Although I'd informed the family of her demise yesterday, Karly Williams hadn't yet heard the news, and she was taking it hard. I gave her a few moments to gather herself, mentally reviewing what I'd learned from her parents.

According to the family, Jessica Cartwright had been living on her own on the outskirts of Cedar Springs for just over a year. She'd just renewed her lease on the apartment, which had been corroborated by the landlord. She was a good girl though not a great student, and she was taking classes at beauty school so she could work in a salon in Dallas.

Karly drew in a shaky breath, eyes still glassy with tears, and turned her attention on me. "It's just so hard to believe. We hadn't talked for a little while but I never dreamed... "

Her breath caught on the last word, and I offered her a

sympathetic nod. "I understand. I was hoping I could ask you a few questions about her."

Karly blinked away her tears, then nodded. "Sure. Anything I can do to help."

"When was the last time you saw her?"

Karly didn't have to think. "We went out for a drink at Flannery's Pub a couple weekends ago." I verified the date with her and she nodded. "We don't—didn't—get to see each other as often as we liked, so we tried to meet up at least once a month."

"What happened that night?"

"We had a couple drinks, talked." She shrugged. "That's about it."

If she was there with a friend, how had the man isolated her? "Did she bring a date with her?"

"No." She shook her head. "It was just the two of us. We talked with some guys there, of course, but she didn't have a boyfriend or anything that I know of."

I made a quick notation. "Did you happen to notice anyone hovering nearby, anyone who maybe stood out for some reason?"

Karly bit her lip and considered the question for a moment. "Not that I remember. I mean, men are—were," she caught herself. Blinking back tears, she swallowed hard and started over. "Men were always coming up to Jessica. She was pretty and fun to be around, and people seemed to be drawn to her."

I nodded. It made sense; in life, she had been a beautiful young woman. "When those men came up to her, did she spend more time talking with any one man over the others?"

Karly slowly shook her head. "No, not that I can think of. But..."

I studied her as she trailed off. Her gaze was faraway, like she was watching the events of that night unfold before her eyes. She blinked a few times, and a delicate red flush crept up her face and neck as she directed her attention to me and shook her head. "I'm sure it was nothing."

"No detail is too small," I told her quietly. "I want to find whoever did this to her."

Karly pressed her lips together. "I didn't actually see her with anyone, but... I think she met up with someone."

I kept my expression clear, despite the confusion I felt. "You mean after the two of you left?"

"No." A guilty expression swept over her face. "I think she may have met a guy there."

"But you didn't see him?"

She bit her lip and shook her head. "I went to the bathroom while she went outside to smoke."

In my experience women tended to move together in packs, for safety if nothing else. "You didn't go with her?"

She made a miserable face. "No, she knows I can't stand it so she told me she'd meet me back inside once she was done."

"What happened then?"

"I looked for her when I came out, but I couldn't find her anywhere. I called and texted, and got a text message back half an hour later that said she went home. I assumed she left with a guy."

A cold chill trickled down my spine. More likely, the man drugged her and used her phone to respond once he'd gotten her home. "Did she do that often, leave with a man she'd met?"

"Well..." She twisted her fingers together in her lap, seemingly reluctant to impart the information. "It wouldn't be the first time. She... liked to have fun."

"So it wasn't out of character for her to disappear?"

She gave a little shake of her head. "Jess loved men, loved being the center of attention. She wasn't a bad person," Karly rushed on as I jotted a note down in the book I carried.

I glanced over the coffee table and met her gaze. "I'm not here to judge her character. I just want to figure out what happened to her that night, so we can find the person responsible."

Karly gave a tight nod and swallowed hard. "Thank you," she whispered. "She didn't deserve..."

"No one does. We'll do everything we can to find this guy. But in order to do that, I'm going to need as much information as possible. Had she had any bad breakups recently, anyone who would hold a grudge or obsess over her?"

An hour later, I left Karly Williams's house with an arm load of information about her personal life, then climbed into the cruiser and headed toward the station. Inside, I found my brother at his desk.

"Hey."

He turned a pair of tired eyes on me as I sank into the chair next to him. "Hey. How'd it go?"

I shrugged. "About as well as can be expected. She did say that Jessica may have gone home with a man that night."

I relayed Karly's story about calling and texting Jessica when she'd disappeared, and Drew held up a packet of papers. "I saw those. I've been going through all of her texts, every post and message on social media..." He gave a little shake of his head. "So far, there's nothing. She was texting a few people suggestive pictures, but each of those men have been cleared."

Damn. I was hoping he'd been making some headway on his end. "Both women were young, early twenties," I said aloud, "but their physical attributes are night and day different. Jessica was blonde with brown eyes, while Kristi has dark hair and hazel eyes."

"Maybe it's more about convenience," my brother mused. "Two different types of women, two different bars. I think it's a crime of opportunity."

I shook my head. "If it's the same guy—and I think it is—he took both women back to their homes. How did he know they were single and lived alone?"

"Hell, I don't know." Drew rubbed his forehead. "Their lives don't overlap at all that I can find. They have different jobs, live on separate ends of town."

Basically, not a single damn thing tying them together, except the fact that they'd been drugged and sexually assaulted. And we still had no idea how he'd incapacitated the women, especially in crowded places like those bars. The only other thing—

"They smoke," I said suddenly.

Drew turned to me, brows drawn. "Huh?"

"Both women are smokers."

He nodded, clearly trying to follow my train of thought. "Kristi said she stepped out back to smoke. But there were other people around."

"But she said she'd gotten it from someone else. I think we need to take a closer look at the men who were there with them. If Kristi bummed a smoke off a man, maybe we can narrow it down. He might be part of that group, or someone may have noticed something."

Drew made a little face. "Great, that should be like trying to find a needle in a haystack."

I knew this part of the job sucked, but if anyone could figure out who'd been drugging the women and how, it was Drew. I stood and placed a hand on his shoulder. "We'll find him."

Sooner rather than later, I hoped for everyone's sakes.

Twenty-Five

CLAIRE

I SAT ON THE COUCH, CURLED INTO GRAY'S SIDE, HIS arm draped over the couch behind me. The TV show we'd been watching rolled over to a commercial, and I felt Gray turn to me. "Can I ask you a question?"

Brows raised, I tipped my head up to meet his curious eyes. "Of course."

He hesitated for a moment. "You haven't really said anything, and I'm not even sure it's my place to ask..."

A trickle of trepidation ran down my spine, and I knew what he was about to ask before the words even left his mouth.

"I'm just curious..." His thumb lightly stroked along my upper arm, light and soothing. "Is there a reason you don't drink alcohol?"

I rolled my lips together and shifted my gaze over his shoulder, pinning it to the wall behind him. I'd known this would come up eventually, but even though years had passed I wasn't sure I would ever get comfortable talking about it. In fact, no one outside of my family even knew the whole story.

I closed my eyes briefly, unable to meet Gray's gaze, and

drew in a fortifying breath. "I used to drink back in college; almost everyone did. We were kids, you know? Thought we had our whole lives ahead of us."

Gray continued to stroke my arm and nodded a little, giving me the courage to continue. "I met a guy my sophomore year in my Chemistry class, and we hit it off, started dating. Bryan was super popular, always getting invited to parties. He was the valedictorian of our class, but in his free time he loved to have fun. He said he worked hard enough during the week that he deserves to unwind a little bit."

I paused, and Grayson tightened his hold on me the tiniest bit. "You don't have to tell me if it's too difficult."

I shook my head. "It's okay, I don't mind. I just..." I swallowed hard. "It still feels like it happened yesterday."

Gray lifted his free hand and laced his fingers with mine. I stared at our joined hands for a moment, drawing on his strength and security. After a beat, I picked up where I left off. "Anyway, over time it all became a little... too much. He'd go out more often than he stayed in, started drinking more and more.

"He was still doing fine in classes, but..." I took a deep breath and admitted out loud what I'd never said before. "He had a problem."

"It's not uncommon," Gray said, his voice quiet.

I nodded, but guilt still weighed heavily on my chest. "The longer it went on, the more I worried about him. I asked him to stop, but he acted like it was no big deal. He'd just tell me to stop worrying so much."

I closed my eyes for a second as the memory of that night washed over me. "He called me one night while I was studying. He wanted me to take him to the liquor store to pick up more booze. I..." I trailed off for a second, lost in a memory five years old. "I thought I was helping him by telling him no. I told him I was busy, and that I couldn't take him. I didn't realize he'd drive himself."

God, I'd never forget that night. "He was about halfway there when he ran off the road and hit a tree. It was dark when it happened, so we didn't find out until the next day when he didn't show up for class. I had texted him that night, but I never got a reply. The police who investigated said it was quick, and hopefully painless," I said faintly.

"I'm so sorry, sweetheart." Gray shifted me closer and wrapped his arms around me.

A tear escaped, and I buried my head against his chest. "I can't help but think of how it could've turned out differently. It was just a couple drinks. What if I hadn't waited so long for him to respond? If I had just gone to the stupid store, would he still be alive?"

"You can't think like that," Grayson softly. "Whatever decisions he made were his own."

Even though he cared for me, loved me even, Gray was never afraid to tell me exactly what he thought. And if he believed the situation was completely out of my control, then I trusted his opinion. Still, that didn't lessen the pain I felt.

"His family came down to... get him." I hated to even think about those couple of weeks following his death. "They were upset, of course. I tried reaching out to them, but they didn't want to see me."

"Had you met them before?"

I shook my head. "No. Even though we'd dated for a couple of years, they lived up in Wisconsin and I never went with him when he went home to visit. I spent the holidays with Jane, and honestly... Toward the end, things were so tense between us that I didn't want to travel with him."

"That's still shitty of them."

I lifted one shoulder. "I can't help but think they blamed me for what happened."

I felt his jaw clench, and his words were low and harsh when he spoke. "You have nothing to feel guilty about. If not that night, it more than likely would have happened at some point in the future. It wasn't your fault."

In some of my more selfish moments, I had considered the same thing. Bryan had an incredibly bright and promising future in front of him, but one moment had ruined that forever. Hearing Grayson validate my opinion made me feel slightly better. He viewed the situation from the standpoint of an officer of the law rather than allowing his emotions to get in the way.

I tipped my face up to his. "Thank you."

He used the pad of his thumb to brush away the remnants of tears before gently kissing my lips. "It's the truth."

"It's never easy to lose someone," he murmured. "I don't think I've ever introduced you to my cousin. You know Bennett Kingsley?"

I shook my head. "I've heard the name, but..."

"It's okay. We're not real close to that side of the family. Bennett's mother is Ma's sister, but she thinks pretty highly of herself. We're not nearly good enough for her to acknowledge."

Although I knew nothing of the woman aside from what Gray had just told me, I wasn't terribly inclined to like her. The Thornes were some of the best people I'd met in my entire life, and it didn't exactly speak well of the woman who deemed them inferior.

"Anyway," Gray continued, "Bennett was our lieutenant when I first started. He and his old partner, Branson, did everything together. They were investigating an abuse case against a defense attorney. His son had been in the hospital several times, and they reported it as suspicious."

My stomach twisted. "Was he...?"

"Being abused? Yeah." Gray's face set in a hard line.

"Branson was trying to find everything he could to put this guy away. One day they got a call that the little boy—Michael —was dead."

My hand automatically flew to the base of my throat, and I swallowed the emotion choking me. How could anyone hurt an innocent child like that?

"Branson blamed himself." Gray sighed. "One night, he just... couldn't take it anymore."

God, how horrible.

"They were the perfect team. I thought for sure Bennett would be the next chief. But after Branson took his life..." He shook his head. "His younger sister Olivia left town, and Bennett was never the same."

We sat in silence for a moment, and I began to understand why Gray had told me this story. Branson had blamed himself, even though it wasn't his fault. In the same way, I'd been punishing myself for years for something that had been completely out of my control.

I snuggled into Gray, loving the way he automatically pulled me in close and pressed his lips to the top of my head. He was my rock, my voice of reason. My everything.

Twenty-Six

GRAY

CLAIRE STOOD IN FRONT OF THE KITCHEN SINK, outlined by the halo of bright light that streamed in through the window. I loved seeing her here, in my house, in my life. I never wanted to let her go.

Slipping up behind her, I wrapped my arms around her waist and pulled her back to me. "Whatcha doing, beautiful?"

She tilted her head to one side and made a little humming noise as I pressed my lips to the side of her neck. "Just thinking."

I trailed my lips higher. "About?"

I could hear the smile in her voice as she spoke. "You. Us."

"Mmm..." Her bottom pressed against my groin, and I swelled at the feel of her. "What about us?"

"I—"

She was cut off by the shrill beep of my phone, and I let out a curse. "Damn it."

I dug it from my back pocket, half-tempted to ignore the damn thing. When I saw the station's number on the screen, a sigh escaped my lips and I stepped away from Claire as I swiped my thumb across the screen to answer. "Thorne."

"Hey, boss," Scott Mackenzie began, "we've got a young woman here who would like to speak to you about the recent incidents involving Ms. Holcomb and Ms. Cartwright."

Damn. I'd just gotten home, and I'd been hoping to spend a quiet evening with Claire. Now that was all shot to hell. "Thanks, Mac. I'll be there as soon as I can."

Even though Drew was technically lead detective on the investigation, I wanted to help in any way I could. We didn't often have situations like this, and I wanted it resolved as quickly as possible. If that meant personally interviewing every person who came into the station, then so be it.

With that I hung up and met Claire's curious gaze. "I've got to go back in for a bit."

She nodded, brows drawn together in concern. "Will you be late?"

"Hopefully not too late." I cupped the back of her head and pulled her in for a quick, hard kiss.

She slid her hands up my chest before releasing me. "Be careful."

"I will."

I studied her for a second, every instinct screaming at me to stay right here with her. The more I was with her, the more I never wanted to let her go. I'd keep her with me every second of the day if I could. This new dimension to our relationship had made me almost crazy with need for her. Even though we'd made love last night, I wanted to pull her under me again already. An all-consuming fire burned inside me that only she could quench.

Finally I ripped myself away from her. "See you later."

I reluctantly forced myself to move toward the garage where I climbed into the cruiser and headed into the station.

My fingers tightened on the wheel, and I tossed a quick look in the rear-view mirror, watching as my house grew smaller and smaller as I drove away. Drew could handle this, couldn't he? I was tempted to turn around and go back to her, climb into bed and pull the covers over our heads. A sigh filtered from my lips. I knew my brother could technically handle the case; he was lead detective. But I was chief of police and it was my duty to the people of Cedar Springs to ensure their safety.

I bit back an oath as I forced my foot down on the accelerator. Damn it. I should have known this would happen. Even though I knew almost everything there was to know about Claire, I couldn't get enough of her. I loved the feel of her next to me, the sound of her breathy little sighs when I kissed that secret spot of hers, loved the way she curled into me when she slept like she couldn't bear to be away from me.

Fuck. I was a complete goner. I'd seen this coming from a mile away but the way I felt about her still had the power to blindside me.

I pulled into my designated parking spot at the station, then headed inside. My mood promptly changed, and all thoughts of Claire were pushed to the side when I saw my brother standing in the doorway of my office.

"Hey." He jerked his chin my way. "I was just getting ready to call you."

"What's going on?"

"We've got another victim."

I swore under my breath as I dropped my backpack on the chair in the corner. "What the hell happened?"

Drew lifted one hand my way, stalling my anger. "She hasn't said much yet, but from what I gather, she might be our first victim."

My brows lifted at that little sliver of news. "Why the hell didn't she come forward before now?"

Drew shrugged one shoulder. "Can't answer that for you. I knew you'd want to talk to her though, so I put her in the conference room."

"Good." I gestured for him to follow along. "Join me."

I forced myself to remain calm as Drew and I headed down the hallway to the conference room. Inside, a young woman waited, looking shifty and nervous. I offered her a kind smile as I slid into a chair across from her.

Drew did the same, then made introductions. "Amanda, this is Chief Grayson Thorne."

"Nice to meet you."

"You, too." Her voice was soft and tentative, and she picked at her nails where they rested on the table in front of her.

"Can you tell me what brings you in today?" I invited.

She licked her lips, her gaze flitting around the room before flicking back to mine. "I, um... I heard about the girl you found the other day. The one who was drugged and... left."

"That's right," I said cautiously. "Did you know her?"

She shook her head. "No, but... I think I might know who did it."

I tried to conceal my surprise. I stared at her. "Did you see the man she was with?"

"No, I've never met him... personally." Amanda shook her head. "But the same thing happened to me. I was at Mason's last month, and the next thing I knew I was in my bedroom at home."

I barely resisted sliding a look Drew's way. Sounded similar to Kristi's story. "Were you with anyone at the bar that night?"

"No." Amanda's gaze dropped away again. "I went out by myself, had an Uber take me there and scheduled to pick me up."

"Did the Uber take you home?"

The hope that had flared to life and my chest died as she shook her head. "The first thing I did the next morning was call the company. The Uber driver said I never showed up, so I think the man brought me back to my house."

"How did he know where you lived?"

She shrugged one shoulder. "I'm not sure. Maybe I told him when I was..."

She trailed off, and I nodded. "It's okay. Can you tell me about the rest of what you remember?"

She drew in a fortifying breath before continuing. "I woke up in bed feeling nauseous. At first, I thought I drank too much and somebody brought me home. But then I heard the man moving around. I pretended to still be sleeping, but I got a decent look at him while he got dressed."

"Did you recognize him?"

Again she shook her head. "No, but I could tell you what he looked like."

Finally, things were starting to look up. Thank God. "Do you remember enough to speak with the sketch artist?

She bit her lip. "I think so."

I tipped my head toward Drew. "Can you give Gen a call, see when she might be able to come in?"

"Sure thing." He pushed back his chair and was gone a few seconds later. I turned my attention back to Amanda. "Genesis Taylor owns the art gallery downtown. Do you know her?"

Amanda shook her head. "I've never been there."

"She's very talented, and she occasionally does some work for us. We'll try to arrange a time for you two to meet up so we can get the sketch done."

"Okay." Amanda licked her lips and nodded nervously. "I'm not sure how much I'll be able to help, but I'll try."

"You'll do great," I assured her. "Besides, anything you can tell us will help. While we wait on Drew, can you tell me more about the man? Did he have any distinguishing characteristics that you remember? Any tattoos or birthmarks that stood out?"

"A tattoo on his left arm." She pointed to her bicep. "It looked like a script letter L."

"Great, that gives us something to start with."

She offered me a little smile that slipped away as quickly as it had come, and I studied her. "Do you mind me asking why you didn't come forward when this happened?"

Her eyes filled with tears, and she dashed them away. "I felt... dirty. I didn't want anyone to know what had happened to me."

I lamented the loss of evidence, but part of me understood where she was coming from. "We're going to do our best to find him and put him behind bars."

One tear trickled down her cheek. "As soon as I heard about the girl who died, I knew it was him. I couldn't let him get away with it anymore."

"I appreciate you coming forward. It was a brave thing to do."

The door swung open, and Drew stuck his head in. "Genesis will be here in half an hour. Is that okay?"

I glanced at Amanda, who nodded. "Send her back as soon as she gets here. And, Drew? Can you grab me a sheet of paper?"

He was back a couple seconds later and passed me a plain white sheet of computer paper, which I slid across the table to Amanda. "Could you try to draw the man's tattoo for me?"

She quickly sketched it out then passed it back to me, and I held it up for Drew's inspection. "Our guy has this tattoo on his left bicep. Let's see if the shop in town remembers doing anything like this."

As soon as Genesis arrived, we got her set up in the room with Amanda to work on the sketch, then Drew and I headed over to the corner of Broadway and Maple. Inside, Lachlan McGinnis tipped his head our way. "What can I do for ya?"

"Need help with something."

I passed the sketch across the counter, and Lachlan studied it for a second before nodding. "This looks like a symbol for a last name."

"Ever done anything like this?"

"Not me." Lachlan shook his head. "But I've got two other artists in the back. Let me check with them."

He disappeared for several moments, then came back carrying a thick binder. "This might be able to help us," he said as he set it on the counter and opened the cover.

Inside were dozens of monograms, and I watched as he flipped to the L. He slowly turned the pages until he found the design he was looking for. Spinning the book our way, he tapped the sketch with a forefinger. "I think this is what you're looking for?"

Drew and I shared a glance. "Looks that way. What does it mean?"

"According to this, Lewis."

I stared at Drew. "Could be first name or last."

I flicked a look at Lachlan. "Thanks."

He gave an abbreviated wave. "See ya around."

"Why don't you pull records for anyone with the name Lewis, say for the past year?" I said to my brother once we were back outside. "I've gotta head over to the ME's office."

Drew nodded, then took off back to the station, and I climbed into my cruiser. Slowly but surely we were closing in. And this time, he wouldn't get away.

Twenty-Seven

CLAIRE

I LEANED AGAINST THE COUNTER, LOST IN thought. Things with Gray had been good—almost too good. For the past several days we'd fallen into a rhythm. After work we would have dinner, then fall into bed and do it all over again the next day. So far, neither of us had mentioned the future, and I couldn't help but wonder what he was thinking. I was almost scared to bring it up. Things right now were amazing, and I didn't want to ruin it by adding any pressure.

Warmth spread through my chest at the memory of last night. It was like the weight I'd carried for the past five years had dissipated. Logically I knew I wasn't responsible for Bryan's death, but I'd blamed myself for all the things I hadn't done, questioned everything I could have said. Who knew if it would have made a difference or not? Maybe, as Gray said, it would have happened eventually anyway.

I could even admit to myself now that things between Bryan and me had been falling apart long before his accident. Our relationship had grown tense, and I'd begun to distance myself from him. In a way, that had compounded my guilt. I felt bad for dragging things out, for not telling him exactly how I felt.

My relationship with Gray was nothing like the one I had with Bryan. Time had passed, and I had changed both physically and emotionally. I was finally ready to move forward with my life, and Gray had given me that gift. I loved him so much it hurt. He was my best friend, but over the past two weeks I'd fallen even harder and faster than I ever could've imagined. He took up a space inside my heart that no one would ever be able to fill. As a lover he was absolutely incredible. He taught me how to embrace my insecurities and be more confident. He loved fully without reserve, never holding himself back.

There was still a tiny part of me that worried he would eventually come to his senses and decide that we were better off friends than lovers. But so far, he'd given no indication that that was the case. He told me every single day, in both words and in the way he touched me, how much he loved me. I felt cherished. Treasured. Adored. I never wanted it to end.

I drummed my nails against the countertop as I stared out the back window. The one thing we hadn't talked about was the future, and nervousness coiled in my stomach like a snake. It was too soon, I knew it was, but I wanted to know exactly how he felt. Did he want to get married? Did he want kids? I bit my lip. Until I knew the answers to those questions, I would need to be extra careful. I was almost out of birth control pills, but I would definitely be needing those. I had a spare prescription at the house, and I debated whether to go pick them up.

There hadn't been any strange phone calls since Monday during lunch, and I even began to question those. In the past, I occasionally got random sales calls from unknown or unlisted numbers. I couldn't help but feel like I was maybe blowing the whole thing out of proportion.

Trent had made no more attempts to reach out to me, and I wondered if he had caught wind of the fact that the police were aware of everything that happened. As far as I knew, they still hadn't seen or heard from him. He probably decided that causing trouble wasn't worth going to jail. Despite everything, I still felt bad for him. Wherever he was, I hoped that he would succeed.

I'd managed to talk Gray into letting me stay here alone while he was finishing up with work, and I bit my lip. Stay or go? It wouldn't take me very long to go to my house, get my things, then come back. Deciding that it was safe enough to venture out, I grabbed up my purse and keys from the hall table, made sure all the doors were locked, then cut through the garage and started my car. While I was at home, I would pack some of the other stuff I needed since it looked like I would be staying with Gray for the foreseeable future. I made a mental checklist as I drove, ticking off toiletries and clothes for both school and the weekend.

At home, I let myself in through the back door and a tiny smile curved my mouth. Though it had only been a few days, it seemed like forever since I'd been here. I loved my little house, but I enjoyed staying at Gray's too. What would happen if things between us continued to progress? Would we move in together? And would we stay at his place or mine? If we decided to start a family, we might even move into a new house, something bigger with more space.

I knew I was getting ahead of myself, but I couldn't help it. The meshing of our lives was both terrifying and exhilarating. I loved the sight of my clothes hanging in the closet next to his, seeing our toothbrushes side by side in the bathroom. Until I knew exactly what the future held, though, I would just have to take it one day at a time.

Cutting across the kitchen, I watered the plants that graced the windowsill above the sink, then gathered the few dirty dishes I'd left behind and put them in the dishwasher. I hadn't bothered cleaning up before Gray and I had gone back to his place last time, so I decided to do a quick once over while I was here. I made my way through the house, straightening things as I went and collecting dirty clothes.

In my bedroom I packed some extra clothes, then grabbed my birth control and some other toiletries. Once I had everything I needed, I got ready to leave. As I passed through the living room, the mailbox came into view in the window, and I realized with a start that I hadn't picked up my mail for the past few days.

Dropping the duffel next to the front door, I walked down the driveway to get the mail. I shuffled the envelopes and flyers as I made my way back up the driveway, and something caught my eye as I stepped onto the porch. A brown box sat to the left of the door, pushed slightly askew from where the door had swung open.

My brows drew together, and I cocked my head as I studied it. I didn't remember ordering anything, but then again, the past few weeks had been so hectic I couldn't remember my own name half the time. I stacked the mail on top of the box, then carried everything into the kitchen.

Flicking through the envelopes, I tossed the junk and set the bills aside to take to Gray's, then turned my attention to the box. There was no return address, nothing to indicate where it had come from. Contemplating what it could be, I pulled a knife from the block on the counter and sliced through the clear tape that had been used to seal it.

My heart stuttered in my chest, and I froze as I flipped open the flaps. There, nestled on top of a bed of tissue paper, lay the picture that had been stolen from my office several weeks prior. My hands trembled as I lifted it from the box and turned it over to inspect it. Thankfully, it was completely intact. I let out a little sigh of relief, grateful that it had been returned to me.

I set the photo aside, then picked up the box to carry it to the recycling bin. The weight told me that I'd missed something, and a sense of foreboding curled through me as I pulled the tissue paper from the box.

A scream suspended itself in my throat and my stomach twisted at the gruesome sight that awaited me at the bottom of the box.

Twenty-Eight

GRAY

I GLANCED ACROSS THE METAL TABLE AT DR. Davison. "Official cause of death?"

The autopsy for Jessica Cartwright was finally complete, and I was champing at the bit to figure out if this was in any way tied to the open cases Drew had.

"Asphyxiation." She gestured toward the young woman on the table. "There were traces of that same GHB-like substance in her system, but that's not what killed her. At some point, she began to vomit and it became lodged in her airway."

I could only hope Jessica was still incapacitated when that had happened. And what about the suspect? Was he there when she aspirated? In a way, this was a boon for us. We now had a murder charge to stick to him in addition to the rape charges that were piling up. It was the final nail in his coffin, and we were going to put him away for a long damn time.

"Any DNA?"

Dr. Davison shook her head. "No. There is evidence of sexual assault but no bodily fluids. I assume he wore a condom, and I didn't find anything on the body. No hair or fibers, no skin cells under her nails. There are no defensive wounds, so my assumption is that she was still unconscious during copulation."

Christ, that was revolting. "You think he gets off on it?"

She lifted one shoulder. "I'm not a psychologist, but I would say yes. More than likely he gets off on the power of it."

I grimaced. "Anything else?"

"Possibly. I found traces of Phenoxyethanol on her skin."

Chemistry had never been my best subject. "And that is...?"

"A substance that kills bacteria." She lifted her blue gaze to me. "But it's also an ingredient commonly found in baby wipes."

I blinked. It was possible, of course, that she'd used them prior to having intercourse. But if she'd been drugged in the same fashion as Kristi Holcomb, she wouldn't have had time. Which meant... "He wiped her down afterward to obliterate any evidence."

Dr. Davison shrugged. "It's a very good possibility."

That motherfucker.

"Thanks for your help, doc. One last question—can you tell if she was a smoker?" We hadn't found any cigarettes in Jessica's apartment, but Karly had admitted that Jessica smoked. I knew it was a stretch, but I was trying to find any possible connection between the two women that I could.

"There was some buildup in her lungs, yes." Dr. Davison nodded. "Judging from the tissue, I would say she was a recreational smoker and probably only indulged from time to time."

I headed out of the medical examiner's office, thoughts swirling through my mind. How was the man choosing his victims? How did he know they didn't have family, no boyfriends, or roommates? I could only assume that meant he knew the women, at least in passing. He'd probably watched them, studied their every move for days if not weeks before approaching them.

We also hadn't narrowed down how he'd been able to drug them, or how he'd managed to pull them aside at the bar. There had been nothing on the cameras, and Kristi said she'd felt fine until she went outside for a smoke. I needed to speak with her again and see if she'd remembered anything new since we wouldn't be hearing this young woman's side of the story. Not only that, but I wanted to see if she remembered anything being applied to her skin. The hospital had checked for assault, but there was no mention of any other substances on her person.

Anger burned in my gut. It pissed me off that something like this could happen in my town, and I refused to let the guy get away with it. If he thought we were just a bunch of uneducated small-town hicks, he had another thing coming. I was going to find this prick and nail his ass to the wall.

The buzzing of my phone pulled my attention away as I slid into the car, and I pulled it from my back pocket. Claire's name flashed across the screen, and I felt a sort of calm descend over me. No matter how bad things were, Claire always managed to ground me. She was such a bright spot in my life, and I was counting down the moments until I could get home to her.

I swiped the screen to answer. "Hey, sweetheart."

"Gray..."

She trailed off, her voice tense, and I immediately went on alert. "What's wrong?"

"A package was delivered to my house, and—"

Her house? What the hell was she doing there? "Don't open it," I ordered as I cranked the engine and threw the car in gear. "Leave it outside and stay away from it."

"But—"

"Trust me," I cut her off. "Do not do anything else. Lock your doors. I'll be there in fifteen minutes."

"Okay."

Her voice was faint and shaky, and it tugged at my heart. "Everything will be fine, sweetheart, I promise. I'll be there as soon as I can."

I hung up and pressed down on the accelerator as I sped down the highway toward Cedar Springs. I navigated through the mid-afternoon traffic, my heart in my throat. What had the bastard sent her? And why the hell was she even at her place? When I left today, I thought she had every intention of staying at my place. It irked me that she'd gone back to her house without me.

I hadn't expressly forbidden it since things had been quiet for the last several days, but I didn't like this. It felt off. He was plotting, waiting for the right moment. I didn't know shit about Trent Jones except that he was troubled and extremely intelligent. If he blamed Claire for all of his recent issues, could he hold enough of a grudge to try to hurt her? It wasn't nearly as difficult to build a bomb as people thought it was.

My pulse thrummed rapidly in my ears, drowning out the soft music on the radio. I pushed the car even faster, and it felt like an hour had passed by the time I slid to a stop in Claire's driveway. I was halfway to the porch before the car door closed behind me, and I fumbled with the lock for a second before I shoved open the front door. "Claire!"

She rounded the corner of the kitchen, her eyes wide in her pale face. One arm was wrapped around her midsection, and she released the thumbnail she'd been nibbling on nervously as she lifted a hand my way. She seemed almost frozen in place, and I rushed forward, sliding my hands up her arms and cupping her elbows. "Are you okay?"

"Yeah." She nodded shakily. "I'm fine, it's just..."

The color drained from her face once more, and I pressed a

kiss to her forehead. "It's okay, sweetheart. Show me what you've got."

She peeled herself away and gestured toward the kitchen counter with one hand. "Right there."

My gaze flitted to a cardboard box near the stove. A knife lay on the counter next to it, along with what appeared to be a picture frame. I slid a look her way. "I told you not to open it."

Her hand fluttered back to her throat. "I'd already opened it by the time I called you," she replied dully. "When I saw…"

She swayed a bit on her feet, and I locked an arm around her waist. "All right, honey. Just take a deep breath."

I maneuvered her to a chair, then poured a glass of water and pressed it into her hand. "Take a drink."

She did as I ordered, her hand trembling as she lifted it to her lips. She took a tiny sip, then set it back on the table, her eyes flickering to mine. "You good?"

She nodded, and I brushed my knuckles along her cheek. "Okay. I'm going to have a look. Where did you find it?" I asked as I cut over to the stove.

"On the front porch. I went out to get the mail and I saw it on my way back in. I didn't remember ordering anything but I never imagined…"

She trailed off, and I focused my gaze on the picture next to the box. I recognized younger versions of Claire and her sister, probably taken sometime during college. Something had obviously shaken her, but I couldn't imagine why. "Was the photo in the box?"

She nodded, her eyes landing on the box for a fraction of a second before sliding away again. "Yes. It came from my office at school—the one that disappeared a couple weeks ago."

I nodded a little. It probably would have been easy enough for Trent to sneak into her office, grab the photo, and hide it away. So why return it now? "Was there a note with it?"

I picked up the knife and used the blade to flip back the flap of the box as she spoke. "I didn't want to look."

As soon as the flap fell open, I knew precisely why. I swore under my breath as the mangled, bloody animal came into view. Yanking open the drawer to my left, I snatched up two potholders, then covered my hands and carried the box outside and set it on the porch. I dug out my phone and called the precinct. "I need patrol over here ASAP."

I gave them Claire's address, then headed back inside to check on her. She hadn't moved an inch, her face still pale, her eyes a little glassy and unfocused. I pressed one hand to her cheek. "We're going to get this taken care of, honey, I promise."

She nodded a little but didn't say a word, and I dropped to a knee next to her. I took one of her hands in mine, silently holding her until I heard the cruiser pull into the driveway. Pushing to my feet, I dropped a kiss on her forehead. "Stay here."

I stepped onto the back porch and greeted Vaughn as he climbed from the car. His dark eyes met mine. "What happened?"

"This." I nudged the box with my foot. "Someone left it for her."

He made a face when he peered inside. "Jesus. Who the hell does shit like this?"

I shrugged, my anger increasing with each second that passed. "I'm not even sure how long it's been here. She's been with me the past few nights and hasn't had any reason to be here."

I flipped open a flap of the box using a pen. "And there's this."

You're next had been scrawled on the cardboard in a bright red ink that closely matched the blood saturating the fur of the small animal inside.

His lips pressed into a firm line. "I'll check with the neighbors, see if they noticed anything."

"Appreciate it." I tipped my head his way. "I'm going to take her home and get her settled."

He waved me off as he went about taking the box in for evidence, and I moved back inside. Claire hadn't moved a muscle, her gaze fixed on the floor. "Come on, sweetheart," I said gently. "Let's get your things packed up."

She pointed with one shaky hand toward the door, and I saw the duffle sitting there. Grabbing it up, I slung it over my shoulder and then extended a hand her way. "All right. Let's go home."

I seethed as I ushered Claire out to the car, keeping one eye on my surroundings the whole way. Trent had gone too far. The next time he stepped out of line, I'd be there waiting for him. And he was in for a rude awakening.

Twenty-Nine

CLAIRE

GOOSEBUMPS PRICKLED ALONG MY ARMS AS another shiver rolled down my spine. The low hum of voices drifted in through the screen door, but I couldn't focus on anything except the wood grain of the table in front of me. Each time I closed my eyes, I saw it. The matted fur. The blood. Glassy blank eyes staring pleadingly up at me.

Bile burned along the back of my throat, and I forced myself to swallow it down even as my stomach threatened to heave. How could anyone do that to a poor, defenseless animal? It was heinous. Sadistic. I couldn't begin to imagine what I'd done to elicit such strong hatred. All I ever wanted to do was help him, but Trent had apparently spiraled completely out of control. There was nothing sane or sensible about what he had done this time. The relentless prank phone calls for one thing. And even though I couldn't stand them, even the creepy crawly creatures left for me to find hadn't even bothered me a fraction. If he could do this to an animal, I could only imagine how he would bend that rage on me.

The screen door closed with a soft stick, and almost immediately I felt the warm strength of Gray's hands settle on my shoulder. "Come on, sweetheart," Let's get your things packed up."

I glanced toward the bag that I'd dropped next to the door, and a shudder rippled down my spine. If I'd never come over here, I wouldn't have found that box. I swallowed hard and pointed to the bag. Gray lightly squeezed my shoulder. "All right. Let's go home."

Though his tone was even and soft, there was no hiding the fury running just beneath the surface. I silently followed him as he lifted my duffel bag to his shoulder then led the way outside. Next to Gray's patrol car, I paused and threw a look at the second vehicle parked along the road.

Gray seemed to read my thoughts as he popped the trunk and dropped my bag inside. "Vaughn is questioning the neighbors to see if anyone noticed where the box came from, or when it showed up."

Made sense. I turned my attention back to Gray. "What about my car?"

"Up to you." Gray framed my face with one hand and inspected me for several seconds. "You've had a shock. Are you sure you're okay to drive?"

I nodded. "I'll be okay." Besides, I didn't want to have to come back here tomorrow to pick it up.

After a second, he relented. "All right. I'll follow you just in case."

Gray brushed his lips over mine in a soft kiss, then held the door for me as I climbed inside. I waited for him to back up first, then I reversed out of the drive and headed toward Gray's house. I couldn't help but think of the phone call I'd gotten that morning. Trent had to have been watching me; was he watching now?

The garage door began to lift as soon as I pulled into Gray's driveway, and I took his silent cue to park inside. He grabbed my bag then passed it to me. I slipped it from his hands and carried it to the bedroom while Gray headed straight for the kitchen. Once I'd dropped the bag off, I trailed behind Gray. I hovered next to the table, staring at his back as he pulled a bottle of water from the fridge then cracked the lid. "I'm sorry."

Gray shut the door then swiveled my way. "What?"

I swallowed hard. "I shouldn't have been there. If I hadn't gone over there today—"

Gray set the bottle on the table, then closed the distance between us. "Stop."

My lips parted, but he pressed one thumb to the underside of my chin and gently pushed it shut, effectively stopping my words. "That wasn't your fault." He shook his head as I stared up at him in question. "I wish you hadn't gone over there without me, but I'm not upset with you. I'm furious with him for doing this to you, but I'm actually glad you found it when you did. A couple more days outside in the elements and we might have lost any evidence. I still can't guarantee we'll get much, but I promise we will find him. You're safe. That's all I care about now. The rest will fall into place."

Gray reached behind him and extracted a knife from the block on the counter, then pressed it into my hands. I stared at it stupidly for a moment. "What's this for?"

"You're going to help me make dinner." One eyebrow lifted as he stepped toward the fridge, never tearing his gaze from mine. "I know you well enough by now that I know you need to stay busy to keep your mind off it."

That much was probably true. But still... "I'm not sure I like you knowing that much about me."

"Sure you do." Gray moved behind me and dropped a kiss on my shoulder as he set the bag of potatoes on the board in front of me. "Start cutting."

I lifted the knife his way, the blade glinting in the afternoon sunlight that streamed through the window over the sink. "Maybe try being a little nicer to the person holding the knife."

A sexy grin tilted his lips as he closed the distance between us. "I'm always nice to you."

One hand settled along my waist, then slipped around to my lower back before pulling me into his huge body. I knew he was just trying to distract me, but he was doing a damn good job of it. I set the knife on the cutting board and sank my hands into his hair as Gray lowered his mouth to my neck. His lips skated along the sensitive cords before skimming along my jaw and finally brushing over mine.

I wasn't sure how long the kiss lasted. Seconds. Minutes, maybe. He knew even better than I did what I needed. I needed to be held, needed to feel secure after the events of the afternoon. But when he finally pulled away, a sense of peacefulness had settled over me that hadn't existed just moments before. He had the uncanny ability to bring my world back into alignment anytime things went sideways.

Wrapping my arms around his shoulders, I pressed my forehead to his chest. "Thank you."

His arms tightened around my back, but he didn't say a word.

A few hours later, I lay reclined on the couch, my legs draped over Gray's lap, and a contented sigh filtered from my lips as he pressed his thumb against the arch of my foot. He did it again, pressing harder this time, and I squirmed beneath him. Gray grinned down at me as he attacked my foot, the pleasure of his fingers kneading into my flesh bordering on pain. He'd been doing his best to distract me all night, first with dinner, then with a movie and a foot massage. His fingers skimmed over my ankle, lightly dancing along my skin, drawing little circles along my calf.

He lifted my foot and placed a kiss on the arch, then

lightly bit down. My back arched at the sensation, and Gray chuckled. "You like that?"

I liked everything he did to me. As much as I loved the way he was touching me right now, I needed more. I wanted to feel close to him, wanted to be in the safe circle of his arms.

Pulling my foot free, I shifted to my knees. Gray's eyes went dark and his hands automatically moved to my waist as I swung one leg over his lap and straddled him. Framing his face with my hands, I pressed my lips to his. It felt so good to take control, to show him how much I wanted him. And I could tell from the hardness pressing upward into my bottom that he liked it too.

His hands slid lower, massaging and caressing, drawing me back and forth over his erection until we were both panting hard. All I could think when we'd finally shed our clothes and he sank deep inside me was how much I loved him—how much I would always love him.

Thirty

GRAY

I SLID MY HAND THROUGH THE LONG AUBURN strands, watching as they slipped through my fingers like silk. Claire lay draped over me on the couch, her fingers dancing across the buttons of the polo I wore. I couldn't help the smile that had taken up residence on my face. We'd spent the morning at the Village Café and had just gotten home half an hour ago. It was a miracle, really, that I hadn't dragged her back to bed yet. Although the couch was as good as anything, and if she kept touching me like this, she was going to find herself naked in short order.

It was so nice to finally be able to relax and just be ourselves. Everything had been so hectic for the past couple of weeks, and I was ready to put that behind us and move on. The phone calls had stopped and the investigation had revealed that the rabbit left in the box on Claire's porch was already dead. More than likely Trent had picked it up off the side of the road. It was a relief to know it wasn't mutilated while alive. While that wasn't great news because Trent was still in the wind, it was better than the alternative.

The one thing we hadn't been able to determine was

precisely when the box had been left on her porch. Vaughn had interviewed each of her neighbors, but no one remembered seeing anything. Since Claire had been spending most of her time at my place, there was a good chance it'd been sitting there for several days before she'd found it. At least, I hoped that was the case. Maybe Trent had gotten the picture and decided he was better off leaving her alone. I sure as hell hoped so, because I was still mad enough to spit nails.

Claire rolled her head to look at me. "What do you want to do today?"

I didn't miss a beat. "You. Repeatedly. Everywhere and every way possible."

Claire playfully rolled her eyes and grinned. "I can't believe you're not tired of me yet."

Every ounce of humor fled as I stared at her. "Won't ever happen."

I couldn't get enough of her. We'd spent the past two weeks together, but instead of sating my need for her, my desire had only increased. I threaded one hand into her hair and tugged her down for a kiss. It'd been far too long since I'd tasted her.

My phone vibrated an alert, and I let out a growl. Hoping it was just a message, I ignored it. The buzzing continued, and I swiped a hand toward the coffee table as I broke the kiss. "One sec."

I'd get back to that just as soon as I murdered whoever was calling right this second. Finn's name popped up on the screen, and my brows drew together as I swiped the screen and lifted the phone to my ear. "Thorne."

"Hey, Chief. Got an update for you. Looks like Trent Jones got picked up for larceny."

"When?" I jackknifed to a sitting position, dislodging Claire from her position on my chest.

She fell to her back on the couch with a little cry of

surprise, and I twisted toward her, an apologetic expression on my face. *Sorry*, I mouthed as I brushed one hand over her hair.

"Booked him yesterday at the county jail," Finn replied. "I just got word, otherwise I'd have let you know sooner."

"What time?"

"Noon."

I glanced at the clock and vaulted to my feet. "Shit! I've gotta get over there before he's released. Thanks for the heads up."

I shoved my phone in my pocket and turned to Claire. "Trent got picked up yesterday for larceny. He's being held over at county for twenty-four hours. I need to get there before it's up."

"Yeah, of course." Claire blinked the confusion from her eyes and immediately pushed off the couch. "I'll stay here while you're gone."

"No." I shook my head. "I don't want you alone, just in case. They might release him before I get there, and I'd rather you be somewhere safe. You can go to my parents. Damn it. No, you can't." I let out a growl. "They're visiting Aunt Mae."

"I can go to Jane's," Claire offered.

Relief rushed through me. "Yes, that's perfect."

It was out of town and I could come get her once I was done. We quickly dressed and I kissed her before she climbed into the car. "Keep your phone on you, I'll call as soon as I'm done."

"I will. Love you." She flashed a tiny, insecure smile like she was embarrassed she'd let that slip out, then started to climb into the car.

Did she really think I was just going to let her go after that? The first time she'd said it, she thought I was asleep. I wanted to hear those words every single day; I would never get tired of hearing them.

Wrapping one arm around her bicep, I halted her movement and gently tugged her back to me. "Say that again."

Her cheeks pinked. "What?"

"Tell me." Threading my free hand into her hair, I caught her gaze and held it for several seconds.

She swallowed nervously. "Love you."

I cupped her face in my hands, my chest swelling with emotion as I stared down at her. "Love you, too."

She melted a little bit at my words, her eyes going soft, and I vowed to tell her every single day exactly how I felt. I dipped my head and brushed my lips over hers in a sweet, lingering kiss before finally releasing her. "I'll be as quick as I can. Be safe."

"I will." She popped up on her toes for one more quick kiss before sliding behind the wheel.

I followed her out of town then beeped the horn once as she headed north toward her sister's while I turned left to head to the county jail. Inside, they led me to a small interview room I'd requested. His eyes widened when he saw me. "We need to talk."

Thirty-One

CLAIRE

I WATCHED IN THE REARVIEW MIRROR AS GRAY turned onto the road that would take him to the county jail. I felt a little pang in the region of my chest as he disappeared from sight, and I rubbed one hand over the spot. I hated not being with him. I felt like part of me was missing, like I didn't quite feel whole without him. He was such a big part of my life—more so now, even—and I was quickly realizing that I wanted to spend every single day with him.

I let out a little sigh as I dug through my purse and pulled out my phone. Gray would yell at me for talking while driving, but he wasn't here right now and I needed to let my sister know I was on my way to her place. I knew where the spare key was, but I didn't like to show up unannounced.

Pulling up my contact list, I tapped my sister's number and waited for the call to connect. Three short rings later, Jane's voice filled the line. "Hey, sis. What's going on?"

"Not much. Gray's busy today, so I was actually just wondering if I could stop by."

"Everything good?"

I hesitated, then debated whether to tell her about Trent

once I got to the house. "Yeah, but Gray doesn't want me to be alone right now, so I figured I would head up your way, get out of Cedar Springs for a bit."

"Hold on one second," my sister huffed on the other end. There was a brief, muffled exchange, and a minute later she was back. "You're a godsend. Allie's got some volleyball tournament going on all day, and I've already been sitting here for four hours bored out of my mind."

I couldn't help but laugh. My sister had never been big into sports, and she definitely hadn't developed a fondness for them despite living in Texas and being married to an ex-college football star. "Don't let anyone hear you say that. You'll start a riot."

"At least then something would actually happen," she grumbled. "Anyway, I'm almost to my car. I can be there in about half an hour."

I glanced at the clock. "That's perfect. I should be there about the same time."

"See you then."

I hung up and turned my attention to the road in front of me. The miles spun away and my thoughts drifted back to Gray as they always did. It still blew my mind sometimes how quickly things had changed between us. Gray was my best friend, but he was also my lover. I could see us getting married, having kids, and settling down. I wanted that so badly my heart ached with need. Gray would be an amazing father. My thoughts drifted to his family, the way they'd welcomed me in, even before Gray and I had taken our relationship to the next level. They were an incredible support system, and I wanted what they had.

Jane and I had never really been close to our parents, even when we were young. It seemed like having kids was some kind of requirement they'd ticked off in their box of life accomplishments, but they'd never really enjoyed being parents. They'd never really enjoyed being married—at least, not to each other, and not for any significant amount of time. My father had remarried four times that I was aware of, and my mother was currently on husband number three.

I knew they were relieved when Jane and I graduated and were officially out of their hair. We corresponded once or twice a year, typically on holidays or birthdays, but never beyond that. They were so far removed from my life that they seemed more like distant acquaintances than immediate family.

I wanted better for myself and my future children, wanted to give them the security and love Jane and I had never received. I felt sad knowing that my future children wouldn't ever see their grandparents, but the love they received from everyone else would more than make up for it. The Thornes welcomed everyone into their home, treated everyone like family. No grandchildren would ever feel unwanted or unloved with them around.

Did Gray even want kids? I wasn't sure. He'd never said anything, and I'd never asked. I think part of me was afraid of the answer, unable to contemplate the idea of him with another woman, with a family that I wouldn't be part of. I knew I was getting ahead of myself, but I couldn't help it. Now that the image had sprung to my mind, I couldn't think of anything else.

What would a child of ours look like? Would they have Gray's hazel eyes or my honey-colored irises? Would they take my auburn locks and fair skin or Gray's darker coloring? Unable to stop it, a smile pulled at my lips. It was craziness to even consider these things, but at the same time... I knew I wanted him, wanted to spend the rest of my life with him.

I turned into my sister's subdivision just after one o'clock then turned down the street that would take me to her house. Her driveway was empty, so I parked in front of the garage then climbed out of the car. I suspected she would be here soon, so I settled against the fender to wait for her to arrive. Less than two minutes later, the hum of an engine drew my attention, and I watched her silver minivan approach, followed by a smaller sedan. As soon as Jane pulled in beside me, the sedan accelerated and swerved around her, then sped down the road.

Jane climbed from the van and threw an angry glare at the car as it disappeared from sight. "Asshole. People drive too damn fast in here."

"I'll say. You need someone to patrol in here. What if there were kids out here playing?"

"Right?" She gestured with her hand, then rolled her eyes. "You'd think they'd be a little more respectful."

I followed my sister inside, where she dropped her purse and keys on the counter, then turned to me. "Spill."

"What?" I affected my most innocent expression as I slid onto a stool at the island.

One dark brow arched upward. "Don't even try that with me. I haven't talked to you for two weeks, but I can tell something is different."

I tipped my head at her, fighting a smile. "Such as?"

Her eyes narrowed. "You're banging him, aren't you?"

A bark of laughter broke from my throat. "Oh, my God. Did you seriously just say banging? Allie would be so embarrassed by you right now."

"Wouldn't be the first time. And for the love of God, please don't ever bring up my daughter's name in conjunction with sex ever again. I am in no way prepared for that yet."

I raised my hands in supplication and fought to get my laughter under control. "Okay, okay. Fair enough."

"Anyway." My sister waved one hand in the air. "Banging, boinking, fucking, whatever the kids are saying these days. You're doing it—with Gray."

I bit down on my tongue but couldn't stop the ridiculous smile that curved my face. "Maybe."

"About damn time!" Jane rolled her eyes heavenward. "I was getting ready to stage an intervention for the two of you."

"Well, I'm happy to report that it's no longer necessary."

"I'm glad." Jane smiled, her face softening as she studied me. "How's everything going?"

I lifted a shoulder, feeling a little tongue-tied. "It's good."

Her head tipped slightly to one side as she inspected me, and I fought the urge to shift nervously. "You look... happy," she finally said.

I couldn't help but smile. "I am. I really am."

"Did you ever tell him about the dream?"

Heat raced over my cheeks. "Actually, he kind of guessed." Jane's brow arched toward her hairline, and I blushed further. "Well, I apparently, like... called his name."

Her eyes widened and a smile slowly spread over her face. "So he already knew you had the hots for him."

I rolled my eyes as embarrassment washed over me. "He had an idea. I almost ruined it, though."

I told Jane all about the week following the dream, how awkward things had become between Gray and me. I told her how he'd misconstrued my dinner with Melissa for a date, then how he'd taken me to his place and kissed me. I wasn't quite ready to tell her about Trent yet, so I glossed over the details that finally brought us together, focusing instead on my relationship with Gray.

The doorbell interrupted us, and Jane flicked a hand in the air. "Probably just a delivery. I'll get it later. So tell me everything. Is he good?"

I lifted a brow her way. "You think I'd tell you that?"

"Um, yeah. You're supposed to tell me everything."

I laughed. "Maybe not everything, but... yes. It's so good."

"Are you guys—"

Jane's words were cut off when the doorbell rang again, and she rolled her eyes as she pushed off the counter. "I'll be right back."

I stared out the window, lost in thought as she padded down the hall toward the front door. Dimly, I heard the low hum of voices, then a second set of footsteps as Jane returned with an apparent visitor. I swiveled my head toward the doorway just as they entered, and my eyes widened when they landed on the woman at my sister's side.

"What are you doing here?"

Thirty-Two

GRAY

I studied the dark-haired kid across from me. Although he had just turned 18, he was damn near as big as I was. The hard look on his face told me he resented my presence and expected me to rip into him. I decided to throw him for a loop. "Do you play football?"

He jerked a little in his seat, surprised by my question. His eyes narrowed in suspicion then he scoffed. "Not anymore."

"Oh, right." I snapped my fingers.

His face set in a mulish expression as he glared over the table at me. "Won't be going to college. And I'm done with football."

I leaned back in my chair and regarded him. "You sure? Seems to me you like to have power over people."

There was a brief flash of emotion in his eyes before dying away again. "Don't know what you're talking about."

Now it was my turn to scoff. "Are you gonna sit here and lie to my face? Are you really going to try to tell me that you haven't been targeting Claire Gates, your guidance counselor? Ex-guidance counselor," I corrected myself. "That's right, you got expelled a couple weeks ago, didn't you?"

A muscle ticked in his jaw. "That wasn't my fault."

I snorted in disbelief. "Of course not. Why would it be your fault?"

Instead of defending himself, Trent slouched insouciantly in his chair. "Just say whatever the hell it is you came to say, then go home."

The kid had a serious attitude problem. "In case you haven't noticed, you're not exactly in a position to make demands or play games. You wanna talk man to man? Let's do it."

"Whatever."

"You've been screaming for attention for the past two years, and the only way you know how to do that is to pick fights and start trouble." I watched as his eyes narrowed, his shoulders tensing. He tipped his head side to side as if stretching his neck.

"If you say so." Trent smirked, but he wasn't looking nearly as confident or unaffected as he had a few minutes ago.

Good, I was getting under his skin already. I wanted to piss him off, needle him until he broke. Because that's when the truth would come out.

"You were too immature to handle what was going on, so you took it out on Claire. You lashed out at her for your own failings. You threatened not only Claire, but Ms. Kramer. But she didn't feel bad for you the way Claire did. She had your ass expelled. She gave you exactly what you deserved because you're nothing but a needy little boy crying for attention—"

"THAT'S NOT WHAT HAPPENED!" HE EXPLODED AS HE launched forward in his seat and slammed his hands on the table.

THE GUARD STARTED FORWARD, BUT I HELD UP A hand to stop him. He warily retreated, and I fixed Trent with a stare. "That's not what happened?" He glared and sat back in his seat.

"If that's how you want to play it." I laced my hands together on the table in front of me and leaned toward him. "Let's start at the beginning. You left the tarantula in Ms. Gates's desk for her to find."

Trent remained silent, so I continued. "The spider was just to scare her. But once you got expelled, you wanted revenge. That's why you planted the snake in her car."

Trent's brows drew together. "The what? I didn't—"

I ignored him. "Then there were the phone calls."

"Phone calls?"

"That's harassment, you know," I said as I leaned back in my chair. "She could press charges for that."

Trent sat up straight and shook his head emphatically. "No. I never called her—I don't even know her number."

"You sure? Because I think you got it from her cell when you put that spider in her desk."

"I didn't do any of that." I leveled him with a hard stare, and he made a little face. "I mean... Yeah, okay, the spider was my idea. But he was harmless. And the phone calls or whatever? I never did that." He raised his hands in front of him. "I didn't have anything to do with that stuff."

"No?" I arched one brow upward. "Because that's exactly what I think happened. I think you enjoy her fear. I think you liked knowing you'd scared her. Stalking her and calling her when she stepped outside her house that morning. Where were you hiding?"

Trent shook his head again. "That wasn't me, I swear. You can check my phone, I never called her. I don't even know where she lives."

He seemed genuinely distraught, but anyone could affect an innocent expression. "You know, all those things I could have written off as childish pranks. But the moment you killed that rabbit and left it for her..."

"What?" Trent paled visibly. "N-no. That wasn't me. That's disgusting." He shuddered. "I know you don't believe me, but..."

He swallowed hard, his contrite gaze dropping to the table between us. "You're right. I was upset about what Mrs. Gates said about my parents. It really got to me, and I wanted to pay her back for that. That's why I left the spider in her desk. It was an asshole thing to do, and I felt bad as soon as it happened."

More likely he was upset he got caught and then expelled, but I let that slide. "Then why have you been hiding?"

Trent lifted one shoulder but kept his gaze fixed on the table. "I dunno."

I didn't say a word when he fell silent, just waited for him to gather the courage to continue. Finally he spoke. "I guess... I mean, my parents are so absorbed with themselves they don't even know I'm around anymore."

I knew from speaking with them that what he said was the truth. "Did you call them when you got picked up yesterday?"

Trent shook his head. "They wouldn't care anyway."

A twinge of sympathy moved through me. Claire was right that he was the product of asshole parents, but he was old enough for a reality check. "This time you got picked up for larceny. What do you think will happen next time?"

Trent didn't say a word, and anger simmered in my blood. "Stealing seems to be a common problem with you. Just like you stole Ms. Gates's photo, right?"

His gaze lifted to mine, more curious than angry. "What?"

"The photo she kept on her window." I lifted it from where it rested on the bench next to me and laid it face up in front of him. "This one."

Trent shook his head. "No, I—"

"You returned it when you left the dead animal for her, didn't you?"

"No, I swear." His eyes rounded as he stared at me. "The last time I saw that picture, it was in her desk."

"It was in Claire's desk?" That didn't make sense at all. Claire said it had disappeared; she certainly would have noticed if it had been placed inside her desk. "Did you grab it when you left the spider?"

"No, not Ms. Gates." He held my gaze, imploring me to listen. "That's what I tried to tell them."

What the fuck was I missing? "So, if it wasn't in Ms. Gates's desk, where was it?"

"Exactly where I told them," he said, his voice tinged with exasperation. "It was in Ms. Kramer's desk."

Thirty-Three

CLAIRE

I blinked at Melissa, who stood in the doorway next to my sister. What in the world was she doing here? And how did she even know where I was?

Melissa offered a tremulous smile and wiped her palms nervously on the thighs of her jeans. "I'm sorry, I know this is a little random, me showing up like this. I hope you don't mind."

I shook off the shock that clung to me. "No, of course not. I'm just surprised is all."

She offered a little shrug, still looking uncomfortable. "I was with Mac when he got the call from Grayson. He heard about Trent getting picked up over in Delton, so I thought I'd come keep you company while he was busy."

"Sure." I nodded slowly as I waved her over. "Come join us."

Melissa took a seat next to me, and Jane leaned her elbows on the counter. "Do you want something to drink?"

"Sure." Melissa smiled her way. "Whatever you have is fine, thanks."

Jane poured her a glass of tea, then slid it to her. "So you work with Claire?"

Melissa took a sip, then nodded. "My position isn't permanent right now. I'm actually just here through the end of the year covering Mrs. Cornwell while she's on maternity leave."

"That's nice. Do you have plans for next year?" my sister asked.

Melissa shrugged. "Depends how things play out."

"We don't have a very high turnover," I explained to Jane before turning back to Melissa. "Hopefully one of the neighboring districts will have a position open up so you can stay close."

"That would be nice." She offered a little smile and lifted one shoulder. "I guess we'll see."

"God, I'm starving," Jane said. "Thank God Claire called when she did. I spent all morning at a function for my daughter and the concession stand food just didn't cut it. I've got some cheese we can munch on, or I can call for a pizza."

Melissa shook her head like it didn't matter, and I waved off Jane's offer. "You don't have to do anything special. Cheese would be fine for me."

Hopefully I wouldn't be here too long anyway. I wondered how things were going with Gray and Trent. Would he admit to the phone calls and pranks, or would he play dumb? I barely suppressed a shudder at the memory of the poor dead rabbit that had been delivered to my house. I still couldn't believe he was capable of such a thing.

"Claire?"

The sound of my sister's voice calling my name jerked my attention back to her. "Sorry. I was daydreaming. What'd you say?"

Jane spoke as she began to pull various blocks of cheese from the fridge and stacked them on a cutting board. "Can you grab some crackers from the pantry? There are some olives in there, too, and anything else you want."

"Let me help," Melissa offered. She climbed from her stool and rounded the island to stand next to Jane. "Do you prefer them cut a certain way?"

"Nope." Jane waved a hand. "Whatever you want is fine."

While they sliced up the cheese, I raided the pantry for snack crackers. I finally unearthed a box and carried them back to the table.

Melissa glanced over at me. "How's everything going with Trent?"

Who's Trent?" I felt Jane's gaze flick between the two of us. "I heard you mention him earlier."

I sighed as I peeled open the package, then set it aside. "He's a kid from school."

"He's a troublemaker," Melissa added. "

Jane's brows drew together. "What do you mean?"

I reluctantly explained everything that had happened recently, and Melissa nodded emphatically. "He could be dangerous. I'm glad they have him in custody."

My sister still looked worried. "But they picked him up for stealing somewhere else, right? What about everything with you?"

I shrugged, downplaying the concern that twisted my stomach into knots. "They're going to question him, see what he says."

"What if he doesn't admit to any of it?" Jane pierced me with her gaze. "What then?"

I bit my lip. "I'm not sure. I'll talk with Gray when I get home and see what happens."

An awkward silence fell for several moments, all of us lost in thought. I could tell the information hadn't appeased my sister at all; in all honesty, it still bothered the hell out of me, too. Something about this whole thing just felt... off. Maybe it was because I didn't want to believe Trent could do something so awful. Maybe it was some sort of female intuition that told me it just didn't jive. I couldn't be sure. All I knew was that I wouldn't rest easy until we had a definitive answer one way or the other. I hoped it would come sooner rather than later, because my nerves were almost completely frayed.

"So you said your husband and daughter are at a volleyball thing?" Melissa finally asked as she chopped away.

Jane nodded. "God knows I love that child, but I could do without the sports that take up every second of free time."

"Yeah, it's a lot," Melissa commiserated. "Is she your only child?"

"Yep." My sister grimaced. "I wasn't brave enough to have a second one after her."

I couldn't help but grin. "Everyone says that raising girls is easier, but they clearly haven't met Allie or Izzy," I said, referencing Gray's baby sister.

"Funny how kids have their own personalities," Melissa mused.

Jane set aside a handful of cheese cubes, and I swiped one off the tray and popped it into my mouth. "It's true. Even with Jane and me, I think we're as similar as we are different."

Melissa nodded, looking deep in thought. "You guys are lucky to have each other."

Jane made a little sound as she rinsed off her knife and set it in the sink, then threw a teasing glance my way. "Some days."

I rolled my eyes. "You don't know what you'd do without me."

She stuck her tongue out at me, and I couldn't help but laugh.

Melissa smiled, but it lacked its usual warmth. "My brother and I were inseparable. We did everything together."

My brows shot up at Melissa's admission. She'd

mentioned losing her parents last year but she'd never said anything about a brother. "I didn't know you had a brother."

"I don't. Not anymore." The knife struck the cutting board with a hard thwack, making me jump. Melissa kept her eyes forward, but a tremor ran through her cheek as her jaw clenched.

Oh. Jane and I shared a wide-eyed look. I wasn't quite sure what to say. I couldn't begin to imagine how it had been for her to lose her parents and her brother. I wasn't sure when he'd passed or how, but that was a lot of loss for one person to deal with. "I'm sorry, I didn't realize."

She drew in a deep breath, then let it out, her gaze focused on the cutting board in front of her. "He was three years older than me, but he was my best friend. He meant the world to me."

I offered a soft smile. "He sounds wonderful."

"He was." Her gaze met mine, and I nearly shrank back at the animosity lurking in the icy depths. Whatever had happened, she obviously still hadn't gotten over it. Before I could say anything, she continued. "My parents' deaths were expected. They were sick, and it was almost a relief to see them finally at peace. But my brother?"

Her entire body trembled. "I will never forget that. A car accident is so quick. One minute they're there and the next"—she snapped her fingers—"they're gone. And you don't even get a chance to say goodbye."

She flicked a look my way, and a chill ran down my spine. I'd never seen her look so... cold. I opened my mouth to speak, but her next words cut me off. "You would know all about that, wouldn't you, Claire? Isn't that what happened to your boyfriend?"

Jane's brow furrowed, her gaze bouncing between Melissa and me. Of course she knew about what had happened with Bryan, but it wasn't exactly common knowledge. Had Melissa gone to school with us? I didn't think so. Only my family knew the true version of events from that night. I'd never breathed a word to anyone, and I knew Jane would never betray my trust by confiding those details, either.

This whole thing was making me uncomfortable, and I wanted no part of it. But how could I ask her to leave without being rude?

Melissa adjusted her grip on the handle of the knife so it faced downward and dug the tip of the blade into the cutting board. A malicious smile twisted her face as she peered across the counter at me. "You lied to everyone. Didn't you, Claire?"

I felt my mouth open in surprise. What the hell was she talking about? "N-no, I never lied. I—"

"You did!" Melissa cut me off as if I'd never even spoken, her expression dark, hatred brewing in her blue eyes. "I lost my entire family because of you. Now I'm going to show you how it feels to lose the ones you love."

The knife was a silvery blur as it whipped through the air, and Jane's mouth formed a small 'O' of surprise as the knife sank into her stomach.

Thirty-Four

GRAY

My mind spun as his words sank in. "Let me get this straight. This picture"—I pointed to the photo on the desk—"was in Ms. Kramer's desk."

Trent nodded seriously, eyes wide. I scrubbed one hand over my face and sat back in my chair. "You seriously expect me to believe that?"

"It's true!"

His eyes flashed with anger, and I pointed a finger at him. "Reel it in. You're already in enough trouble as it is."

He slouched in his chair and crossed his arms over his chest. "Whatever."

I bit the inside of my cheek to keep from snapping at him. His story didn't line up. Why the hell would Melissa Kramer have Claire's photo in her desk? Trent had been thrown out of school for getting into an altercation with the teacher, so it made sense that he would want some sort of retribution for that. And what better way than to blame both Claire and Melissa for him getting into trouble?

His accusations were outlandish to say the least, but this was the only thing I had to go on at the moment. I drew in a deep breath and pinned Trent with a stare. "Start from the beginning."

He snorted. "You wouldn't believe me anyway."

Maybe, maybe not. "Try me."

"I went into Ms. Kramer's room during her free period while she was gone." I lifted a brow his way. Trent rolled his eyes, but his shoulders dropped a fraction in defeat. "Fine. I was pissed because she wouldn't let me retake the test we'd just had. I'd bombed, and she told me I could retake it, then changed her mind."

"So you planned to do... what?"

"I dunno." He shrugged. "I was gonna do something to Ms. Kramer, just like I did with Ms. Gates. Nothing bad, just... you know. Something to scare her a little for being such a bitch."

I bit my tongue and nodded for him to continue. Fighting with him now wasn't going to help matters, so I decided to keep my mouth shut and bide my time. Maybe he'd eventually give me something I could use.

"Anyway. I was poking around her desk, trying to find something I could use against her. But then I found the answers to the next math test in one of the drawers. I decided what the hell. She wouldn't let me retake the last test, then I was gonna ace the next one."

Well, not the worst thing in the world, I supposed. I didn't condone it, but at least he hadn't done anything destructive or hurtful. "Okay. Then what happened?"

He eyed me warily, then continued, "So, I grabbed the score sheet so I could make a copy then sneak it back in before she'd notice. But that's when I saw the picture."

I gestured toward the frame again. "This one?"

"Yep." He nodded. "It was right there under the test. I remembered Ms. Gates had been looking for it the other day."

"She told you that?"

"No, not exactly. But I've been in her office enough recently." He rolled his eyes heavenward. "I have the damn thing memorized by this point. She had two pictures on her windowsill. This one was missing the last time I was in there."

Interesting. "What happened then?"

He sighed. "Ms. Kramer came in and saw me with the photo. That's when she freaked out. She ripped the photo and the test answers out of my hands and started yelling at me. I tried to ask her why she had the picture, but she was going crazy. Started crying and screaming that I was harassing her, and a whole bunch of the kids overheard."

The back of my neck prickled. "Which is how you ended up in the principal's office."

"Yeah." He blew out a harsh breath. "I never touched her. She's fucking crazy."

"What happened to the photo after that?"

"Not sure. By the time I went to the principal's office, she'd gotten rid of it. She told him I'd been stealing"—he held up one hand—"I know. That part was true. But she never explained about the picture. And every time I tried to bring it up, she cut me off, started crying all over again. He didn't believe me. No one did."

I had to admit—it sounded insane. But over the course of my career, I'd learned that some shit was too crazy to make up. "Anything else?"

He mulled it over for a second, then shook his head. "Not that I can think of."

I drummed my fingers on the metal table, a million thoughts running through my head. "I don't know what I can do about the larceny charges"—I held up a finger in his direction when his mouth dropped open—"but I'll try to work something out. I need to check on a few things first. Hang tight."

He crossed his arms over his chest again, his lips a firm

white line as dejectedness tugged at his features. "Not like I'm going anywhere."

"Listen." I planted my hands on the table and leaned toward him as I stood. "I believe you. But you throwing attitude around isn't going to help anyone right now. Ever hear the phrase, 'you'll catch more flies with honey?' Dial down the anger a little bit and let me help you."

After a few tense seconds, his posture relaxed. "Sorry."

For the first time since I'd entered the room, I saw a glimmer of the bright young man he'd been before his world had turned to shit. "Have you eaten yet?"

He blinked and his mouth opened then snapped shut again before he gave a tiny shake of his head. I stared at him. The kid had a ton of potential, and he'd been thrust into a situation where he had to take care of himself because his parents had let him down. He'd been doing his best to survive a shitty situation, and he deserved a break. "Burgers okay?"

"Sure."

His wide eyes studied me like he wasn't sure how to act, and I offered a little smile. "It's not a trick. I'll have one of the guys grab something to eat, or I'll DoorDash it if no one's available."

He swallowed hard, his gaze darting over my shoulder. "Thanks."

"No problem." I stood. "I need to make some phone calls. I'll be back to check on you in a few."

I retreated from the room and found a patrolman at his desk. "Can you call in an order for me?"

I told him what I needed for Trent, then made my way outside where it was quiet. Drew was still tied up with his case, so I called our other detective, Finn Murphy. He picked up on the second ring. "Chief?"

"Hey." I rubbed my temples, wondering if I was crazy for even considering this. "Are you in the office by chance?"

"Yep. Whatcha need?"

"I need a favor. There's a teacher that Claire works with—Melissa Kramer."

There was a long pause on the other end, and I could practically hear the wheels turning in his head. "The one who's...?"

"Yeah." The very same woman one of my men was currently dating. "I need you to run background on her, see what comes up?"

There was a soft scuffling sound on the other end, and Finn came back several seconds later. "She stopped in to see Mac for lunch and left not that long ago. Do I need to have her brought in?"

I quickly discarded the idea. "Not yet. For now, just run her name and see what comes up."

"You got it. I'll be in touch."

He disconnected, and I tapped my foot impatiently on the sidewalk, my mind spinning. Why would Melissa have any reason to take Claire's picture, let alone harass her? She was new to the area and had seemed nice enough. I briefly considered calling Claire to see if she could think of any reason, but I didn't want to bother her while she was with Jane.

She'd texted just a little bit ago to let me know she'd arrived, and I already missed her like crazy. I wanted to get this shit wrapped up so everything could finally go back to normal.

A sedan pulled up and parked in front of the jail, and one of the corrections officers climbed out, takeout bag in hand. She passed it to me. "I think this is yours."

"Thanks. I really appreciate it."

A niggle of worry tugged at the back of my brain as I made my way back to the interview room. Trent would be free to leave soon, and I wanted to make sure I had all the information before he slipped off the hook again. I studied him as I handed the food across the table. "You sure you don't remember anything else?"

He shook his head as he dug into the hamburger. "Nope. I don't think so."

My lips pressed into a flat line as I leaned back against the wall. I fucking hated this game—waiting for leads, waiting for information. My phone buzzed, and my heart jumped at the sound. "Excuse me."

I ducked from the room and swiped a thumb over the screen. "What'd you find?"

"Not entirely sure," Finn replied, his voice low and cautious. "Looks like Melissa changed her name last year, citing harassment charges from an ex-boyfriend."

Well, that was interesting. Could explain how she'd ended up in a small town like Cedar Springs. "What was her given name?"

"Krantz."

I froze. Why did that sound so familiar? "What do we know about her life before?"

"Lived in Killeen before she moved to Cedar Springs a couple months ago. Graduated from UT two years with a degree in education, but this is her first position." He paused for a second. "That's interesting."

He waited so long I wanted to rip my hair out. "What?"

He made a little humming sound before continuing. "Looks like both parents are deceased, as well as a brother."

A chill ran down my spine. "What was the brother's name?"

My heart thudded heavily in my chest as I waited for his response.

"Here it is." I knew what he was going to say even before it left his mouth. "Bryan. Bryan Krantz. Deceased at twenty-two..."

Everything went out of focus for a second as the world spun beneath my feet. Melissa was related to Brandon Krantz, the boyfriend Claire had lost in college.

"Chief?"

I forced myself to tune back in to what Finn was saying. "I need to ask her some questions. See if you can find her. And, Finn—be discreet."

The last thing I needed right now was for Mac to find out and lose his shit.

"I'll take care of it." His voice was low and solemn.

I ended the call, and immediately swiped to my contacts to try Claire as I pushed out of the jail at a fast clip. Two rings rolled into three, then four.

"Come on, baby, pick up," I urged.

Her voicemail picked up, and I let out a low growl as I punched the button to end the call. Until I figured out what the hell was going on, I didn't want her talking to Melissa. I climbed into my car and headed toward Jane's house, dialing as I went. Her phone rolled over to voicemail too, and my heart lodged in my throat. I didn't want to blow things out of proportion, but...

Shit. All of my guys were busy working with Drew on the sexual assault case, and I was still half an hour from Jane's house. Did I know anyone closer?

Shit, shit, shit.

Dread curdled in my gut. Something was wrong—I could feel it. I palmed my phone, then flipped through my contacts until I found the person I was looking for. Connor Quentin owned a personal protection agency but lived just outside of Cedar Springs. If anyone could understand my plight, it would be him.

The call connected after two rings. "Quentin."

"Con, it's Grayson Thorne." I didn't bother with niceties. "Listen, I have a huge favor to ask."

"Shoot."

I briefly explained the recent incidents with Claire and how Melissa could potentially be involved. "I'm just leaving county, so I'm thirty minutes out. Is there any way you can swing up to check?" I could call the local police, but I didn't want to waste their time if it was a false alarm. "I wouldn't ask, but... I just have this gut feeling something's wrong."

"I understand." I heard the shuffle of movement in the background. "I'm leaving now. I can be there in fifteen or so."

Relief rushed through me. "Thank you, I appreciate it."

"No problem. Besides, I owe you one."

Several months ago, Con's wife, Grace, had been targeted by a stalker. He'd nearly succeeded in poisoning her father, and Con had been shot when the man tried to kidnap Grace. "You don't owe me shit. I was just doing my job."

"And I'm just doing mine," came his no-bullshit reply. "Now, anything else I need to know going in?"

I gave him a brief overview of Melissa's background and her brother's ties to Claire. "She just moved to Cedar Springs a few months ago, shortly after her parents passed."

"Could be the trigger that set her off," Con said, echoing my thoughts. "Sounds like she blames Claire for what happened to her brother."

"Yeah, that's what I'm afraid of." My lips pressed into a grim line. "I'll feel better once I know she's safe."

"You got it."

I rattled off Jane's address, then disconnected the call. Part of me felt bad sending Con on a wild goose chase, but I couldn't shake the icy sensation that formed along my spine.

I clenched my hands on the wheel and pressed down on the accelerator, knowing deep down that shit was about to go sideways.

Thirty-Five

CLAIRE

A SCREAM CUT THROUGH THE AIR, AND I DIMLY realized that it was coming from me. I lunged to my feet as Jane gasped and clutched her side, her eyes wide with fear, face creased with pain. Time slowed and everything around me disappeared, caught in a sort of demented tunnel vision, my gaze fixed on Melissa. I watched in horror as she pulled the knife free and Jane collapsed to the floor. Blood thrummed hard and fast through my veins, and hysteria reared swiftly. I started to move toward them, but Melissa pointed the knife my way.

"Don't move!"

My heart raced, but my feet froze at her command. Anger and fear swirled in my stomach, my mind still struggling with the events of the past several minutes. "What the hell is wrong with you?"

"Me?" One brow ratcheted toward her hairline. "I think we should talk about you."

My mouth opened and closed, and my mind spun. I grasped the back of the chair beside me as the world tilted beneath my feet. "You just stabbed my sister! Are you crazy?"

She snorted. "Not hardly. You have no idea how long I've waited to do this."

"What the hell are you talking about? Why are you doing this?"

"You really don't get it, do you?" Melissa gave a slow shake of her head. "I should have killed you a long time ago."

She lunged toward me, but I threw the chair into her path, blocking her. I leaped backward, intending to round the island and make a run for it, but Melissa retreated in the opposite direction. She narrowed her gaze and took a step to her right, toward the end of the island. I automatically stepped to the right, keeping the island between us as we circled each other. Damn it!

"You're insane!" I shrieked. "You killed her!"

From the opposite side of the island, Jane let out an agonized groan. I moved toward her, but Melissa countered my steps with two of her own. I was backed into a corner, literally. With the counter at my back, I had to pass the island to get to the sliding door that led to the patio, or I could cut down the hallway and make a run for the front door. Either way, I had to get past Melissa. She lifted the knife and twirled it idly between her fingers. I couldn't see my sister where she lay ensconced behind the island, and I prayed she was okay.

"You still don't get it, do you?"

"That you've lost your damn mind?" I let out a stifled laugh. I couldn't believe I thought this woman was my friend. "That's pretty obvious."

"No, you idiot!" She slammed the handle of the knife against the counter, and I flinched as light glinted off the blade. "Do you know who I am?"

I stared at her, dumfounded. She stared right back, head tipped slightly to one side. "You killed everyone I loved. And now I'll do the same to you. I'll make you watch your sister die, then I'll kill you, too."

I blinked rapidly, trying desperately to process her words. What the hell was she talking about? I'd only just met her. She'd started at Cedar Springs High just last month, so I knew I'd never seen her before that. I shook my head. "I haven't killed anyone."

"Maybe not personally, but you were responsible just the same."

My mouth dropped open, then I snapped it shut again as a familiar guilt came rushing back over me. The last time I'd felt this way was when... I froze. I studied her features, really stared at her, and trepidation streamed through me as my mind slowly connected the dots. The car accident that claimed Bryan's life. Melissa's brother dying in a car accident.

Bryan.

His sister *Melissa*.

Oh, God. I shook my head. It couldn't be. "No. You can't..."

"Yes." Melissa's lips twisted into a mirthless smile. "It's me."

When we were in college, he'd mentioned his younger sister a couple of times, but we'd never met. I'd even seen pictures of her, but she'd been a teenager, and she looked vastly different than she had five years ago.

"How do you like it, Claire? How does it feel to lose your sibling—the one person you know will always be there for you?"

"N-no." I shook my head. "He made the choice to get in that car. He—"

"It was all your fault! He never would have done it if it weren't for you!"

A wave of nausea rose up, and tears stung the backs of my eyes. I opened my mouth, but before I could say anything, Gray's voice floated back to me. It's not your fault. I shook my head again and stood a little taller. "I didn't make him drink that night. He made the choice to get in the car. Had I known, I would have told him—"

"It never should have happened!" She brandished the knife in my direction and waved it wildly. "You were supposed to drive! He asked you to drive him, and you didn't!"

Everything inside me stilled, and bile crept up my throat. "How... How did you know that?"

I'd never told anyone that before Gray. I'd carried that guilt with me for the last several years. There was no way she could know.

Melissa glared at me, hate emanating from her in waves. "If you'd driven him like he asked, he would still be here. He asked, and you told him no like the bitch you are. Want to know how I know?"

I shook my head, but she continued anyway. "He was on his way to the store when he called me. He said you'd refused him—again."

"He had a problem!" My voice broke on an anguished cry as tears crept into my eyes. "I was trying to help him!"

"You were being a selfish bitch!" She thrust the knife in my direction. "He needed your help, and you turned him down!"

"I—"

"Do you know what it's like, Claire? Do you?" Her voice rose several octaves. "I heard *everything*."

My stomach twisted, and I wanted to cover my ears to block out the rest of her words. I couldn't bear to think of it.

"One minute, we were talking, the next..." She shook her head. "I'll never forget that sound. The glass shattering, the metal crunching. I hear my brother's cries, listen to him take his last breaths every night in my dreams."

Oh, God. "I'm so sorry, I—"

"No!" She shrieked the word, her eyes burning with a wild fury as she glared at me. "You don't get to apologize! You didn't just take my brother that day. You took everything. My family, my life. My parents gave up after we lost him. They stopped caring, stopped living. I watched them slowly deteriorate before my eyes until they were shells of the people they'd been. You killed them all."

There would be no rationalizing with her, that much was painfully obvious. Her judgment had been clouded by grief and resentment. She believed I was responsible, and no one would ever be able to convince her otherwise.

Fear clutched at my throat, and I quickly debated my options. If I could just get outside, get someone's attention... Melissa seemed to know exactly what I was thinking, because she leaned over the island, knife slashing through the air as she swiped at me. I dodged the blow and as fast as I could, I threw myself toward the living room. I heard the pounding of feet as Melissa ran after me, but I kept my gaze forward, my only goal to make it to the front door.

The edge of the rug flipped up as I raced across the room, and my feet tangled just as Melissa slammed into me from behind. We crashed to the ground, and pain radiated throughout my body. Adrenaline coursed through my veins, and I fought to keep going. I kicked and punched at the woman on top of me, trying to throw her off. Melissa drove the knife downward, and I threw myself to the side just as the blade whipped past my face. It sank into the floor, and Melissa's face twisted into a grotesque grimace as she yanked it free.

I used the distraction to shove her off balance, then rolled to my knees. Melissa whipped the blade my way, and a burning sensation slashed across my forearm as the blade cut through skin. I hissed at the contact and pulled my injured arm in close to my chest. Fury rippled across her face, and she swung the knife in an arc once more. Using all my strength, I brought my knee up between us and drove it into her stomach. Her mouth opened on a grunt of pain, and the knife clattered to the floor and slid out of reach.

Melissa leaped forward, grabbing my shoulders and pinning me to the ground. She howled as I scratched at her face and neck, grabbing her hair and pulling anything I could reach. Her hands slid downward and closed around my neck. She slammed me backward once, twice, and the air left my lungs, stars dancing before my eyes. Blood coated my hand and arm, and it smeared over Melissa's face as I fought to hold her off.

The doorbell rang, catching us both off guard, and we momentarily froze. I recovered quickly. "Help!" I screamed the word as loud as I could, and Melissa's hold tightened.

Her eyes glowed with anger as her grip tightened. Black spots crept into the edges of my vision, my lungs burning in need of oxygen. I scratched at her face, clawed at her eyes, but my movements were jerky and uneven. A cruel smile twisted her lips as she stared down at me. She opened her mouth and froze.

Her eyes went wide, and her grip slackened. Her body jolted several times in rapid succession, then she slumped forward. I scrambled away, dragging much needed breath into my lungs. My vision cleared, and I saw Jane on her knees behind Melissa, knife in hand.

The pounding of footsteps drew our attention, and Jane brandished the weapon at the dark-haired stranger. He held his hands up as he approached. "Gray sent me."

It took a second for his face to register, and I laid my hand on Jane's arm, stilling her. "It's okay."

Slowly he approached Melissa, sidestepping the pool of blood that seeped outward. Lowering himself to a knee next to her, he pressed his fingers to her neck to check for a pulse. Connor Quentin's dark eyes met mine, and he gave a tiny shake of his head.

A breath filtered from my lips as I turned toward my sister. She met my gaze, and the knife slipped from her fingers. The echo of the clatter bounced off the walls, startling me into action. With a broken cry, I launched myself toward her. Tears came hard and fast as we wrapped our arms around each other and held on tight.

Thirty-Six

GRAY

M y h e a r t l o d g e d i n m y t h r o a t, a n d I p r e s s e d m y
foot down on the accelerator, my heart thudding hard in time
with the blue and red lights pulsing up ahead. I slid to a stop
behind one of the cruisers and had already thrown open the
door before the car was in park. My gaze honed in on the two
ambulances parked in front of Jane's house, and a sick sense of
dread welled up, threatening to choke me. I held up my badge
as I ducked beneath the yellow tape encircling the scene.

"Sir, you can't—"

I waved my badge in the patrolman's direction, my gaze
never leaving the vehicles in front of me. Fear clutched at my
throat as I rounded the first ambulance and my gaze landed on
its occupant. Jane. She was covered in blood from head to toe,
some of it bright red, other patches brown and crusty. But she
was awake and alert, and her eyes clashed with mine. She lifted
a shaky hand and pointed toward the second ambulance.

I started forward at a dead run, terrified at what I might
find, but needing to know nonetheless. I paused at the back of
the ambulance and braced one hand against the glossy red

enamel, then drew a deep breath. Stealing myself, I stepped forward. Claire sat at the back of the ambulance, her gaze fixed somewhere in the distance. I couldn't move. Couldn't breathe. I was terrified that I was dreaming, that this wasn't real. I quickly skimmed her body for injuries. Drying blood marred her hands and shirt. A bandage covered her left forearm, but I could see nothing else.

Slowly, as if feeling my eyes on her, Claire turned her head. I took a wary step forward, then another. Like they belonged to someone else, my hands lifted to her face. Her skin was soft and pale beneath my fingertips, and I tipped her head first one way, then the other. I skimmed her face, her neck, and chest. I trailed my hands lightly over her shoulders and inspected the bandage on her arm. All the while, her eyes stayed locked on me. She didn't move. Barely even breathed.

She was okay. *Thank God.*

Once I'd ascertained for myself that she wasn't truly hurt, I grasped her elbows and guided her to her feet. As soon as she was steady, I looped my arms around her and pulled her close. "You're okay."

She gave a little nod, the top of her head brushing my chin. She held herself slightly away, her body rigid. I squeezed her even tighter, one hand sliding up to the back of her head and pressing her face to my chest. "I don't know what I'd have done if..." I couldn't complete the thought.

I felt her lungs hitch as she drew in a sharp breath. There was a brief pause before she melted into me, fingers clutching at my neck. A sob ripped from her throat, muffled by her face pressed to my chest. I held her even tighter, absorbing her entire body weight. I murmured to her as she cried, gently rocking side to side.

My heart finally began to return to its normal pace, though I felt suspiciously like crying myself. I'd come so damn close to losing her. I brushed my hand over her hair, up and down her back. I couldn't stop touching her; I never wanted to let her go.

Claire's tears finally slowed, and I pressed my lips to her temple, still not relinquishing my hold on her. She cuddled even closer, melding into me as she turned her head to the side. We stood that way in silence for a few moments, activity bustling around us. Her chest rose and fell, then she spoke. "It was Melissa."

"I know, baby." I rubbed small circles over her back. "I found out just as I was leaving the jail."

She sniffed, then pulled back to look at me. "How'd you find out?"

I laced my fingers together at her lower back, still not ready to release her. "Trent, believe it or not. Remember that day he got kicked out of school?" She nodded. "Melissa only told half the story. Trent did steal the test paperwork, but he also found your photo in her desk. That's why she freaked out."

She swallowed hard and gave a little shake of her head. "I never..."

"I know." She'd fooled everyone, Mac included. I hadn't had a chance yet to speak with him, and I wasn't looking forward to it. As soon as Claire was situated, I'd have to deliver the news personally.

Sliding one hand up her spine, I cupped the back of her neck. "You had no reason to suspect her. I wasn't even sure myself until I got here. When I saw the ambulances parked out front..." I closed my eyes and my arms automatically tightened around her waist. I couldn't tell her all the horrible things that had gone through my mind on the way here. I dipped my head and brushed a kiss over her forehead. "I'm just so fucking glad you're okay."

"Me, too."

I lightly grasped her wrist and pulled her arm down so I could inspect the bandage. I kissed her hand, then laced our fingers and pressed our joined hands to my chest. "Can you tell me what happened?"

"I got cut."

I lifted a brow, and Claire rolled her lips together. I'd understand if she wasn't ready to talk about it, but I was dying to know.

"She..." Claire's gaze darted away before fixing on our hands suspended between us. "Melissa showed up out of the blue. I should have known then because I never remembered telling her where Jane lived. She was acting... strange. I was getting ready to ask her to leave when she stabbed Jane." Her chest rose and fell on a deep breath as she gathered herself. "She just... snapped. At first I didn't even realize what was happening. She had the knife in her hand and then..."

A shudder racked her body, and I curled my fingers into her lower back where I still held her. "I couldn't see Jane, and I... I thought she was dead," she whispered brokenly. A tear slipped from the corner of her eye and rolled down her cheek, and I released her hand to wipe it away.

"I ran, but Melissa grabbed me. We fought and..." She swallowed hard. "All of a sudden, she just stopped. I didn't see Jane behind her with the knife. She stabbed her." She blinked up at me, her eyes glassy with tears. "She saved me."

My heart twisted in my chest as emotion rocked through me. Thank God for Jane. I framed her face with my hand and touched my forehead to hers. "I'm so sorry you had to go through that. I'm sorry I wasn't here for you. You're two of the bravest people I know."

Her mouth twitched a tiny bit as she attempted a weak smile. "Thank you."

I slid my hand under her jaw to cradle her face, then lifted it to mine. "I mean it. I'm so proud of you."

My gaze slid over the top of her head as a familiar face came into view. Con dipped his chin at me, and I shifted Claire to my side as he approached. "Thank you."

"It was nothing." He shook my outstretched hand, then turned his attention to Claire. "How's your arm?"

"It'll be okay." She forced a smile. "Thanks for coming to help."

"You ladies had it all under control," he demurred. "I'm just glad to see you're both okay."

"I appreciate you coming on a whim." I glanced down at Claire. "I just had this bad feeling, and I didn't know who else to call. Con happened to be the closest person."

"You'd do the same for me." His dark gaze flicked to mine. "Always trust those instincts."

That was true. We all watched each others' backs, and we all had that cops' sixth sense, that feeling of foreboding when something wasn't quite right.

"I gave my statement to the police," he said. "You need anything else?"

"No." I shook his hand once more. "Thanks again. I'll be in touch."

With that he was gone, and I glanced down at Claire. She was still pale, and I couldn't begin to imagine what she was feeling right now. I grasped her chin and tipped her head up. "I love you."

Her eyes turned liquid soft as she melted into me a little more. "Love you, too."

I pressed a kiss to her lips just as a paramedic rounded the ambulance. I nodded his way but kept my arm looped around her waist. "Sir."

He glanced at Claire. "Your sister is being transported to Cedar Springs General. We really recommend you get stitches as well."

She nodded solemnly as she shifted on her feet. "I will."

"I'll take her," I offered. I wasn't about to let her out of my sight again so soon.

Thirty-Seven

CLAIRE

THE NEEDLE PIERCED MY SKIN AGAIN, AND I instinctively squeezed Grayson's hand. Though they'd given me a local anesthetic for the pain, I could still feel the slight pinch of the needle, the pull of the thread as the doctor bound my wound. The laceration wasn't terribly deep, but it was nearly three inches long. Still, I was lucky that I was walking away with a mere cut. Jane had been admitted to the ER several hours ago and was taken back for surgery to repair the damage from her stab wound.

A shudder racked my body at the memory, and Gray squeezed my fingers. I turned and offered him a tired smile. Even though it was early evening, I felt like I'd been up for days. I was exhausted mentally and physically, but I couldn't go home until I'd seen Jane.

"There you go," the doctor said as he tied off the last stitch, then covered it with a bandage. "I'll have the nurse get you aftercare instructions, then we can get you released."

"Great." I offered a little smile. "Thank you."

He gathered his things then left the room, and Gray

shifted to the bed so he could wrap an arm around my waist. "Are you doing okay?"

"I'll be fine." I lifted my arm. "Could have been worse."

Gray didn't say anything, he just pulled me closer and pressed my face to his chest, then rested his chin on the top of my head. We stayed like that for several minutes, neither of us knowing exactly what to say, until the nurse came in. She passed me instructions for the wound, then discharged me so we could go check on Jane.

Monitors beeped as I pushed open the door. Dex sat in the chair next to the bed, and he threw a little smile my way as Gray and I entered. "Hey. All patched up?"

I held up my bandaged arm, complete with fourteen stitches. "It's just a scratch." My gaze slid toward Jane. "How is she?"

A combination of worry and relief filled his eyes as they flitted over his wife. "The surgeon said she'll be fine. It didn't hit any organs or major arteries, but she'll be sore for a while."

"I'm sure. I just wanted to stop by to apologize."

Dex pulled me into a hug. "I'm glad you were with her, and I'm just grateful you're both safe."

It didn't erase the guilt I felt at having led Melissa right to my sister, but his absolution helped. Tears sprang to my eyes. "Thank you."

Gray rested one hand on my shoulder and pulled my back against his hard chest. "Why don't we head out, sweetheart? You both need to get some rest."

Gray led me to the elevators, and I leaned into him as we rode down to the lobby. "Are you tired?" he whispered against my hair.

The prospect of sleep made me yawn, and I covered my mouth as I nodded. "Yeah, a little."

He kissed the top of my head just as the doors whooshed open. "Let's go home."

I started to nod, then tipped my head up to him as something occurred to me. "What about my car?"

"We can get it later. Is there anything inside that you need?"

Gray had the foresight to bring my purse with us to the hospital, so there was nothing of vital importance that couldn't wait. I shook my head. "Nope."

"It'll be safe enough there," he replied. "You can take a little nap on the way home if you want."

The drive to his house wasn't far, but I wasn't sure if I'd actually be able to relax enough to fall asleep. I was still worried about Jane, still a little baffled about the whole situation with Melissa. I couldn't believe she'd gone so far off the deep end.

Gray led me to his car and held the door as I slid inside. Once he'd settled in the driver seat and pulled out of the parking space, he reached over the console and slipped his hand into mine. It was warm and reassuring, and my heart swelled until it felt like it would burst. I stared out the window as we drove, my mind flitting through images like a movie reel.

I blinked as we pulled into Gray's garage, surprised that the drive had passed so quickly. He glanced at me. "Do you need help getting out?"

I couldn't help but smile at his attentiveness. "No, I'm good, thanks."

He closed the bay door and waited for me to precede him into the house, then pulled me into his arms. "Why don't you go on up to bed, and I'll be there in one second."

I trudged upstairs, already missing him as I brushed my teeth and climbed under the covers. Gray appeared barely a minute later and slid in next to me. His strong arms wrapped around my waist, and I let out a contented sigh. The tension drained from my muscles as I finally began to relax.

Thirty-Eight

GRAY

HER NOSE NESTLED INTO THE CROOK OF MY NECK, and my heart finally began to calm. I breathed her in and clutched her tighter to me. Claire melted even closer, her legs tangling with mine. I never wanted to let her go. I wanted to keep her wrapped up in my arms right here with me, where I knew she would always be safe.

I wasn't sure I'd ever be able to forget what had happened today. She'd been hurt because I was too busy chasing the wrong lead, and I never wanted to feel like that again. I'd handled a lot of cases with the PD, but with Claire... It had hit me on a deeply emotional level.

The words poured from my mouth before I could stop them. "God, baby, I was so fucking scared."

Claire pulled away the tiniest bit and tipped her head up at my admission. "I can't begin to describe all the things that went through my head walking onto that scene," I continued. "It killed me to think that I wasn't there, that you needed me and I'd let you down."

"You could never let me down. You figured out it was Melissa."

"You were hurt because I—"

"No." Her hair brushed my chin as she shook her head. "I was hurt because Melissa was broken inside. She'd carried a grudge for years and losing her parents finally tipped her over the edge."

I understood that, but it didn't eliminate my guilt. "If I hadn't sent you to Jane's, none of this would have happened."

"Of course it would have." Claire stroked my chest as she spoke. "Melissa trailed me all the way to Cedar Springs and got a job at the school so she could insinuate herself in my life and get close to me. Do you really think she'd have given up when things didn't go her way?"

Objectively, I knew what she said was the truth. I just didn't like it. I drew in a deep breath. "Seeing you hurt..."

"I have a few stitches, that's all. I'm fine."

Her voice was soft, meant to comfort me. It didn't help. "I know. But I should have protected you."

"You did," she insisted. "You were there when it mattered. Besides"—she tilted her face up and pressed a kiss to my chin —"I don't need you to protect me every second of the day. I can take care of myself."

I tightened my hold on her. "I know, but that makes me worry even more."

"Why?"

Because I loved her so fucking much, I had no idea what I'd do if I lost her. "Because I should have been there with you. I kept thinking that the whole way there. I was so focused on Trent that I completely missed—"

"Don't blame yourself." Claire slid her hand up my neck. "You think I don't feel the same way? I saw her every single day. She pretended to be my friend. I should have seen the similarities, should have noticed something. But she hid who she was, who she'd become. She was so twisted by grief that she would have done everything in her power to accomplish her goal."

I hated that she was right. Hated that no matter what we'd done, the end result probably would have been the same. If only we'd found Trent sooner. If only the principal had listened to his story in the first place.

"Wondering what could have been won't help," Claire said softly, seeming to read my thoughts. "All that matters is everyone's safe."

Thank God for that. I still couldn't stop thinking about how very close I'd come to losing her forever. I needed to feel close to her, needed her to know I was never going anywhere ever again.

I slid one hand under the thin tee shirt she wore and gently worked it up. She arched into me as her breasts were exposed to the cool night air, and her nipples pebbled to firm points. Levering up on one elbow, I took one in my mouth and sucked hard. Claire gasped as I lightly bit down, and her hands clutched at the back of my head, silently urging me to continue.

Taking care to not jostle her injured arm too much, I stripped the shirt over her head, then attacked her panties. Once she was naked, I pushed off my own boxers and maneuvered over her. Sliding one hand under her bottom, I lifted her hips until I found the slick folds of her core. I let out a little hiss as I eased my shaft inside, and it was immediately enveloped by her wet heat. I wanted to bury myself deep inside her, stay there forever.

"Fuck, Claire..."

She arched upward, curling into me, and I sank in to the hilt. Our mingled gasps filled the air, and I clutched at her hips as I tried to clamp down on my control. The urge to move hard and fast was overwhelming, but I beat it back as I stared down at her. I pulled out a few inches, then slowly slid back in.

Her tits bobbed with each shallow thrust, and I cupped one, feeling its familiar weight. Her nipple strained against my palm, tight and erect, and I brushed my thumb over the sensitive peak, eliciting a low moan of pleasure from her. Keeping the pace slow and even, I tweaked and teased the tiny point until she writhed in my arms and begged for more.

I bit down on the space where her neck met her shoulder. She let out a soft cry, and her pussy clenched around me. Fire burned low in my belly, and I knew it wouldn't be long. Bracing my hands on the bed beside her shoulders, I pulled out then changed the tempo and plunged back in hard and fast.

Claire sucked in a breath and dug her nails into my shoulders, her face twisting under the exquisite mixture of pain and pleasure. Two more deep thrusts and she came apart with a stifled cry, her body going completely lax under the force of her orgasm.

A tingling shot up my spine, and I knew I was getting close. "You're mine, Claire." I threaded one hand through her silken locks and pulled her down to me. "Forever."

She made a sexy little sound as I rolled my hips, and I claimed her mouth, curling my tongue over hers. She ripped herself away, panting as she lifted her hips with each hard thrust, giving me everything she had. "Come for me, baby... Need to feel you one more time."

As if my words spurred her on, I felt her walls clench around me, and she let out a keening cry. Her pussy clamped down on me, and I gritted my teeth, trying to stave off my orgasm. I started to lift her off me, but her knees gripped my thighs like a vise.

"Claire... Fuck, baby, I—"

I shoved deep one more time then let out a ragged groan. "Fuuuuck!"

Hot cum spurted deep, filling her up, and I pumped up

into her twice more before collapsing over her. My cock still seated firmly inside her, our bodies sealed by the combination of our sweat and lovemaking, it was the most perfect thing in the world.

Thirty-Nine

~~~~~

CLAIRE

Peeking my head around the doorway, I saw my sister lying in the stark white hospital bed, eyes closed. Dex sat in a chair by the side of the bed, phone in hand.

"Hey." I pitched my voice low so I wouldn't wake Jane.

His head jerked toward us and he climbed to his feet as Gray and I quietly stepped inside. Dex pulled me into a quick hug. "How are you feeling today?"

The stitches felt tight and uncomfortable, but it was nothing compared to what my sister had been through. I forced a little smile. "I'm okay."

He gestured to the chair he'd just vacated. "Here, have a seat."

"Where's Allie?"

"She's with my mom. They stopped by for a few minutes this morning, and they got to talk to Jane while she was awake.

"Good." I sank into the uncomfortable chair and glanced at my sister before returning my gaze to him. "How has she been today?"

"Everything seems to be fine, just really tired and sore.

She'll be weak for a bit, but she should be out of here in a couple days."

That was a reassurance, at least. Gray tossed a look at Dex. "Do you need me to grab you something to eat or drink?"

"You guys can both go."

"If you don't mind." Dex smiled, but his eyes looked tired. "I feel like I've been sitting forever."

"Of course not." I waved one hand at them. He deserved a break.

Gray grabbed my good hand and squeezed. "Do you want anything?"

"No, thanks. I'm good."

He leaned down and brushed his lips over mine, then disappeared, Dex in tow. I turned back to my sister. She looked so pale, so frail lying there that it stung my heart. This was all my fault.

Suddenly, Jane shifted on the bed and her eyes fluttered open. A small smile crossed her face. "Hey."

I stood and leaned over the bed to pull her into a gentle hug. "How are you feeling?"

Jane pressed a hand to her stomach. "Like I got stabbed," she deadpanned.

"Oh, my God, stop." The laugh that bubbled up at her dry humor turned hysterical, and tears burned the back of my throat. Heat raced over the bridge of my nose, and I hiccupped a sob as they broke free. "I'm sorry. I'm so sorry."

"Oh, honey." Jane grabbed my hand and pulled me close.

Covering my face with my hands, I buried my face in the thin white blanket that covered the bed as the tears came faster.

"Don't cry," Jane urged, her voice cracking. That only made me cry harder. She rubbed small circles over my back until we'd both calmed enough to speak.

Wiping the moisture from my cheeks, I pulled back to

study my sister. "I never meant to hurt you," I whispered. "If I'd known..."

Jane swiped at a lone tear that clung to her chin. "None of that was your fault, so don't you start."

"She came after you because of me," I said fiercely. "I practically led her right to you. And if..." God, I couldn't even fathom. If the knife had pierced Jane just a couple centimeters to either side, it would have been so much worse. She was all I had left, and I could have lost her.

"You didn't do anything," Jane insisted. "You didn't invite her. Melissa found her way to my place. She's the one to blame. Not you."

She was right; Melissa was hell-bent on revenge, and nothing would have deterred her. Except Jane did. And now she had to live with that. I swallowed down the bile that crept up my throat. "I wouldn't be here without you. You saved me. You—"

My sister grabbed my hand and squeezed. "And I would do it all over again. You're my baby sister. I will always look after you."

I offered a watery smile. "I love you."

"I love you, too."

A throat cleared behind me, and I tossed a look at Gray. He watched us with concerned eyes, and they narrowed slightly in silent question, asking if I was okay. I nodded, and a smile curled my lips as he visibly relaxed.

Jane released my hand, and I moved to Gray's side so Dex could take his place by my sister once more. "Thank you," Jane said, her gaze fixing on Gray. "For taking care of her."

He dipped his head in acknowledgment. "I'll always take care of her."

"Good." Jane smiled. "But don't you dare think of having the wedding until I'm up and about."

"No, ma'am." I heard the smile in Gray's voice as he

wrapped an arm around my waist and pulled my back firmly against his chest.

My mouth dropped open as I regarded my sister. "Jane!"

She just shrugged. "We all know it's coming. Stop fighting it."

I twisted my head to look at Gray over my shoulder and lifted a brow. "I don't get any say in this?"

"Nope," came the unanimous reply from everyone in the room.

I couldn't help but laugh. "I didn't say I wanted to," I grumbled good-naturedly before pointing at Jane. "But he hasn't even asked yet."

Gray turned me in his arms, and my heart rate kicked up as his hazel eyes met mine. "Do you want me to?"

Was that a serious question? "Of course I do," I said quietly. "But I don't want you to feel obligated, or—"

One huge hand slid up my spine to cup the back of my neck. "You're the only woman I've ever wanted. I will ask you right here in front of everyone if that's what you want." He paused and studied me for a long moment. "Is that what you want?"

I bit my lip, the hope and happiness swelling in my chest and threatening to burst. I nodded. "Yes."

One brow lifted, and a teasing smile quirked his lips. "Yes, you'll marry me, or yes, you want me to bare my soul in front of everyone?"

"Yes," I said again, a huge smile curving my mouth.

Gray shook his head as he stared at me. Slowly, he dropped to a knee, eyes locked on mine. Even though I knew it was coming, tears gathered in my eyes. He lightly grasped both of my hands in his. "Claire Gates, I love you more than anything in this world. I want to spend the next seventy years making you happy."

"Seventy years? You think you'll be able to put up with me that long?" I teased.

Gray shook his head with a smile. "Seventy lifetimes wouldn't be enough."

I tugged on his hands, and he climbed to his feet. I wrapped my arms around his shoulders and leaned into him. "Then I guess just this one will have to do."

His arms went around my waist and he lifted me off my feet as he hugged me close. I dimly heard Jane in the background, but I was focused completely on Gray as he kissed me, then touched his forehead to mine. "I can't wait to marry you."

GRAY

THE FIGURE SITTING ON THE FRONT PORCH STEPS caught my attention as soon as I turned into the drive. Claire must have seen too because she sat forward in her seat. "Is that...?"

I threw an arm across her chest automatically, halting her movement. "Stay here."

I put the car in park, then threw open the door. I was halfway to the house before it closed behind me. Trent popped up from his seat, and I studied him with narrowed eyes. "What are you doing here?"

He shifted nervously, his gaze flitting over my shoulder. Behind me I heard Claire climb from the car, her footsteps nearly silent as she pulled even with me. I didn't tear my gaze from Trent as I wrapped one arm around her waist and tugged her against my side.

She placed one hand on my chest as if the slight touch would physically restrain me. "Trent?" Her voice significantly softer than mine, more curious than suspicious. "What are you doing here?"

Trent's eyes slid over the two of us before he spoke. "I

heard what happened. After Chief left yesterday..." He hesitated for a second. "It was all over town that Ms. Kramer hurt you. I wanted to make sure you were okay."

Even as I fought the urge to roll my eyes, I felt Claire melt a little bit. "I'm okay. But what about you? Where have you been?"

She extracted herself from my hold, and I suppressed a low growl as she approached Trent. "Come on, let's go inside and you can tell us everything."

She unlocked the door and ushered Trent in, then threw a disapproving gaze my way. So maybe I hadn't been so quiet after all. Reluctantly I followed them into the house, keeping a closed eye on Trent.

Seated at the kitchen table, he told Claire about running away from home. He'd couch surfed for the past couple of weeks, hanging out with a couple of kids who'd graduated last year.

Claire shook her head. "I wish you'd said something."

Trent lifted one shoulder. "I deserved it."

I lifted a brow. Was he actually trying to take responsibility for his actions, or was this just a way to save face? Probably the latter.

I studied Trent as he gazed across the table at Claire, his expression somewhere between adoring and lustful. Well, that wasn't gonna fucking fly. I draped my arm over Claire's shoulders, and his gaze immediately slid to mine.

Yeah, I silently conveyed, *I caught you looking. And yeah, I know how damn lucky I am.*

Trent turned back to Claire with a little smirk. "Good thing Chief Thorne was here to make sure you were safe."

Kiss ass. Even though he wasn't responsible for harassing Claire, I still didn't trust him. He was a little too cocky, and his attitude, though improving, still needed an adjustment. I had to admit, I would be glad to see the back side of that kid.

"Well, I should head out." Trent stood, and I felt compelled to follow as Claire trailed him to the door.

"Are you sure you'll be okay? Do you have somewhere to go?"

"I'm good, thanks." He smiled and opened the door, then turned back. "By the way, Ms. Gates, I know what I want to do now."

A smile spread over her cheeks. "I'm so happy for you. What did you decide on?"

"I'm going to go to the academy." Trent tipped his head my way. "I want to work with Chief."

I knew my face was a mirror image of Claire's when her mouth dropped open in shock. A tiny smile tugged at the corner of Trent's mouth. "See you soon."

With that, he was gone. I reached out and closed the door, almost in slow motion. I turned to Claire, who looked just as surprised as I felt. My gaze slid back to the door and the young man who'd just vacated it. One I'd apparently be seeing a lot more often.

"Well, shit."

CLAIRE

GRAY LACED HIS FINGERS WITH MINE, THEN TUGGED me toward the living room. "Come with me."

He sank down in the corner of the couch, then settled me across his lap.

It was strange to think that the entire ordeal with Melissa was over now, and I wasn't entirely sure how I felt about it. I was relieved, of course, that I no longer had that threat hanging over my head. But now my focus was solely on my relationship with Gray, and I wasn't sure how to proceed.

He'd asked me to marry him less than an hour ago; I should be thrilled. Instead I was worried that things were moving too fast. We'd only just established our relationship; what if he was only offering out of obligation?

"What are you thinking, sweetheart?" Gray's voice cut through my thoughts.

"Oh, it's nothing."

He lifted one hand to stroke the side of my face. "Must be something. You're looking very serious."

I should've known I could never lie to him. I let out a sigh. "Just thinking about us... What we're going to do now."

Gray studied me for a second. "What do you mean?"

One huge hand settled on my thigh, and I played with his fingers as I contemplated exactly what to say. "I don't know." I shrugged. "I kind of like the way things have been the last couple of weeks."

"I like it, too," he offered quietly. "I like knowing you'll be there when I get home from work, and I like that you're the first thing I see every morning. I'm looking forward to a lot more of that."

I blushed at his words, and Gray tucked a lock of hair behind my ear. "Is that what you want?"

Mutely, I nodded. I bit my lip, disappointed, as Gray shifted me off his lap and stood. He pointed at me, his face stern. "Don't move."

He pinched my chin between his thumb and forefinger and gave me a hard kiss before pulling back. "I mean it. I'll be right back."

A tiny smile curled my lips as Gray strode quickly from the room. I heard the front door open and close, then a few moments later he re-entered the house. His footsteps moved closer, and I turned my head to look at him. "You good?"

"I am now."

Gray slid his hands under my thighs, then scooped me onto his lap. I snuggled close as he wrapped his strong arms around me and held on tight. For several minutes we sat that way in companionable silence.

"Remember what happened the last time we were right here?"

I could hear the smile in his voice, and I rolled my eyes as I sat up to look at him. "Maybe I wouldn't have freaked out about the dream if you'd given some sort of indication that you felt the same."

Gray shook his head. "You know what's absolutely crazy? I was going to tell you that morning. I wanted to take you to breakfast, then tell you everything. After we woke up together, I thought I'd ruined everything."

A pang of guilt sliced through me. "I'm sorry. I overreacted and—"

He pressed a finger to my lips. "That's not why I'm telling you this. The reason I brought it up is because I knew then how crazy I was about you, I just hoped you felt the same. In a way, we've kind of come full circle."

I let his words sink in for a second. It was true. Just a few weeks ago we each thought we'd ruined our relationship. "I just don't want you to feel..." I searched for the best word. "Pressured... to do something you're not ready for?"

"You think I'm not ready to settle down with you?"

I pressed one hand to his chest. "That's not what I mean. It's only that... We've been friends for so long, I just want to make sure you're doing what's best for you."

Gray stared at me for so long that I grew uncomfortable. Finally he shook his head. "I think I know what's going on here."

My heart rate kicked up. "What?"

"You're scared."

My mouth dropped open. "I'm not scared!" Not exactly.

"Okay," he amended. "You're worried that me asking you to marry me was just the next logical step in our relationship, right? You're afraid that someone better suited for me will come along and you'll be holding me back."

My throat tightened. "I—"

"That will never happen." His voice was firm. "Do you know why?"

I shook my head.

Beneath me, Gray shifted slightly and pulled something from his pocket. A gasp escaped at the sight of the small black box. Was that...?

Gray flipped it open, revealing the sparkling diamond

inside. "Because I love you, and I can't imagine my life with anyone but you."

My mouth dropped open as I eyed the ring. "You've just been carrying that around?"

"Yep."

My mind was blown. "For how long?"

Gray shrugged. "A couple months."

"A couple months?!" My mind went blank, and my mouth opened and closed several times before I was able to form words. "But... we weren't even together then. You... I can't believe you've had it all this time."

"Of course I did." Gray took my hand in his. "I knew I wanted you the moment we met. It wasn't a matter of whether I was going to propose, I've just been waiting for the right moment."

"Gray." Tears filled my eyes as he slid it on my finger.

He cupped the back of my head. "I don't care where we live, or what we do. I just need you."

He lowered his head and brushed his lips over mine. It felt as if all my dreams had come true.

Epilogue

GRAY

SHE WAS THE MOST BEAUTIFUL THING I'D EVER SEEN.

Claire stood next to the refreshment table talking with my mom and Jane, and I couldn't pry my gaze away from her. She wore a blue sundress similar to the one she'd had on the day we met, a huge smile curving her lips, her eyes bright and happy. It was absolutely perfect.

"About damn time."

I rolled my eyes as Drew appeared by my side. "Whatever."

"Seriously. I'm happy for you two." He gave me a one-armed hug. "I'm glad it all worked out."

"Me, too."

A few familiar faces appeared at the edge of the yard, and I waved to Con and his family. I recognized his wife, Grace, next to him, along with his younger sister, Abby, and another taller man who I assumed was her significant other.

Con lifted a hand in greeting, and I waved back. Claire caught sight of them and excused herself, then headed our way. I extended one hand to Con. "Thanks for coming."

Claire reached my side at the same time the small group

did, and she greeted Con with a hug. "It's good to see you again."

"You, too." He patted her back affectionately before releasing her. "How's your sister?"

"She's good." Claire gestured toward the table where Jane and my mother stood talking. She's here today, and I'm sure she'd love to see you."

"Of course." Con inclined his head, then looped an arm around Grace's waist. "Have you met my wife, Grace?"

"I haven't. It's so nice to meet you." Claire extended her hand, and Grace shook.

My gaze was automatically drawn downward to the swell of the woman's rounded stomach. I couldn't wait to see Claire like that, couldn't wait to watch her hold our baby. It sparked a sense of urgency and also terror. There was so much evil in the world. How would I protect them from all of it?

I glanced up at Con, whose knowing eyes met mine. Normally stoic and reserved, around Grace he seemed almost relaxed. Happy. I settled a hand on Claire's hip and drew her closer to me.

"This is my sister, Abby," Con continued, "and her fiancé, Clay."

Drew, Claire, and I shook their hands. "Thanks for coming."

"How's your case coming along? Have you found him?"

"Not yet." Drew shook his head. "We'd like to set up a sting to lure him in."

"Not a bad idea," Con murmured.

"Except that we only have two women in the department, and everyone recognizes them."

"What about someone else?"

I shook my head. "We can't use a civilian."

"What about me?"

Everyone whipped toward Abby, including her fiancé. "I'm sorry, what?"

"What?" She turned a not-so-innocent look on him.

"Not a chance." His gold eyes snapped with fire, and Abby rolled her own eyes at him.

"Why not? You could help. Both of you could." She gestured between Con and Clay. "No one recognizes me, and—"

"I swear to God, woman..." Clay trailed off, his face furious, but Con looked contemplative.

"It's not a terrible idea—as long as you're onboard."

"What the fuck?" Clay exploded. "You're not using my wife as bait."

"Not your wife yet," Abby shot back.

He growled. "Only because you refuse to set a date."

Abby grinned and, realizing everyone was watching their interlude, focused on Claire. "I'm making him work for it."

I felt a tiny tremor run through Claire's body, and I fought the urge not to laugh myself. Clay murmured something that sounded suspiciously like, "Damn woman's going to be the death of me."

Abby was clearly leading him on a merry chase; and just as obviously, he was so smitten with her he didn't even care.

"Tell you what," I spoke up. "Why don't Drew and I stop in next week and we can discuss it?" Maybe that'd give them some time to cool down.

Clay still looked ready for murder, but Con nodded. "Works for me."

"There's a ton of food," Claire said. "Please, help yourselves."

With a final promise to talk next week, the group moved toward the tables set up next to the porch. Claire leaned into me, and I pressed a kiss to the top of her head. I skimmed the backyard, scanning the familiar faces of everyone who had come to wish us well. A smile stretched my face as I turned to her. "Just like the day we met."

"It is," she agreed. "Funny how things had come full circle."

Two years ago I met the woman of my dreams; now she was going to be mine forever. Surrounded by family and friends, the woman I loved by my side, it was more than any man could ask for. It was absolutely perfect.

Also by Morgan James

QUENTIN SECURITY SERIES

Twisted Devil – Jason and Chloe

The Devil You Know – Blake and Victoria

Devil in the Details – Xander and Lydia

Devil in Disguise – Gavin and Kate

Heart of a Devil – Vince and Jana

Tempting the Devil – Clay and Abby

Devilish Intent – Con and Grace

*Each book is a standalone within the series

RESCUE AND REDEMPTION SERIES

Friendly Fire – Grayson and Claire

Cruel Vendetta – Drew and Emery (Fall 2022)

RETRIBUTION SERIES

FROZEN IN TIME TRILOGY

Unrequited Love – Jack and Mia, Book One

Undeniable Love – Jack and Mia, Book Two

Unbreakable Love – Jack and Mia, Book Three

Frozen in Time: The Complete Trilogy

DECEPTION DUET

Pretty Little Lies – Eric and Jules, Book One

Beautiful Deception – Eric and Jules, Book Two

*Each book can be read as a standalone, but are
best read in order

SINFUL DUET

Sinful Illusions – Fox and Eva, Book One

Sinful Sacrament – Fox and Eva, Book Two

*Books should be read in order

BAD BILLIONAIRES

(Radish Exclusive)

Depraved

Ravished

Consumed

*Each book is a standalone within the series

STANDALONES

Death Do Us Part

Escape

About the Author

Morgan James is a USA Today bestselling author of contemporary and romantic suspense novels. She spent most of her childhood with her nose buried in a book, and she loves all things romantic, dark, and dirty. She currently resides in Ohio and is living happily ever after with her own alpha hero and their two kids.

CPSIA information can be obtained
at www.ICGtesting.com
Printed in the USA
LVHW101512240922
729196LV00016B/131

9 781951 447243